TRUE BEAUTY

BY

PRISCILLA C. WU

Copyright © 2014 Priscilla Wu
All rights reserved.
ISBN: 1500653276
ISBN-13: 978-1500653279

DEDICATED TO

My Mom and Dad,
now you'll have something else to brag about.

ACKNOWLEDGEMENTS

To Hannah, for reading my stories without complaints ever since I was ten years old, and for being my longest fan.

To Aileen, for being the first one to find out about my publication goal, and for providing me with moral support along the way.

To Ashley, for putting up with my constant complaints and internal struggles over this book, and for not being afraid to be painfully honest with me.

To Ru, for keeping me company during my late night editing, and for providing me with moral support by being the cutest dog anybody could ever ask for.

TABLE OF CONTENTS

CHAPTER ONE: BEAUTEOUS

Beauteous [byü-tē-əs] adj. - Beautiful, especially to the sight

A small smile graced itself onto Hana's face as she stared at the swaying tree branches through her car window. A slight breeze caused cherry blossom petals to flutter through the air and tall stems of grass waved to Hana as she drove by. True, the sights were restricted by the thick tinted glass of the car window, but she still appreciated it all the same.

The world was a beautiful place.

The car turned an abrupt corner and Hana's smile quickly disappeared as the sights of nature vanished to be replaced by a series of large grey buildings.

It was the people living in it that were ugly.

Hana tore her eyes away from the window to stare at her hands that were resting on her lap. She didn't want to see what the world had to offer any longer, because those things were anything but beautiful.

"Are you excited?"

Hana lifted her gaze from her lap to her father, who was seated across from her.

"Are you excited?" he repeated, assuming that Hana hadn't caught his earlier words.

Not at all. "Very," Hana's soft voice answered.

Her father seemed pleased with her short reply, and turned his gaze out the window. Unlike Hana, he appreciated the sights that he saw; he had already become immune to the indecencies life had to offer.

The corners of Hana's lips twitched downwards as she stared at her father with disappointment. He was relatively young in age, but the grey in his hair and the wrinkles on his face had intensified from the stress that had built up over the past years. He was a successful business owner, and with success came worries and problems. Despite the aged features of the man's face, however, he could still pass off as relatively handsome.

In Hana's eyes, however, he was ugly.

Today was Hana's 18th birthday, and as a reward for being the best daughter anybody could ever wish for, Hana's father decided that she was old enough to follow the customs of the upper class.

She was finally mature enough to receive a Noye – a slave.

"We'll be arriving in a few minutes and you'll finally get to pick one out," her father smiled. "You can brag to all of your classmates since they won't be getting one for a couple of more years."

It was customary for adolescents to receive a Noye from their parents on their 21st birthday as a coming of age present. Hana's father, however, decided to give Hana hers a few years early; after all, she deserved it.

Hana knew better than that, however, she knew it was simply another way for her father to flaunt their wealth.

The car rolled to a stop, and so did Hana's heart. She hadn't properly prepared herself for the horrifying sights she would soon see. Her father, on the other hand, laughed merrily as the car door opened for him to step out. "Come now, daughter."

"Ah, Chando, you've arrived! We've been waiting for you all day! This is the birthday girl, I presume? She's beautiful!"

Hana stole a quick glance at the person who had praised her.

Hideous.

"Thank you, Michael," Hana's father laughed as he clapped the man merrily on the shoulder. "Let's give the birthday girl her present as soon as possible, alright? Please escort us to the hallways."

Hana cringed at the word. The hallways. It was there that Noyes would be lined up, each of them attempting to be on their very best behavior due to the fear of not receiving dinner if they weren't.

"Come, Hana," her father called. He followed his words with a light scold, "Don't just stare down at your feet."

Hana hid her small fists behind her back, and nodded her head. She turned to what she assumed was the owner of the Noye house and smiled apologetically. "I apologize for my rude behavior." *Sorry, not sorry.*

Michael laughed, "You've raised your daughter perfectly, Chando!"

The group of three soon arrived in front of a set of grand, wooden doors and Hana quickly inhaled a deep breath.

"Here we are! Choose carefully, Hana." Michael showed off his yellowing teeth in a smile as he pushed open the doors.

It was horrible.

It was absolutely horrible to see all those faces staring back at her.

They weren't ugly faces, not at all, but they weren't beautiful either.

Hana suspected that once upon a time each one of those faces radiated valiant beauty, but after being tainted by the ugly aspects of humankind, they lost their shine. They were now blank canvases with tinges of hope and anguish painted across their features.

Hana stood frozen in front of the row of Noyes. It all got even worse when she was suddenly met with a chorus of broken voices.

"Welcome, Master Hana."

"Well, Hana, go on. Make sure you choose carefully," Hana's father stated as he gave her a gentle push forward.

Hana hadn't gotten any farther than midway through the hallway when the sound of a slap caught her attention. She stared straight ahead to see a worker in his early 20s standing in front of a Noye with an angered expression on his face. The worker had silky blond hair that sat perfectly on his scalp. His eyebrows had been perfectly plucked and there was not even the slightest blemish on his porcelain skin. To others, he would have been considered as handsome, prince-like, almost.

To Hana he was revolting.

"Henry!" Michael barked angrily, embarrassed that his valued customer and his daughter had witnessed such a sight.

Henry's head shot up and he opened his mouth to shout angrily at the person who dared to spout his name in such a scornful tone. He stopped, however, once he got a glance at the man. "Father!"

Hana mentally scoffed: like father, like son.

"Did I not tell you earlier that we would be having valuable guests today?" Michael scolded as he gestured to Hana and her father.

Henry's eyes turned briefly to Hana's father before resting onto Hana.

She quickly became uncomfortable with the man's intense stare, and shifted her gaze to look at the Noye Henry had just attacked.

He had a childish face, complete with a button nose and a pair of doe eyes. There was a red imprint on his cheek and Hana wanted nothing more than to permanently tattoo a similar feature onto Henry's face.

"I apologize, father," Henry responded, not sounding very sorry at all. "Sean was mouthing out again. Seeing as how he doesn't seem to care about blows to himself anymore, I decided that he might shut his mouth if his precious friend was the one to pay the price."

Henry proudly glanced over at Hana to gauge her reaction. He was briefly stunned when the awed expression he was expecting was actually one of scorn and disdain.

Hana turned her gaze to the boy that was sitting next to the red faced one. His eyebrows were furrowed in, his jaw was angrily clenched, and his hands were clasped into tight fists at his sides

This must have been Sean.

Sean's angry eyes drifted from Henry and onto her. To her surprise and amusement, his orbs seemed to turn even angrier. She didn't blame him for his hard expression, however, because she understood what the other was thinking. To him, she was just another petty high class civilian looking for a toy to use during her free time.

"I see. Although that is a clever method, you must restrain yourself until our guests have left. It is rude to do such a thing in their presence," Michael stated as he patted his son on the shoulder. He turned to Chando with an apologetic smile. "I apologize for my son's careless actions."

"There's no need," Chando responded as he held up a hand. "Do whatever needs to be done. Noyes need to know their place."

Henry smiled at the words of approval and raised his hand to strike Chris's face. Sean's jaw clenched and he darted forward to stop the man from attacking Chris, but froze when somebody reacted quicker than he.

"Please stop," Hana's quiet voice sounded, contrasting against the strong grip she held on Henry's wrist.

As quick as it had come forward, Hana retracted her hand. Sean could have sworn that he imagined the whole thing if it wasn't for the red imprint of her thin fingers around Henry's wrist.

An awkward tension quickly captured the room and many faces gaped at Hana with mixed expressions of fear and admiration.

"W-Well, shall we continue browsing the selection?" Michael coughed as he gestured towards the end of the hallway. He gave his son a sharp look, and slightly jerked his head to signal his dismissal.

"There's no need," Hana replied calmly as she brushed a few strands of stray hair from her face. "I've already made my decision."

Brief expressions of surprise captured the faces of the three men, before a pleasant smile spread across Chando's face. "Which one?"

There was a beat of silence before Hana announced her decision. "The boy named Sean."

"Are you sure?" Michael gaped with furrowed eyebrows.

"Perhaps you should continue to look around?" Chando suggested.

"No. I've made my decision," Hana responded firmly, her eyes trained on the Noye in question. "I would like Sean."

Sean opened his mouth to shout something close to "Over my dead body!" but reluctantly decided against it. He instead forced a stoic expression onto his face, and stared at her with a set of cold eyes.

"Why me?" Sean asked blankly.

"Because," Hana responded slowly as her eyes raked the other's face. "You're still beautiful."

A blanket of silence engulfed the room.

All eyes were trained on the small, mysterious girl, and the filthy Noye she had just claimed.

Beautiful?

Sean could have laughed. How could *he* be beautiful? He, with his coarse hair, harsh eyes and calloused hands. How could he be beautiful with Chris sitting right next to him? Chris, with his precious doe eyes, soft skin, and delicate fingers.

"Sorry," Sean stated slowly as the corners of his mouth twisted upwards into a crude smirk. "I'm not for sale." He didn't even flinch when a hand roughly struck the side of his face.

"It seems like you haven't realized the fact that you belong to us!" Henry growled with flared nostrils.

"Excuse me," Hana's sharp voice cut across the air. "What do you think you're doing to someone who doesn't belong to you?"

Henry's eyebrows furrowed, offended that she had the audacity to reprimand him. He opened his mouth to retort, but was cut off by Sean.

"I won't leave Chris," Sean stated stubbornly as he reached over to envelope the said boy's hand into his own.

To the surprise of everybody in the room, Hana let out a soft chuckle.

"I was right," Hana stated softly. "You certainly are beautiful."

For some unknown reason, Sean felt blood rush to his cheeks at the stranger's words.

"Father," Hana called softly as she turned to look up at Chando. "I know it might be too much of me to ask, but may I have two?"

"Two?" Chando was taken aback by his daughter's question. His instinct was to immediately say no, but he held his tongue. Never had he known an individual who possessed two Noyes, even more one who had just turned 18. Nevertheless, he knew that it wasn't impossible, although complicated, to grant his daughter her birthday wish for two Noyes. He mentally smirked at the idea, knowing well that others would gaze at their wealth with envy.

"It will take a month's time," Chando answered as he slowly nodded his head. "But I will be able to get additional papers for another Noye."

"Please file a reservation for both Chris and Sean under the Acacia family name, Henry," Michael ordered his son.

"But—" Henry protested with outrage.

"You will do as I say," Michael snapped. He turned to Chando and clapped his old friend on the shoulder. "What do you say we go grab a cup of coffee like old times?"

"You're making a bad decision," Henry growled after making sure the old men were gone. "You're going to regret this."

Hana blinked. "If that's the case then I'll suffer my consequences at a later time." She turned her back to him as a way of saying that the conversation was over.

Henry let out a growl and left the hallway with pounding footsteps.

"Why did you do that?" Sean asked with narrowed eyes, suspicious of the girl's motives. "We don't want to be your Noyes."

"You have a bad temper," Hana responded simply. "You're very easy to anger, aren't you? But I can tell that you care greatly for those that you love. Perhaps that's what makes you so beautiful."

"Stop calling me that," Sean spat as he glared at her. "I'm not beautiful. What part of this face makes you think that I'm beautiful?"

These words caused Hana to fall silent and Sean smirked victoriously – at least until she spoke once again.

"I'm not sure. Perhaps it's the scars that litter your face – the scars that represent the beatings you've taken to shield your friends. Or maybe it's the way your bones protrude out of your shirt from all the meals you have skipped so the others would have enough to eat," Hana answered slowly as her eyes scanned the other's body. "It's also possibly the dark circles under your eyes that symbolize the sleepless nights you've suffered to watch over the others."

Sean was left speechless at the girl's words and he felt utterly vulnerable underneath the intense gaze of the stranger.

"I can see that you don't trust me, but it's quite alright. I don't expect your trust so easily, and would be quite disappointed if you did give it to me so quickly," Hana shrugged. She stared down at their injuries for a few seconds before beginning to rummage through her bag. Hana withdrew a small tin canister, and placed it into Sean's hand. "This is ointment; please apply it to both of your wounds."

"Why won't you do it yourself? Are we too dirty for you to touch?" Sean spat, eyes filled with a mix of pain and contempt.

Hana shook her head and calmly responded, "I assumed that you would not want a stranger to touch you. Especially Chris."

Sean didn't know what to say.

"One month," Hana stated. She stared at the pair and repeated herself once more. "One month. I'll get you to trust me in one month."

Sean's eyes narrowed at her confidence. "What makes you so sure?"

"Because I think you're like me," Hana answered with a shrug, her hidden arrogance beginning to take a hold of her words. "I think you're capable of looking at people and deciphering their true intentions."

Sean was at a loss for words once again.

"Well, I have to go now, but I will be back tomorrow," Hana stated as she turned to leave. She stilled for a few seconds, and turned back to stare at Sean with hesitance, as if she was mentally debating on whether or not her next action would be appropriate.

"Thank you," Hana released a small smile as she brushed the tip of her finger against a faded scar on Sean's face.

Sean held his breath at the sight of her smile. The curve of her lips was so slight that it was debatable as to whether or not it was really there.

"For what?" Sean finally asked, mentally scolding himself for remaining silent for so long.

"For allowing me to see the beauty in people again."

* * *

"Are you happy with the Noyes you've chosen, Hana? It is still not too late to change your mind, you know. Michael told me that the ones you've chosen aren't really the best he has to offer. The tall one, Sean, is rash and violent and the small one is a mute," Chando informed his daughter as he rubbed his chin thoughtfully, his lips curved into a frown.

"I am sure of my decision," Hana responded firmly as she turned her gaze out the window.

Chando nodded in satisfaction. "You should spend some more time with Henry too. Apparently there are quite a lot of girls after him."

Hana nodded her head once more, but offered no words expressing her opinion. She'd rather die, is what she thought.

Chando was content with his daughter's action, and let the car ride continue in silence.

* * *

True to her word, Hana returned to the Noye House the next day.

The dingy residential building that the Noyes lived in completely contrasted the one she had visited yesterday. Noyes were scurrying all over the place, working hard to complete the jobs assigned to them so they could return to their homes later to rest. There was a large courtyard in the front of the building, blockaded from the outside by thick metal gates.

The receptionist informed her that Sean and Chris were most likely residing in their cages, and granted her access to the lower floor.

Hana cringed at the word. Cages. She was even more disturbed at how the woman said it, as if there was nothing out of the ordinary; as if the people living in those cages were animals instead of humans.

The cages were just as horrible as she had imagined.

The "rooms" of the underground floor were separated by iron bars that ran vertically from the ceiling into the ground. The ground was made up of dirt – thick layers of it; Hana wondered if actual concrete was lying beneath all the filth that nobody bothered to clean.

"Hell is more like it," Hana muttered under her breath, flinching when a spider web brushed against her hair.

Each "room" possessed a sink, a small table, and 4 lumpy blankets spread across the dirt grounds. There was an almost pungent stench in the air, but that too had been expected. The Noyes were hardly given any food, let alone the chance to bathe on a daily basis.

"You're looking for Sean, aren't you?" a sudden voice called out, causing Hana to jump slightly in place. "You're the girl who bought Sean, right? He was going on about how some rich girl claimed she was going to visit every day."

Hana turned to her right and met eyes with a lanky male. His face was smudged with dirt and the grime that layered his black hair gave it a grayish tinge. He continued, his voice hinted a European accent, "If you're looking for Sean and Chris, they're not here. It's going to be a while until they get back."

"Where have they gone?" Hana asked as she approached the tall boy.

"I think they're on kitchen duty today. Hey Luca! Luca! Are Sean and Chris on kitchen duty today?" he turned his head to call out to the boy sleeping behind him.

"Yeah," Luca's voice croaked back in return.

Hana's eyebrows furrowed at the sound. She glanced behind the tall boy, and spotted another sprawled out across the ground, his dirty blond hair peeking out from underneath a layer of sheets. "He's sick, isn't he?"

The boy's face fell. "Yeah. He has been for a while now, but the guards keep stealing Luca's medicine so he just stopped requesting it."

Hana paused. "Can I come in?" she asked with a cocked head, using her hand to gesture towards the open gate.

His eyebrows furrowed at her request. "I… I mean, I guess," the boy responded, uncertain as to why she would want to enter.

Hana pushed open the gate, and winced when the hinges screamed sharply in protest. After kneeling down beside Luca, she laid the back of her hand against his warm forehead.

"Who… Who are y-you?" Luca asked weakly.

"My name is Hana Acacia," Hana responded as she slipped her bag off of her shoulders to rummage through it. "And you should know better than to go this long without medicine, Luca."

"W-What's the p-point of… of asking f-for it if the g-guards are going to st-steal it?" Luca's bitter chuckle quickly escalated into a cough.

Hana uncapped a bottle of water and pressed it gently against Luca's cracked lips. "Drink."

Obediently, Luca greedily gulped down the water as if he hadn't consumed liquids in a long time; Hana suspected he hadn't.

"What have the guards been giving him in return?" she turned to ask the taller boy who stood silently at Luca's side.

He bitterly responded, "Nothing. They haven't been giving him anything because they say that he's going to die soon anyways. I've been sharing my meals and water with him, but they aren't enough."

Hana's eyes softened at the sight of the angry other and she asked, "What's your name?"

"Aiden," he answered.

"You're a beautiful person, Aiden," Hana smiled softly.

Surprise filled Aiden's eyes and he fell silent at Hana's words, not knowing exactly what to say in return.

"You won't die, Luca," Hana reassured him as she pulled him into a sitting position. She pressed the palm of her hand against Luca's back as support, and gestured for Aiden to come over. "Prop him up, please."

Hana pulled a silver canister out of her bag along with a plastic spoon. A delicious scent wafted through the room once it was opened and Aiden had to swallow his saliva to hold in his hunger.

"Open your mouth, Luca," Hana stated as she carefully slipped a small spoonful of warm porridge through the other's lips. She had initially brought it as a peace offering for Sean and Chris, but she could always bring another tomorrow. Hana continued to spoon feed the other until the canister was half empty.

A tinge of red managed to flow back into Luca's cheeks, but he still remained a sickly color. Hana frowned at his appearance, and rummaged through the contents of her bag. She had caught a fever herself a few weeks ago, and hoped that she still had the medication on hand. She smiled in satisfaction once she discovered the bottle of red tablets.

"What is that?" Luca frowned as he watched her shake the bottle into the palm of her hand.

"It's medicine," she answered as she handed him two tablets.

Luca eyed the pills warily; suspicious as to how convenient it was that she happened to have medication in her bag. "If I die..."

Hana raised an eyebrow, "If you die, what good would come to me?"

Luca thought over her words for a few seconds and shrugged his shoulders in agreement. He popped the pills into his mouth and took a swig of water, scrunching his face in displeasure as he did so.

Hana rewrapped the silver container of porridge and the medicine before slipping it under the table. "Feed him the rest of the porridge at dinner time, along with two more tablets," she instructed Aiden.

"You should get some rest, Luca," Hana smiled as she gently helped the male lay down. "You will feel better tomorrow, so rest well."

"Thank you," Luca whispered softly before closing his eyes.

Hana checked her watch and saw that it was about time to go. She climbed to her feet and notified Aiden of her departure.

"You aren't going to wait for Sean and Chris?" Aiden asked, hoping that she wouldn't leave so soon.

Hana shook her head. "I can always see them tomorrow."

Aiden nodded his head reluctantly, and gave Hana a bright smile. "Thank you, Hana. If Luca died… I would… I wouldn't…"

"You're welcome, Aiden," Hana smiled, relieving Aiden of his trouble to find the right words to say. She lifted a hand and gave Aiden a small wave goodbye before disappearing up the stairs.

* * *

Sean and Chris immediately noticed the brightened atmosphere of the cage when they returned. "What happened here?"

"The angel came to visit," Aiden answered with a dreamy expression on his face as he brushed Luca's bangs aside.

"What angel?" Sean asked with raised eyebrows.

"An angel that healed Luca of his sickness," Aiden smiled as he gestured to the sleeping male.

Sean had to admit that the other appeared a little healthier with the color he now possessed in his cheeks. "Such an angel exists?"

Aiden nodded and pressed his hand against Luca's forehead to feel his friend's decreasing temperature. "She goes by the name of Hana."

* * *

"Is the angel here?" Luca asked as he propped himself up on his elbows.

"Not yet," Aiden informed him as he helped Luca sit up properly. "She said she'd come back today, so don't be disappointed. It's still morning."

Sean stared at the pair with amusement. The two others that he and Chris had shared their cage with for two years had been waiting for the arrival of his supposed "master" all morning. It was ridiculous, really. How could they have become so infatuated with a woman they had known for hardly an hour? He wasn't at all impressed, however. The pair always trusted others much too easily.

Despite these thoughts, Sean's head unconsciously shot up at the sound of a light tap on the cage entrance. Chris, who was at his side, stared at him curiously before turning his head to see what had caught his attention.

"Ang- Hana!" Aiden called out gleefully as he ran to meet the small girl at the door. "You've come!"

"I said I would, didn't I?" Hana responded as she followed him through the door. She still hadn't gotten used to the foul stench in the air, but she didn't let herself think about it too much. She met eye contact with Sean and gave him a nod of acknowledgement. Chris quickly averted his gaze so she wouldn't do the same with him.

"Are you feeling better, Luca?" Hana asked as she pressed her hand against Luca's forehead.

A small surge of jealousy erupted in Sean's chest and he was surprised at the emotion. Why would he feel jealous towards his roommate for simply being touched by the girl? She didn't mean anything to Sean, yet he still unconsciously developed a bit of longing for her to treat him as she did Luca. He immediately scolded himself for his thoughts, however; he refused to give her that satisfaction.

"You're still a little warm. Has Aiden been feeding you your medicine on time?" Hana asked with a raised eyebrow.

Aiden frowned at Hana's accusations and her eyes smiled in amusement as she patted the other's arm. "I'm just teasing."

Sean stared at his friends with slight bitterness; his earlier mental scolding was immediately discarded. If Sean was the one she had claimed, why wasn't she trying to get on friendly terms with him? He was the one who would be under her care within a month's time, would he not? Did she like Aiden and Luca more? Sean bit down on his lip. Sure Aiden and Luca were much friendlier than he, but they weren't too bright.

Sean was taken away from his thoughts by a sudden tug on his shirt and he glanced down to see Chris staring up at him with confusion. Chris used his finger to write out characters into the ground. *What's wrong?*

"Nothing's wrong," Sean reassured him as he patted Chris's head.

Hana glanced over at the pair and smiled at the brotherly affection they showed for one another. At this close proximity, Hana noticed the number of old scars that were scattered across Chris's entire body. She understood now that they must have applied make up to cover the old wounds during Chris's appearance in the hallways. She was curious, however, as to why they hadn't even bothered to cover up Sean's past injuries.

"I thought I'd find you here."

Everybody in the cage froze at the sound of the familiar voice.

"Why would you be looking for me in the first place?" Hana asked in return as she calmly turned around. "I can't imagine that there would be any reason for you to meet me."

"My father wants me to court you," Henry stated with a small smirk plastered across his face. He leaned against the iron bar of the cage door, and ran his hand through his hair in what he assumed was a 'cool' manner. "He thinks you fancy me. Isn't that amusing?"

"It would be if it was true," Hana responded monotonously as she trained her attention back onto Luca. She pulled a thermometer out of her bag and commanded Luca to part his lips. Luca stared hesitantly at her and glanced at Henry, but opened his mouth in the end.

"Don't turn your back on me," Henry hissed as he wrapped his hand around Hana's upper arm to jerk her towards him.

"I don't believe my father would appreciate it if I told him that you treated his daughter with aggression and disrespect," Hana calmly responded. "Please restrain yourself. Now, what exactly do you need? If there is nothing in particular, I will request that you leave."

"Excuse me?!" Henry's crude laughter echoed against the walls; his eyes narrowed and his nostrils flared. "You're asking me to leave when my father is the one who owns this place? Are you stupid?"

Deciding that talking to the other would simply be a waste of her time, Hana turned her attention to a more important matter. She pulled the thermometer from Luca's lips and checked his temperature, "Your fever isn't too high, so you should be fine in a few days."

"I told you to look at me when I'm speaking to you!" Henry shouted as his hand flew forward. His motion was suddenly stilled from the grip Sean held on his wrist and he trained his angry gaze on the Noye.

"What the hell do you think you're doing, dirty trash?" Henry growled as he tore his arm away from Sean's hand.

Sean didn't know how to answer, for his defense had surprised even himself. He had saved her unconsciously. Sean was too preoccupied with his thoughts to notice how Henry pulled his arm back to attack him.

"If you touch a single hair on his body I will not hesitate to sue," Hana stated firmly as she trained a strong glare onto Henry. "According to the contract, both Sean and Chris are now registered under my family's name, and attacking one of them would be like attacking a member of the Acacia family. You will suffer severe consequences and most likely cause your father to lose this place. Are you willing to accept the punishments?"

Henry's fist froze mid-air and Hana mentally smirked victoriously. "I would recommend that you lower your hand."

Henry growled at the humiliation Hana caused him, and swore that he would pay her back. While leaving the cage, he released his anger by slamming his fist against a Noye who had been innocently walking by.

"That bastard," Hana muttered as she knelt down beside the Noye. She offered him an apologetic smile, "I'm sorry about that."

The brown haired boy shrugged in response, "It's my fault for being nosey. I wanted a glimpse of the angel Aiden had been going on about all night and I guess this is what I get in return."

Hana cocked her head with amusement at his words, "Angel?"

A blanket of red fell over Aiden's cheeks and he immediately stammered out a defense, "I j-just said… something like that."

"Well then," Hana's rare chuckle floated through the room as she held out a hand to help him to his feet. "I'm Angel."

The Noye took her offer with a bright smile, "I'm Kai." His eyes lit up in realization and he held up a finger to signal her to wait a minute. "Hold on, let me get Haru; he wanted to meet you."

Before Hana could ask who Haru was, Kai had already disappeared into a nearby cage. She watched in slight amusement as Kai reappeared, now dragging a boy along with him. He was tiny in structure, and looked no more than 15 years old, his baby fat still clinging to his cheeks.

"Hana, this is Haru," Kai smiled as he presented his roommate. "Haru, this is the angel Aiden was talking about."

"H-H-Hel-Hello," Haru stammered as he stared down at his fiddling fingers. "I-I-I'm Ha-Har-Haru."

Hana stared at Haru for a long time, causing him to become twice as flustered under her intense gaze.

"K-Kai," Haru whined as he tugged on the other's sleeve.

"Hi Haru," Hana finally greeted. "It's very nice to meet you."

A crimson blush crept onto his face, "Y-Y-You don-don't have t-t-to lie t-to m-m-me-me."

"I always tell the truth, Haru," Hana answered as she turned to head back into the cage. She paused momentarily, and gestured for the pair to follow her in.

The blush that had captured Haru's cheeks had now spread to the tips of his ears. He shuffled into the room behind Kai with his head ducked down in an attempt to hide the color of his face.

The cage was now beginning to get a little crowded with the new additions. It had already been a tight squeeze with just the four of them alone and three additional occupants swallowed up even more space. Despite the stuffy air and the lack of room, however, the seven of them felt completely at ease.

By the time Hana had left, she didn't even notice that she could no longer detect the stench of the air.

CHAPTER TWO: DAINTY

Dainty [dān-tē] adj. - Delicately beautiful or charming

The next day, Hana had arrived for barely five minutes before all of the Noyes except for Chris were called out to bring in a few shipments.

"I'll be back soon," Sean whispered into Chris's ear as he climbed to his feet, a bit hesitant to leave the boy alone with Hana. Still, it wasn't as if he had any other choice. Sean gave Chris another small smile of reassurance before following after the others.

"The two of you care about each other a lot," Hana's voice caught Chris's attention. She gave him a gentle smile, attempting to soothe his nerves with her words. "I admire your relationship a lot. To have a mutual bond of affection must be one of the best things in the world."

The corners of Chris's lips slightly twitch upwards. She opened her mouth to ask Chris a question, but quickly closed it once again. There was only one question that corrupted Hana's thoughts and she knew that it wasn't appropriate to ask. With a small sigh, she forced the notion from her head and instead formulated another topic of conversation.

She would find out why Chris was mute another day.

"Ah!" Hana eyes lit up as she recalled the present she had hidden in her bag. She quickly rummaged through its contents, searching for the item she had brought for him. "I have something I wanted to give to you."

Chris's eyebrows rose curiously at her words and he crept forward the slightest inch to find out what it was.

She pulled out a pair of gloves and shyly tossed them onto Chris's lap. When he stared down at them with a blank face, she explained, "I noticed that your hands shake whenever it starts getting a little chilly. They're coated on the outside, so they won't get dirty when you write."

It was the smallest token, really, but Chris appreciated the present. Admittedly, he didn't like the girl at all when he first met her, but this gift managed to melt his icy walls just the slightest bit. He stared at the badly stitched *"Chris"* that was sewn onto the exterior with blue thread.

"I bought the gloves, but I thought they should be more personalized," Hana explained when she caught Chris's line of sight. She paused as an afterthought and admitted sheepishly, "I'm not the best at sewing..."

Chris found it utterly ridiculous that she couldn't sew. He now noticed the small bandages that were wrapped around Hana's finger tips. The corner of his lips perked upwards as he imagined the girl constantly pricking herself in the efforts to spell out his name. It made him feel warm; the fact that Hana had spent so much time doing something as meagre as writing out Chris's name for him. It was a nice feeling.

Chris traced out *Thank you* into the dirt of the ground to express his gratitude. Hana was too far away to see what had been written, so he gestured her forward with the crook of a finger.

A bit too eager to see Chris's reply, Hana scrambled to her feet. Her sudden motion caused her leg to trip over the other and she fell forward before she could stop herself. A soft body broke her fall and Hana's eyes immediately flew open in realization.

"I'm so sorry Chris! It's my fau—"

The rest of her words got caught in her throat as she stared down at the scars that decorated Chris's skin. She had acknowledged the marks before, but never until now had she been able to actually get a good look at the dark fragments.

Were those *bite marks?*

Her eyes trailed further down the boy's scarred skin; they definitely were. It would have been hard to distinguish the overlapping scars from far away, but now at such a close proximity, she could easily make out spots where dentures had clamped onto repeatedly.

Chris registered the look in Hana's eyes and he followed her line of sight to a particularly large bruise that he was sporting on his upper arm – a bruise in the shape of a hand print.

Bewildered, Chris's hand shot out and he pushed Hana away from him with all of his strength. Once the girl landed backwards, he scuttled to the corner of the room to be tucked away and enveloped by the darkness.

Hana winced at the pain that jolted up her arms when she fell back onto the palms of her hands. She glanced over at Chris, and swallowed hard at the pure look of horror and fear that stretched across his face. She should have known better than to let her gaze linger on the dark marks.

Feeling immensely apologetic, she opened her mouth to call out his name, but was interrupted by an angry shout that came from Sean.

"Chris!" Sean exclaimed as he came running into the cage. He skidded to a halt, and dropped to his knees to pull the now sobbing boy into his arms. His head turned to stare at Hana and she flinched under the strong glare of contempt.

"What did you do to him?!" Sean barked angrily, practically seething as he rocked the crying boy in his arms.

Hana opened her mouth to defend herself, but no words came out. She didn't know what to say. She hadn't meant to harm the other on purpose, and felt horrible for the mental anguish she must have caused the elder.

"Get the hell out of here!" Sean growled as he rubbed Chris's back soothingly. "Leave or I'll throw you out!"

Hana gave the boy a small nod before climbing to her feet. She wanted to explain herself to Sean, but she knew that wouldn't be such a good idea; the tinge of madness in his eyes told her so.

"Don't you dare come back," Sean's cold voice hissed. Once he registered her fading footsteps, Sean spun back around to face the nearly hyperventilating elder, "What did she do to you?"

"Sean? Chris? Chris what's wrong?" Luca asked as he entered the cage with the others following closely behind him.

"Chris! Tell me what she did to you!" Sean exclaimed as he shook Chris by his shoulders.

"What are you doing?!" Luca exclaimed as he pulled Sean away. "How do you expect him to calm down when you're not calm yourself?"

Sean let out a loud growl as he pulled away. He knew that Luca was right; he being angry was only making it worse for Chris. It was just... he wanted to know what Hana had done. In all honesty, he kind of liked Hana. He saw that she was a good person, and although he wouldn't show it on the outside, he believed in her. That's why he was so frustrated to see that his trust had been betrayed. He wanted to know if it really was Hana that had caused harm to Chris, because a little part of him didn't want it to be true. He wanted to continue his growing fondness for the girl, and would have no reason to do so if she really did harm the elder.

"Good, you're calm now," Luca smiled after gently coaxing him to relax. "Now tell us what happened."

With a slow, shaky finger, Chris gradually wrote out an explanation on to the ground. *It wasn't her fault.*

Sean felt relief consume his body as he stared down at the messily written words. His anger and frustration immediately vanquished.

"What made you so upset?" Luca asked gently.

Chris remained unmoving for several minutes before he finally held out a trembling finger. Five pairs of eyes watched carefully as he carved out shaky letters into the dirt.

She saw my scars. She knows.

They fell silent as they read the messy words, and exchanged eye contact with one another. Chris's quivering finger engraved another message into the ground.

She probably thinks I'm dirty.

"Silly," Sean chuckled as he crouched down in front of him. "That's it? That's why you cried as if you had been stabbed?"

Chris's bottom lip jutted out at Sean's scolds. As an afterthought, he might have over reacted just the slightest bit.

"Hana doesn't care for your scars, Chris, at least not in the way that you think," Sean assured the other as he gently wiped his tears away with his thumbs. Ironically enough, he was lecturing him on Hana's good nature despite screaming at her just minutes earlier. "And she definitely doesn't think you are dirty. Do you understand me?"

Chris let out a small nod and Sean smiled as he patted his head reassuringly. Chris closed his eyes and enjoyed the gentle touch, exhausted by the effects of his mental breakdown.

Sean sighed, already regretting his rash actions. He should have calmed down to see what the problem was first, rather than blame the girl right off the bat. He would apologize and explain himself to the girl tomorrow, definitely. He just hoped she wouldn't be too angry with him.

Unfortunately, such an opportunity never came.

* * *

Three days had passed since Sean had falsely accused Hana and she hadn't been able to make it to the Noye house ever since.

She cursed her bad luck; why had a pile of work hit her at that particular moment? Sean probably saw her absence as her admittance of guilt from attacking Chris, or if Chris had explained everything to him, he probably saw her as a coward.

Hana Acacia was not a coward.

"Do you think they hate me, Jay?" Hana asked in a quiet voice as she twiddled her thumbs together.

Her personal driver, Jaymes, let out an incredulous scoff, "What right do they have to be mad at you, Miss Hana? If they say anything just call me and I'll come and beat—"

"You're not helping," Hana huffed childishly.

Jaymes glanced at her through the review mirror with amusement, "Excuse me for asking, Miss Hana, but are you *pouting* right now?"

Hana straightened herself up, "No."

Jaymes climbed out of the car to open the passenger door for her. He clucked his tongue and arched an eyebrow. "You've been in here for fifteen minutes. I think it's time you go inside."

Hana contemplated his suggestion for a split second before shaking her head, "No, I think I should spend another good ten minutes in here before making that decision."

Jaymes rolled his eyes and held out his hand to help her out. Hana sighed and reluctantly took the offer. She stumbled out of the car when he pulled her with too much strength. She shot him a dirty look and he simply laughed it off.

"Have fun, Miss Hana. I'll be back to pick you up soon," Jaymes smiled cheekily as he climbed back into the car before driving off.

Hana watched the car disappear before turning to stare up at the Noye House. She inhaled a deep breath of air, and confidently strode into the building, muttering words about how she was not a coward under her breath.

She was moving so quickly that she would have missed the familiar patch of blond hair amidst a group of guards if it wasn't for the squeal of a voice. She froze mid-step, and slowly turned in a clock like motion to face the group of offenders attempting to hide in the dark shade of a hall. Her ears perked once she heard one of the guards murmur, "Be a good boy, Chris", and her eyes immediately narrowed in anger at the name.

"Let go of him," Hana's cold voice cut across the air like a knife. "You will let go of him or I swear to god I'll kill you."

The guards spun around, guilty from being caught in the action. Hana's eyes widened when they caught sight of the naked boy that had been forced to his knees in the middle of their man made ring. Her blood boiled in fury; were they the ones responsible for the marks that served as permanent symbols of suffering for Chris? A hundred thoughts cluttered her mind all at once and she forced them out to concentrate on the current situation at hand. One of the men opened his mouth to shout angrily at the girl for interrupting, but another quickly held him back.

"That's the daughter of the Acacia family, hold your tongue," Hana heard him whisper quietly.

Hana walked towards them in an almost calm manner. The guards would have let out breaths of relief if it wasn't for the look of pure death in Hana's eyes. Shivers ran down their spines.

Hana stared down at Chris's bare body and he averted his eyes in shame, embarrassed to have been caught in such a situation by his master. If she hadn't before, surely she would view the older now as tainted goods, dirty and filthy from the touch of other men. His eyes widened in realization and horror; what if she didn't want him anymore? What if she took back her words, and only purchased Sean instead? His body began to tremor at the thought.

To his uttermost surprise, Hana knelt down and pulled the boy's pants up for him, not even blinking when she met eye contact with his private area. She looked around for Chris's shirt and her eyes zeroed in on the ripped scraps of clothing that littered the ground. She pulled off her own jacket and placed it around Chris's shoulders. Hana then gave him a small comforting smile, so quick that Chris had to mentally debate as to whether or not he had actually seen the curve of her lips.

The hall was silent, and the tension was so thick that the sharp look of Hana's eyes could have cut it in half. She slowly gazed at all of their faces and the guards felt beads of sweat roll down their foreheads with every passing second. Why wouldn't she say anything?

"You all must not value your lives very much," Hana finally muttered under her breath. She gave them no chance to process her words and spun sharply on her heels.

"Come, Chris," she ordered as she continued down the corridor, ignoring the cries of protest that followed her. The guards must have realized what she meant.

The two walked in silence. Sean had been pacing when they arrived, and spun around once Hana announced their presence.

"Chris!" Sean exclaimed with relief as he wrapped his arms around the boy's torso. He had heard that Chris had been taken away by the guards again, and had been waiting stoically for his return. He was relieved to see that Chris had arrived relatively untouched.

"Please take care of Chris," Hana's soft voice stated. Sean looked up from over Chris's shoulder and stared into the girl's knowing eyes. "I have matters to take care of, so I'll be leaving for now."

"Wait," Sean called out as he stepped forward to stop her.

Hana wearily glanced back at him. "What is it?"

"Did you... did you save him?" Sean asked in a quiet voice as he timidly glanced at her.

Hana stared at him in silence for a long time. Finally, she gave him a curt nod before turning to leave the cage. Again, her footsteps made no sounds. She registered the soft plea of Sean's voice telling her to come back soon before she left the cages completely.

Sean's thoughts for the girl disappeared when he registered the tight grip Chris had on his shirt and he wrapped his arms even tighter around the elder's shoulders.

Sean had never been as thankful in his entire life as he was at that moment. Four years. For four years he had to watch Chris get dragged off with those disgusting men with the inability of doing anything.

Chris let out a soft, broken sob into Sean's chest, and Sean immediately began to stoke his head in an attempt to soothe his nerves.

He still remembered the first time it had happened as if it was no more than a day ago. It was in the middle of the night when he had been awoken by the sudden cries of his name. His eyes flew open just in time to see Chris being dragged away by a handful of guards. Sean attacked them without hesitation. He was obviously outnumbered, and was taken down in almost an instant. All Sean could do was watch under the blows of fists and flashes of blood as Chris got dragged off to a corner. The last thing he saw were Chris's wide eyes before he blacked out.

When Sean finally regained consciousness, Chris was at his side, silently tending to his wounds. He sat straight up, and stared at Chris in a panic, ignoring the pain that shot through his body.

"What did they do to you?!" Sean exclaimed as he clasped his hands on to the boy's shoulders to inspect his injuries. Chris didn't answer, but he knew he didn't have to use words to explain what had happened.

"Chris," Sean's strained voice sounded. "Are those... bite marks?"

He got his answer when Chris shamefully averted his eyes, tears threatening to spill down his cheeks.

Sean didn't say anything after that, and neither did Chris. He simply engulfed the older, fragile male into his arms, and rocked him back and forth, swearing that he would never let them touch Chris again.

Chris limped the entire week.

He broke his own promise two weeks later when the sound of cries and whines awakened him. He didn't want to open his eyes, for he was scared of what he'd see when he did.

The guards were different this time, but they still had similar intentions as the last ones. Chris screamed for Sean and Sean darted forward without failure, hoping to this time come to the rescue. He threw his fists blindly and scratched and bit everything that came in contact with him, but it still wasn't enough.

The events of that night replicated the one from two weeks ago, and again, the last thing Sean saw before he blacked out was the look on Chris's face as he got dragged away. Sean didn't know who he was angrier with – the guards or himself.

Sean woke up to gentle hands as they bandaged his wounds. He laid there silently, staring up at the elder's fatigued face. His eyes traveled down to Chris's neck, flashing in anger when he saw that the bite marks had doubled in quantity.

"Don't look," Chris whispered, ashamed of the marks that blemished his skin. A single tear slipped from his eye.

That week, Sean had nearly killed one of the other Noyes with an iron bar when he had playfully slapped Chris's butt, causing the other to wince in pain.

A month passed by eventless. By then, Chris had already calmed down, and had forced himself to forget all the things that happened on those two nightmares of nights. Sean was smarter than that, however. He stayed awake every night, refusing to let the weakness of sleep consume him.

Finally, they came.

Sean was prepared for them. With a single blow, he managed to knock one of the guards unconscious with the metal pipe he was equipped with. He shouted for Chris to wake up and run away, but it was too late.

As a punishment for actually getting the nerve to prepare himself with a weapon, the guards decided to give Sean a gift before they knocked him out with brutal fists.

That night, they made him watch.

The next day, Sean couldn't even meet Chris's eyes.

A few months passed by and Sean finally allowed himself to feel at ease once again. Perhaps the guards had gotten tired of Chris, and had gone to prey on some other innocent Noye. Sean didn't care who it was, as long as it wasn't Chris.

Sean soon realized how naïve he had been. After waking up one night to relieve himself, he stumbled upon Chris and the guards.

"That's right, you're a good boy, Chris. You're such a good boy, aren't you? A good boy with a pretty little voice."

He stood there for a few seconds in shock, unable to process what was happening before his eyes. Chris's face was completely expressionless. His eyes were closed and his face was stoic – as if he had already grown used to the rough treatments, and was simply waiting for the end. It wasn't until one of the guards acknowledged Sean's presence that his eyes flew open in horror.

"Sean, no," Chris's cracked voice rasped. "Please, leave."

Sean's hand curled into a fist, but before he could attack, a searing pain shot through his abdomen. He staggered a few steps forward, and stared down at his torso to see the stalk of a knife jutting out of his body.

Chris's screams were the last thing he heard before he blacked out.

He woke up the next day with a throbbing pain in his stomach and a tearful Chris seated beside him.

"Chris, are you okay?" Sean exclaimed as he shot upwards, letting out a low hiss of pain at the sudden strain the action caused his wound.

Chris calmly wiped his tears away from his eyes and nodded as he gave Sean a small, forced smile. "I am fine, Sean."

Sean realized that he was lying on something that completely contrasted the hard floor of the cages and his eyes darted around to observe the white walls and curtains.

"You're in the hospital," Chris explained.

Sean's eyes widened in surprise; a hospital? Never before were Noyes sent to the hospital, even if they were on the brink of death.

"Sean," Chris stated quietly, catching the boy's attention once more.

"Sean, I want you to stop fighting them," Chris continued in a low voice. "No matter what they do to me, I want you to stop fighting them. I want you to turn a blind eye and ignore them."

When Sean's mouth opened in outrage, Chris held up a hand to silence him. "Please, do this for me. Do this as a favor for me."

"L-Look, I know I haven't been able to save you yet, but I will! I swear to god I will! Don't lose hope in me," Sean exclaimed in protest.

Chris shook his head with a sad smile. "I haven't lost hope in you, idiot. I just... I just hate seeing you get hurt. It's worse than what they do to me. Please, Sean."

Before Sean could even reply, Chris climbed to his feet and quickly made his way to the door. "I want you to abide by my wishes, Sean. This is the last thing I will ever ask of you, please. I will see you tomorrow."

Sean's protest died on his tongue once Chris vanished from sight. Tears sprung to his eyes and he fisted the sheets of his bed angrily. "Damn it!"

Chris didn't come back to visit him the next day, nor did he the next.

Finally, a week later, Sean was able to leave the hospital and be returned as a Noye to the cages. He had been waiting for that day the entire week and the doctors found it strange that the boy would willingly leave the nice comfy bed and decent food to return to a life of horror.

Sean ignored them. They didn't know about Chris.

When Sean returned, a wide smile spread across his lips once he spotted Chris sitting calmly in the middle of their cage.

"Chr--!" Sean's happy cry of Chris's name died in the air once the other turned to look at him. His smile wiped off his face and he fell to his knees, ignoring the pain that jolted through his body from the rough impact. "What have they done to you?"

Chris kept his promise. That was the last thing he would ever ask.

Sean never heard his voice again.

* * *

Hana returned to the cages the next day at an ungodly hour of the morning and she greeted the sleepy Noyes with drooping eyes.

"You look exhausted," Luca yawned.

"I've just been busy, that's all," Hana murmured sleepily as she stumbled towards them in small strides.

Sean stood next to the girl's swaying figure, ready to catch the weak body if it was to collapse. "You should have gone home to rest."

"You told me to come back soon, didn't you?" Hana mumbled.

Sean was both embarrassed and grateful that she had heard his silent request. Still, he refused to let his glee show on his face and he forced his eyes to narrow at the exhausted girl. "Not if you were going to come like this." *No, don't leave.*

"I can't leave, I've already sent my driver away for the night," Hana murmured as she sunk to the hard ground. She pulled her knees up to her chest and rested the side of her face against her knee caps.

It was beginning to get even harder for Sean to force the frown on his face. "You like being so much trouble, don't you? Well, since there is no choice, I guess you can slee—"

"You can come sleep with me, Hana!" Luca piped up cheerfully as he patted the open space beside him.

Sean's jaw dropped. Was Luca not capable of reading the situation?

"It's alright, Luca," Hana responded as she closed her eyes. "I would take up too much room. Just return to sleep, alright?"

Luca opened his mouth to protest, but through the dim moonlight that came through the barred window, he accidently met eye contact with Sean. The other's threatening orbs were enough to tell him to shut his mouth. "I... I'll be getting to sleep then. Goodnight."

His fake snores that sounded seconds later were painfully obvious and Sean resisted the urge to face palm himself. Luckily, Hana was simply too exhausted to care for distinguishing the differences between real and fake snores.

"Come," Sean stated silently as he scooped the small girl into his arms. He ignored her weak protests as he transported her over to his scrap of a blanket. Sean frowned when she shivered. He lied down next to Hana, and slid his arm under her neck, transferring her head to his chest for a better source of warmth. Sean was overjoyed when the girl didn't protest against the new sleeping arrangements; she actually curled closer to him for warmth. Her quiet, even breaths that sounded seconds later told him that she had fallen asleep.

' He couldn't see much except for a nest of hair, and internally cursed himself for positioning her at such an angle. Now how could he admire the girl's delicate, doll like features?

Sean's eyes widened in realization and he would have slapped himself if his arms weren't all too comfortably wrapped around Hana's small shoulders. He let out a long, quiet groan as he thought about the current situation. He was giving in to the girl much too quickly, and that scared him. He had never cared for anybody other than Chris before and the fact that those that he needed to watch over and protect had doubled in numbers, scared him.

Sean decided, however, that he would erase the thoughts from his mind, and simply enjoy life as it was; life in the present, life with Hana.

Little did Sean know that he wasn't the only one who had changed so quickly after the introduction of a new character into his life. Hana had transformed in an even more dramatic way than Sean had. No longer did the petite girl speak in soft tones of such few words at a time. Although her character remained rather monotonous at home, she seemed to slip under a whole new persona when she was with the boys. Hana was still soft spoken of course, and wasn't fond of too much excitement, but she enjoyed herself a lot more. She spoke complete sentences, stringing several of them together at a time. She found herself actually making an effort to talk to the boys, to sneak them food and medicine, to care for them. Most importantly, she found herself smiling with them.

The boys had made her smile more in the past few days than she had in almost her entire life.

It seemed as though fate was working rather quickly in turning the gears of their relationship; as if to make up for all the time that had been lost.

* * *

Sean woke up the next, or to be more exact, later on that morning from the hushed giggles and whispers that flew across the room.

"What the hell is going on?" Sean grumbled as he rubbed at his eyes. He tried to get up, but a light weight against his chest reminded him not to do so. His face softened as he felt the warm puffs of air from Hana's lips skitter across his thinly clothed chest. Due to his restraint, he had to strain his eyes to see the faces of the giggling others.

"You got cozy with the angel pretty quickly," Kai stated with a smug expression and crossed arms. "The two of you look as if you're glued to each other with the way you're sleeping."

If it wasn't for the fact that Sean didn't want to interrupt Hana's peaceful sleeping, especially with how tired she had looked earlier that morning, he would have thrown the girl off to strangle Kai to death.

"S-S-Sor-Sorry S-Se-Sean," Haru stammered as he fiddled his thumbs together. "I-I t-t-told th-th-them to b-be qu-quiet, b-b-but th-they would-wouldn't li-listen to m-me-me."

Aiden chuckled at Sean's reaction, and chimed out, "Sleep, sleep!"

"Come on Haru; I'll help you with your speech," Kai stated as he wrapped an arm around Haru's shoulders to lead him out of the cage.

"Chris, do you want to get breakfast with us?" Luca invited the elder as he and Aiden prepared to depart the cages.

Chris bit down on his bottom lip in hesitation. He never ate without Sean, but now he saw that Sean was too preoccupied to go with him. Chris gave Sean one last glance before agreeing to leave with the pair.

"Chris's coming with us, Sean," Luca called out to the younger as the trio made their way out of the cages.

Chris glanced over his shoulder, and smiled when he saw that Sean hadn't even noticed the other's notification.

Chris was surprised that he didn't feel any sort of bitterness or jealousy towards the figure that was lying in Sean's arms. He had always pictured himself as the sole figure of importance in Sean's life and now that another one had come butting in, he thought that he would hold the girl with contempt. He honestly had no such feelings, however, and was actually happy that the younger had found another person to protect.

After all, the protection that Sean offered Hana was different from the kind that he offered Chris. Sean's loyalty towards Chris was to some extent, almost mandatory in Sean's eyes. He saw Chris as the last of his figurative family who obviously needed protection, and therefore provided it. Hana, however, Hana was somebody that Sean *chose* to protect and that made Chris happy. He was happy that if something, someday, were to happen to him, he wouldn't have to go through the guilt of leaving Sean all alone. Sean would have something else to live for, even if the younger didn't realize it yet.

Honestly, Sean was at that point wide awake, but he made not even the slightest movement in fear that it would cause Hana to wake up. He would never admit it, but he liked the radiating warmth of the small girl.

"Alright, it's time to get up now," Aiden's loud voice announced after what seemed to be only seconds.

Sean let out a small growl when Hana was tugged off of him, but immediately bit it back once he saw how she cutely rubbed her fists against her eyes. She stretched her arms above her head, and let out a small yawn that resembled a puppy.

"How late is it?" Hana murmured through closed eyes.

"Late enough for you to be up, that's for sure," Luca replied as he plopped down next to Hana. "You were gone for so many days and you look so tired, what happened? I was worried that you were never going to come back." At the latter part of his words, several dirty gazes were shot towards Sean.

"I had meetings to attend," Hana answered as she finally opened her eyes, blinking several times to get adjusted to the light. She turned to Sean and smiled, "Thank you for being my personal cushion, Sean."

Sean flushed a light red and mumbled, "You're welcome."

Chris quietly made his way over to Hana's side, and sat down next to her. Hana felt a tug on her sleeve and she glanced down to see Chris staring up at her. He pointed down at the ground and her gaze followed his outstretched finger to read what he had written in the dirt.

Will those guards be punished?

Hana fell silent for a few seconds, "They won't bother you again."

Chris appeared satisfied with that answer and he cleared the message from the ground to replace it with a new one.

Thank you for saving me.

Hana stared down at the message for a few seconds before training her gaze onto Chris. Her expression softened when he cocked his head curiously at her, wondering what exactly was going through her head.

"You've had a hard life," Hana murmured under her breath as she gently stroked Chris's hair. Her eyes swam with empathy and pain and she offered him a small, comforting smile.

Chris inhaled a sharp breath of air at her words, and a sudden pain shot through his chest. He froze and stared at her, feeling a flood of emotions immediately wash through his system. A single, stray tear slipped from the corner of his eye and he immediately wiped away the evidence with the back of his hand.

Hana could feel her heart cracking in two at the sight. She swore to herself that she would never let such a painful expression cross his face again. Wordlessly, she pulled Chris into a tight embrace, providing him with the protection he had needed his entire life.

CHAPTER THREE: HUMAN

Human [hyü-mən] adj. - Subject to or indicative of the weaknesses, imperfections, and fragility associated with humans.

Two weeks had passed since the date they had all first met, and already the six Noyes accepted Hana as one of their own. They would smile when she smiled, frown when she frowned, laugh when she laughed, and all the rest. It was nearly frightening how infatuated they could have been with the girl within only two weeks of time.

The more time Hana had spent with the boys, the more work began to pile on top of each other, and finally it came to such an extent that Hana could no longer afford such leisure visits.

She awoke the next morning lying on her bed when she knew she had fallen asleep at her table. She stared at her ceiling with blurry eyes, sighing as the ringing of the alarm shot through her ears.

"Miss Hana, would you like me to bring your uniform, or will you be skipping school again today?" Jaymes asked as he stepped into her bedroom. Although Jaymes was officially titled as her chauffeur, he took it upon himself to take care of her throughout the day.

Hana ran her fingers though her messy locks and blinked repetitively in an attempt to get rid of her fatigue. "Yeah, I'll go," she answered.

Jaymes frowned at the weariness of her tone; he could practically see the exhaustion that decorated her face. "Perhaps you should skip it?"

Hana shook her head, "I've skipped school too often these past few days. It wouldn't look good if I continued my bad attendance."

The two departed for her school soon after and Hana immediately regretted not giving in to Jaymes's words when they arrived at the noisy campus. The loud voices did nothing to aid her throbbing headache and she gave Jaymes a weak goodbye.

As she moved down the hallway, she caught sight of a crowd of familiar boys and quickened her pace, hoping she wouldn't be noticed.

"Hey Dustin, look who's back," one of the boys whispered as he eyed Hana. "Why don't you go see if she's willing to take you up on that date?"

Dustin frowned. "C-Come on guys," Dustin laughed as he punched his friend gently on the arm. "She's been gone for a couple of days and she was probably sick. I don't want to catch diseases from her, you know?"

"Don't be such a girl," his friend laughed as he shoved Dustin forward.

"Hey, Hana!" Dustin called out with reluctance.

Hana sighed and closed her eyes when she heard the call of her name. She reluctantly stopped, and pressed her lips into a firm line.

"Is there a reason for you to be calling me, Dustin?" Hana asked wearily as she turned around to stare her class mate in the eyes. Dustin's eyebrows furrowed with concern at the fatigue that decorated Hana's face. With his friends behind him, however, he wouldn't voice his worry.

Dustin arched an eyebrow, and curved his lips into the nasty smirk Hana only saw when he was with his "friends". "Is that the way the Acacia Corporation's famous daughter should be speaking?"

Hana twitched, but refused to let any emotion of irritation form on her face. She turned to him and blinked twice, "Yeah."

"You never fail to amuse me, Sweetheart," Dustin laughed as he threw his arm around Hana's shoulders. He glanced back at his friends for support and his smirk broadened when he was met with approval.

Hana clenched down on her jaw in annoyance. She and Dustin were acquainted in a relationship that wouldn't be classified as friendship, but over the point of being simple schoolmates. She thought Dustin was internally a good person, even if it didn't show when he was with his friends, and Dustin liked her because she didn't question his friendship with the other douchebags.

Hana understood why Dustin remained friends with the other boys, even if they wouldn't provide him with any benefits in the future. All teenagers was looking to fit in, weren't they? Dustin had found his acceptance among his peers, even though it required him to act like somebody he wasn't. The faux persona Dustin claimed while under the public eye certainly wasn't praiseworthy, but Hana didn't hold it against him. He was only human, after all, and one of the utmost desires of a human was to find a place where they belonged; she only wished that Dustin would realize that the place he was in right now wasn't the right one.

"If you'll excuse me, I have a class to attend," Hana stated in a hostile tone as she pulled away from Dustin's grip. She paused for a few seconds, "Please refrain yourself from speaking to me in the future."

Dustin's eyes widened slightly in surprise and his eyebrows furrowed; he was afraid that she had taken his words to heart. Dustin opened his mouth to apologize, but realized that he could do no such thing in the presence of others, and pressed his lips together.

Hana rubbed her temples as she walked away from the group of boys and to her classroom, ignoring the cries of triumph from Dustin's peers.

By the end of the day Hana had gotten a decent amount of work done, and was pleased that her day spent at school wasn't too useless after all.

As she sat down on the front steps of the school waiting for Jaymes to arrive, Hana mentally sorted out everything that needed to be done.

A sudden shout interrupted her thoughts. Her head snapped up at the sound and her eyes narrowed at the familiar voice. She pulled her bag over her shoulder and climbed up to her feet to investigate the cry. A few thumps met her ears and she slipped past some hedges to eye the ring of boys that were standing in a small clearing hidden among the shrubs.

Hana gazed at the faces of the boys, engraving both them and the names on their ID tags to her memory. She sighed when she saw Dustin standing amongst the ring with his eyebrows furrowed in with worry. She then eyed the boy kneeling in the middle of the circle, and quickly understood why Dustin looked the way he did.

She recognized the boy as Nathan Lane, Dustin's older half-brother who was regarded as quite the nerd by the school population. Dustin never publically acknowledged the relationship between the two of them, so their blood remained a secret to everybody other than the pair and Hana.

Hana pulled out her phone, and sent Jaymes a quick text, requesting for him to come to her aid. She wasn't all too fond of the idea of playing the damsel in distress, but Hana wasn't a fool – she knew her limits. She had taken self defense lessons as a child, but even that wouldn't protect her against the handful of muscled boys that stood before her.

'I'll be there in 5 minutes' was the reply she received.

Hana glanced up at Nathan who had earned another hard kick to the chest for remaining silent, and then another to his head when he had 'made to much noise' from coughing. She contemplated on whether five minutes was enough for them to actually impose any harm on her.

"I assume that you are all having a decent amount of fun?" Hana called out as she stepped into the clearing.

All heads whipped around to face her and she gauged the different emotions she was met with; some expressed annoyance and irritation while others displayed amusement and interest.

Hana knelt down in front of Nathan to help him up. She clucked her tongue against the roof of her mouth as she wiped the blood away from his lips with the pad of her thumb.

"What do you think you're doing?" a voice hissed and a hand jerked her backwards. She grimaced when her bottom hit the concrete ground, but refused to give the bullies any satisfaction of her pain.

"I'm helping him," Hana replied simply as she calmly climbed back onto her feet. She shot a reproachful look in Dustin's direction. "Because nobody else seems to be."

Dustin was taken aback by her sudden hostility and he gazed shamefully down at his feet to escape her judging eyes.

"Kids should learn not to stick their noses into the business of others. Should we teach this little girl a lesson?" one of the guys hissed.

Hana cocked her head. "But I'm not a child." She eyed the bronze colored name tag that was pinned to his uniform, and pointed to her own, silver colored tag. "Look, I'm even older than you."

"Don't try to get smart with us," a foreign voice snarled into her ears.

Before she knew it, Hana was shoved to the ground with both of her wrists pinned to her side. The student straddled her waist and Hana almost rolled her eyes when she felt a hard bulge press against her stomach. How barbaric of a man, to be aroused by simply over powering a girl.

"H-Hey, Jason, maybe we should just let her go," Dustin tried to offer. He immediately backed down when a hand smacked him against the back of his head.

"Are you crazy? That's Hana Acacia! Do you know how hard it would be to shack up with her? We're not passing up this chance, so if you're going to chicken out you better tell us now," another growled.

Hana scoffed at the way Dustin cowered – some friends he had.

Hana counted the passing seconds in her head, wondering how much time had already passed. She smiled in satisfaction when she heard quiet rustling sound from the side.

"You deserve everything that is to come to you," Hana stated simply, attracting the attention of the ring of boys once more.

Before any of them could ask her what the hell she was talking about, a figure darted through the greenery, swiftly striking down one of the boys with a fist before moving onto the next. The student that had been straddling her quickly climbed off to help the others of his group.

Hana smiled proudly as Jaymes easily beat the bullies, not earning a single scratch to his own skin. He hadn't been positioned as practically her guardian for nothing. He reached almost 30 years of age, but the additional years only added to his intense strength. Hana often thought about how much of a pity it was to have a fighter as great as Jaymes protecting her when he could be off watching over the president. Whenever she voiced her concerns, however, Jaymes simply laughed it off, insisting that he wasn't as strong as she claimed.

"Spare that one," Hana called out when Jaymes had pulled his fist back to attack Dustin's face. Jaymes asked no questions, and pushed him lightly aside before moving on to the rest that were attempting to flee.

"Nathan Lane?" Hana called out as she knelt beside the injured student.

Nathan's bottom lip quivered in fear as he slowly gazed up her. A glint of recognition sparked in his eyes.

"H-Han—" He cut off his words when he met eyes with another familiar face. Dustin immediately averted his gaze, ashamed of his actions.

"Come with me, Nathan," Hana called out as she pulled him up to his feet. She glanced around the clearing for a few seconds before bending over to pick up his discarded glasses.

"The frame is broken, but it shouldn't be too hard to fix. Let's get out of here for now," Hana offered as she helped him exit the greenery. She stopped momentarily to call out over her shoulder, "Follow us when you are finished, Jaymes."

"How do you know who I am?" Nathan asked quietly. He flushed when he accidently made eye contact with the girl, and averted his eyes before mumbling a soft, "Sorry."

"Why wouldn't I? You're a year three student who ignores his academic potential and scores straight Bs' and Cs' in an attempt to persuade everybody that he isn't the nerd they say he is," Hana answered.

Nathan expected no less knowledge from the girl who claimed the top spot in academics. He felt slightly bitter towards the girl despite the fact that he sincerely respected her. How was it that she was the academic star, yet was an exception to the taunts and jeers that he had received from simply scoring in the top 50? Nathan parted his lips to respond, but was interrupted by the sudden rustling of bushes. Hana smiled up at Jaymes who was brushing stray leaves out of his hair.

"I apologize for not arriving earlier, Miss Hana," Jaymes murmured as he wiped his hands clean with a small cloth.

"You arrived just in time," Hana reassured him. She caught sight of Dustin peeking at them from behind a tree and smiled knowingly, "I'll be leaving now then. Will you be alright finding your own way home?"

Nathan nodded his head, shyly thanking Hana once more.

* * *

The high tension that radiated through the cage wasn't exactly the warm welcome Hana had been expecting.

"Has something happened?" Hana asked as she stared at Aiden who was angrily moping in the corner of the room.

All heads darted up at the familiar voice and the atmosphere lightened just the slightest bit by her appearance.

"Why does Aiden look like a mix of a murderer and a lost puppy?"

Hana asked curiously. "And where have the others gone?"

"He and Luca got into a fight," Kai informed her. "So Luca left and dragged Chris along with him. Sean went too, just in case."

"What did they fight about?" Hana questioned with a raised eyebrow.

"Something really stupid," Kai sighed, shaking his head at the memory of the argument. "They'll make up again soon."

"Hey Aiden," Hana called out as she crouched down beside the male who was prodding at the ground with a stick. "What are you doing?"

"Drawing Luca," Aiden spat as he stabbed his stick bitterly into the ground.

"I don't think Luca has three eyes," Kai piped up as he crouched down in front of the drawing to inspect the other's work.

"That's not an eye, that's a second mouth because he obviously doesn't know when to shut up," Aiden sneered as he proceeded to carve the other a uni-brow. "Either that or he just likes hearing himself talk a lot."

"Obviously it's because I like hearing my own voice," Luca growled as he walked into the cage with Sean and Chris at his side.

Sean's weary face immediately brightened at the sight of Hana, but he made no movements to acknowledge her, worried that he'd seem overly eager. Chris, on the other hand, feared no such thing, and didn't waste any time before he engulfed the girl into a tight hug.

"What are you doing here, Hana? I thought you had to finish all your work?" Luca asked after greeting Kai and Haru but not Aiden.

"I needed to talk to somebody," Hana responded.

"Who? Me, possibly?" Luca grinned brightly, completely contrasting the deadly aura his better half was emitting.

"Sorry Luca, but I need to talk to Sean this time," Hana answered as she sent Sean a smile.

Sean's eyes widened slightly in surprise at the sound of his name and he couldn't resist the upward twitch of the corner of his mouth. He cleared his throat and stared at Hana with what he hoped was a stoic expression. "What did you need to speak to me about?"

"I just needed some advice," Hana responded as she walked to his side. She gestured for the two of them to leave the cages to speak in private. "Can you spare a few minutes of your time?"

Sean opened his mouth to agree almost immediately, but restrained the eagerness of his tone. "Yeah, I have some time to give you."

"Hey Sean," Luca chortled as he leaned in to whisper into Sean's ear. "You need to work better on hiding your schoolboy crush. It's written all over your face."

"And you need to work on minding your own business," Sean

muttered under his breath.

Hana pretended not to hear the exchange and she slipped her hand into Sean's larger one to pull him out the door. She stopped briefly and cocked her head at Luca and Aiden, "You two better make up."

Kai and Haru exchanged glances and hastily bolted out of the room. Chris tried to follow quickly behind them, but was caught by Luca who grabbed a hold of his upper arm.

"I don't think so. You're going to stay here and make sure I don't kill this idiot," Luca scoffed as he forced Chris to sit down. Chris reluctantly obeyed Luca's command and sent Sean and Hana a pitiful wave.

"Come on, I know a good place," Sean spoke up as he dragged Hana down a series of pathways. "There's a little bench that faces the outskirts of the walls. It isn't great, but it's the most private area here."

Hana nodded her head and allowed Sean to pull her along until they finally arrived.

"What did you want to talk to me about?" Sean asked as he plopped down onto the dirtier end of the bench.

"There is a friend that I have," Hana began to explain as she seated herself next to the boy. "He's in a bit of trouble, but I don't know what to say to him. I was hoping you could help me."

Sean stared silently at the trees in front of them, not offering any words in response. Hana was beginning to think that he wasn't willing to listen to the petty story of a stranger until he finally parted his lips, "Well? Continue on."

The corners of Hana's mouth curved slightly upwards and she continued to explain Dustin's predicament to Sean, the other offering small nods every few words to show that he was listening.

"Your friend sounds like an asshole," Sean commented when she concluded her explanation.

Hana chuckled, "He seems like one, but I know he's good at heart. He just needs a little help seeing it, I guess."

"A lot of help," Sean nodded in agreement. He leaned back to stare up at the clear sky. "It's kind of like he adopts a whole new persona; a whole new identity to protect him from society."

"So what do you think?" Hana urged him to continue.

"He sounds like a coward," Sean scoffed as he ran his fingers through his hair. "Hiding behind some character he created, but…"

A small smile formed on Hana's lips. "But?"

Sean glanced uneasily at her before stretching his arms towards the sky. "But… I don't blame him… Sometimes…. Sometimes you have to do what you have to do in order to survive in this cruel world."

He thought about his own walls that he had set up around himself and Chris to prevent anybody from hurting them. His cold behavior had prevented so many others from befriending him and Chris. The other four only stuck around because they were too stubborn to stay away.

"Even if that isn't how he truly is, he has to live under some made up character to survive. In this world... in this world that destroys the weak immediately... sometimes..." Sean's voice drifted away. How could he hold Hana's friend with disdain when he was exactly the same? When Hana had first explained the story of her friend, he immediately hated the guy, and saw him as weak and cowardly, but now... how could he?

A bitter smile spread across his face as he recalled the days of his childhood, back when he still retained untainted innocence. He envisioned the younger Sean who always had his lips spread into a bright smile. The Sean who had enough kindness to share with everybody.

A knowing smile slipped onto Hana's face. She had made the right decision in questioning Sean of Dustin's methods.

Almost ten minutes passed by before Sean snapped out of his thoughts. "S-Sorry, Hana. I was just thinking, and I—"

Hana held up a hand to cut him off and he stared at her with a confused expression. "You don't have to tell me, Sean. Let's go back, okay?"

"Wait, I haven't-" Sean called out as he grabbed onto the girl's upper arm. He immediately let go when she flinched in pain. His eyes narrowed at the reaction and he pulled up the sleeve of her shirt, growling at the marks scattered across the pale skin.

"I just got into a bit of trouble, that's all," Hana explained quickly.

"I thought you knew how to fight!" Sean exclaimed as he examined the dark bruises that decorated her wrist.

"I'm five feet tall, Sean," Hana sighed as she pulled her arm away from his grip. "There's a limit to how much power I am capable of possessing; I'm not super woman, you know."

Sean fell silent at her words and he gently caressed her injuries with his thumb. Her bruises opened his eyes to just how normal Hana really was. Sean had always envisioned her as almost hero like, always willing to sacrifice her wellbeing for others and rescue them whenever they were in need. Now he saw how human she really was.

"Sorry," Sean murmured as he released her arm.

Hana cocked her head at his apology, genuinely confused as to what he was apologizing for. "What for?"

Sean glanced up, and quickly averted his eyes in embarrassment once he met eye contact with her. "Sorry for... it's nothing."

Hana didn't pester him for an answer, and instead suggested that the two of them return to the cages now that their discussion was finished. Sean nodded in agreement, and stole a glance at her before the two climbed to their feet. *Sorry for making you into something you're not.*

* * *

Hana pressed her cheek against the cold window, enjoying the cool touch of the glass. She tightened her grip around the mug of hot tea that served as a small hearth of warmth in her hands.

Hana took a deep, shaky breath as she tried to breathe all of her frustrations out of her body. Her chest constricted with pain and she raised the rim of the mug to her lips to take another sip. The mental and physical stress she was undergoing was beginning to take a toll on her and she wanted nothing more than to abandon everything.

But she wouldn't.

She couldn't.

For she was Hana Acacia, successor of the Acacia family name, top student of her academy, protector of Noyes – the so called 'bright light of the future'.

A quiet, bitter laugh escaped her lips and she ran her clammy fingers through her long hair; she had nobody else to blame except for herself. She had just been notified that she was expected to speak at the corporate meeting that would take place in two days, and had nothing prepared for the event. A glance at her work table deepened the crease of her furrowed eyebrows even more. Her grip on her mug loosened just the slightest bit and the cup came crashing to the floor, shattering on impact. She felt the hot tea splash against her leg that had been hanging loosely from her position on top of the large window sill and grimaced.

"Miss Hana, are you alright?" Jaymes called out with worry as he burst into the room.

Hana's lips curved into a faux smile almost automatically and she raised a hand to stop the male from coming closer. A single step further and he would be able to see the current mess she was in.

"It's nothing, Jaymes. I can take care of it myself," Hana's voice floated out. Jaymes nodded his head with uncertainty before shutting the door behind him. Her smile dropped at the click of the closing door and she heaved a sigh as she crouched down to clean up the spilt drink.

It was hard.

She knew others assumed that she saw everything as simple to complete, but truly it wasn't. She was only human too, just like everybody else, but it seemed like everybody chose to forget that fact. Hana was what everybody considered as their safety net, always expecting her to come to the rescue if they were to fail at anything they did.

She clucked her tongue against the roof of her mouth, and scolded herself for her thoughts. Truthfully, Hana had nobody else but herself to blame. It was her own fault that she created such a reputation for herself; what started off as trying to please people with small favors and actions escalated into her being the go to person for help.

People, she quickly realized, would never be satisfied with the things they had. If she were to help somebody with a simple math problem, they would return seeking help for a couple more, and then again for the entire sheet. It felt good at first, to be able to relieve people of their worries, but soon the expectations kept building higher and higher, and it was up to Hana to outdo herself every time.

The real reason she had asked Sean for his help was because she thought Sean would gain from his words. She didn't find herself suited to give advice to Dustin when realistically, she too was hiding behind a faux facade in order to gain her place in the world. Sean was suffering the same identity crisis, but the reason she had gone to him was because she knew he wasn't in too deep. He could still change himself with a bit of self-reflection. He wasn't as stuck as Hana was.

To the world she was Hana Acacia, the girl who could take on any problem and come to the rescue of anyone in distress. To herself, she was Hana Acacia, the girl who was always biting off more than she could chew.

In the eyes of others, she might have seemed like the nearly perfect human being, but she knew she wasn't even close to achieving such a utopian ideal. It was all an act; she had her fair amount of blemishes.

Hana exhaled a long, shaky breath.

Her perfection was her greatest flaw, and her biggest enemy was herself.

CHAPTER FOUR: INTREPID

Intrepid [in-ˈtre-pəd] adj. - characterized by resolute fearlessness, fortitude, and endurance

"Your father has returned from his trip and is waiting downstairs for you. He said that he wanted to eat breakfast together since it has been quite a while," Jaymes informed Hana the next morning.

"He'll probably just scold me for visiting the Noye house too often again," Hana sighed as she gestured for Jaymes to come forward and tie her neck tie; she always had problems with where the fabric was supposed to loop through. "Let's go down; we can't keep him waiting."

"Ah, Hana," Chando greeted her daughter when she entered the room. She returned his greeting with a small smile before taking a seat in her respective spot at the dining table.

"How is school? Do you still have first place in your grasps?" Chando asked as he placed down the newspaper he had been reading.

"Yes," Hana answered politely as she took a bite of her toast.

"Jaymes?" Chando called out as he stared at the man expectantly.

"Miss Hana scored perfectly on the last exam. In their overall rank, the student in second place is still over a hundred points away from beating Miss Hana," Jaymes immediately stated.

A satisfied smile spread across Chando's lips and he let out a bellowing laugh. "My daughter is always so modest."

"Thank you for your praise," Hana responded quietly. Her eyes caught sight of the headline of his newspaper, and widened in surprise. "Father, may I…?"

Chando's eyes lowered to follow Hana's line of sight. He picked up the newspaper and handed it to his daughter. "Such a horrible event, wouldn't you think so? I hope this doesn't ruin business. Those rodents are always causing trouble for the rest of us; you would think that they knew their place in society by now."

Hana remained silent as her eyes quickly scanned the inked text, mentally retaining all the information that was present.

"Well, I must leave now or I'll be late," Chando excused himself as he put on his coat. "Be safe today, and don't stay too long at that dump. It's especially dangerous now."

All Hana spared was a nod as she continued to read the article.

"We must go or we'll be late," Jaymes stated the second Hana placed the newspaper down. She nodded her head and followed Jaymes to the car as she thought over the things she had just discovered. A small smile slid onto her face and her eyes gleamed as she thought of an idea.

"Change of plans, Jaymes," Hana announced as she slid into the car; the words she had just read in the newspaper were still fresh in her mind. "Looks like we're going to be paying an early visit to the Noye house."

* * *

"There's been a revolt," Hana whispered in a hushed voice of excitement as she stared into the eyes of the six Noyes.

"What do you mean?" Aiden asked with a raised eyebrow of confusion. "What kind of revolt?"

"A Noye revolt, there's been one a few days ago not too far from here," Hana stated. Her eyes darted over her shoulder every so often to make sure no others were eavesdropping on their conversation.

Sean got a bad vibe from the look on her face.

After deeming her next words safe from foreign ears, she added in a hushed whisper, "What if we had a revolt ourselves?"

Dead silence captured the cage, and her eager smile slowly slid off as she gazed at the unenthused faces that stared back at her.

"Are you crazy?" Luca finally stated. "We wouldn't make it ten minutes."

"Hana, I'm thankful that you're so eager to help us fight for our freedom, but… a revolt?" Kai murmured hesitantly as he scratched the back of his head. "I don't think… I don't think that's the right path for us." Haru nodded along with his words.

"Then what exactly is the right path for you, Kai?" Hana demanded, a sudden anger capturing her chest. "What? I'd like to know. Are you going to be chosen during the next hallway showing and spend the rest of your life serving an ungrateful, snotty daughter of a noble? Is your goal in life to simply serve the same person over and over again without the respect each and every one of you deserve? To be constantly ridiculed among the elites and spat at and taken advantage of? Why are you allowing your pathways to be deemed by society's unjust standards? This cycle, this cycle of cruelty and inequality is just going to continue year after year after year. A Noye is born, a Noye is bought, a Noye is killed – it'll never end. You are all simply seen as pawns and tools of society; why will you not fight for what you deserve?!" Hana was nearly in tears by the time she finished her words.

She knew it wasn't her position to say such things to them, and that they were within their rights to be offended by her words. Despite this, she didn't regret them. If she, a complete outsider who was situated at the prosperous end of the social ladder, was willing to fight for the freedom of those at the bottom rungs, why weren't they? They had their reasons, of course, but she couldn't help but feel disappointed with the lack of motivation and determination. Did they not want change?

The boys remained speechless around her, not knowing what to say in return. They knew that ultimately, she was right, but still they wouldn't do anything. To stage a rebellion against the Noye house would be no easy feat. Not only would they be against hundreds of guards, but they'd also be fighting against the state. They'd be considered fugitives, and if found, they'd be killed on the spot. They weren't willing to lose their lives for the freedom they no longer missed.

They also weren't willing to sacrifice Hana's name. They knew she was willing to help them whole heartedly, which is why they had to reject the idea even more. The girl had presented them with nothing but kindness and protection – how could they repay her by risking her life?

And perhaps they were just selfish. Perhaps they believed that if they had to go through this suffering for so many years, why would others get to escape? Why would they have to go through the hardship of fighting for another's freedom?

"I'll be taking my leave now," Hana stated as she picked her bag off of the ground to throw over her shoulder.

Luca opened his mouth to protest, but the look in her eyes told him that he should let her go, so he said nothing.

Hana glanced at them for a final time before briskly making her way out of the cages. She left them in a silence that would haunt them for the rest of the night.

* * *

Sean's eyes darted to the door with uncertainty. It was nearly three in the afternoon; did Hana plan to never come back? He chewed hard on his bottom lip and tapped his foot impatiently.

Sean's uneasiness didn't go undetected by Chris. He tugged at Sean's sleeve to grab his attention. *Are you thinking about her?*

Sean's face flushed, embarrassed to have been caught. Chris grinned in amusement and carved another message into the ground.

Do you love her?

Sean's eyes widened at the question. "Of course not! I do like her as a person and I certainly respect and admire her, but to *love* her?"

Chris pursed his lips, disappointed that Sean still hadn't realized his feelings. Now it was true that they had only known Hana for a couple of weeks, but even he wouldn't turn a blind eye to the tight bond she had formed with each and every one of them.

Chris had trust issues. Sean had trust issues. Each and every person who was ever labeled with the word "Noye" had trust issues, yet Hana was so easily able to break down those barriers. Chris didn't understand how she was capable of slipping past the walls that protected their hearts, but it wasn't as troubling as he thought it would have been.

He was happy.

For the first time in a long time, Chris was happy. He was happy that the new female character was able to steal their hearts so easily.

He was happy for Sean.

Sean wouldn't admit it, for he probably didn't realize it yet himself, but Chris knew that the younger loved the girl. He assumed that Sean was in denial of his feelings because he would feel weak if he did accept them. Despite being the youngest, Sean was also the strongest, and falling for a girl within a mere few weeks was not strength. In Sean's eyes, it was a weakness and he didn't need any more weaknesses.

"What are you thinking about?" Sean asked as he nudged Chris gently on the shoulder.

Chris simply gave him a small smile. Sean frowned, unsatisfied with Chris's lack of response, and was about to speak in protest until he was interrupted by a familiar voice. Chris almost laughed at how eagerly Sean jumped to his feet; like a puppy greeting his master at the door.

"Sorry I'm late," Hana apologized with a shy smile as she stared cautiously at the boys, worried that her harsh words from the day prior were still lingering in their heads.

She was met with silence. She opened her mouth to give them a sincere apology, but was interrupted when a sudden figure ran into her.

"Haru?" Hana asked the boy who had his arms wrapped around her.

"I-I th-thought you we-were never c-coming b-ba-back!" Haru cried as he fisted the back of her shirt. The boy looked so torn that even Sean didn't mind the closeness of the two.

Hana cocked her head in confusion. "Why would you think that? I would never suddenly disappear without informing you guys."

"B-But yo-yo-you we-were-were an-ang-angry ye-yes-yest-yester-day-day!" Haru cried, his stuttering becoming twice as worse with the tears that rolled down his cheeks.

Hana clucked her tongue against the roof of her mouth, "Do you take me as somebody who would abandon you just because I was frustrated?"

Haru bit hard on his bottom lip and let out a loud sniffle. "N-No."

She pressed each of her fingers into the sides of Haru's mouth to pull his lips up into a smile. "Then you shouldn't cry."

Haru swiped at his eyes with the back of his dirty sleeve and nodded his head. His lips curved into a small smile of relief.

"Then you... you aren't angry with us anymore right?" Luca asked in a timid voice. He folded his hands behind his back and rocked on the balls of his feet.

Hana chuckled at the adorable sight and stretched upwards to dishevel the boy's bangs, "No, I am not angry anymore. It was unreasonable of me to throw this onto you all so quickly, so I apologize for that."

Aiden quickly shook his head, "Don't be sorry! It's not your fault!"

"Don't be mistaken, however," Hana clarified. "I'm not apologizing for my suggestion. I'm simply apologizing for the fact that I expected you all to jump on board right away, and that I got angry when you didn't."

"What do you mean?" Kai asked with a cocked head of confusion.

"I mean that I haven't dropped the idea just yet," Hana shrugged, ignoring the looks of disbelief that were thrown her way. "I don't want to argue, so I would suggest that you guys keep your words on this matter to yourself, or at least until I've departed for the day."

The Noyes exchanged uneasy glances, but abided by her words and kept their silence.

A smile broke across Hana's face and her eyes shaped into small crescents as she gazed at the boys in front of her. "Now then, who wants to try some of the pastries I've snuck in for you all?"

* * *

"Are you outside the school, Jaymes?" Hana asked as she tucked her phone between her ear and shoulder. It had been a few days since she had seen the Noyes, and was looking forward to their reunion. "I'll be outside soon, just wait a few more minutes."

She caught a glimpse of Dustin out of the corner of her eye and stopped mid-step, crouching over to pretend to tie her shoes while she secretly observed the other.

To her uttermost disappointment, it seemed like Dustin and his friends were deciding on which unlucky soul would be their next victim.

"How about Nathan? I didn't get to beat him to my heart's content since that dumb bitch had her body guard come," one of them snickered.

Dustin's eyes widened at the suggestion and he opened his mouth to protest, but quickly shut it, afraid of the taunts he would receive in return.

Hana sighed as she pushed herself off the ground - maybe some people were just incapable of changing.

"Hey guys, why don't we just go out and eat instead? My legs are aching from the laps Coach Hazlet made us run, and I could really use some burgers. What do you guys say? My treat?" Dustin spoke up finally, his eyes nervously darting around to observe the others' reactions.

Hana froze mid step as she processed his words. Her lips curved into a small smile of satisfaction and she glanced over her shoulder to get a look at Dustin's face. He was staring at them all with a hopeful expression, his hands curled into tight shaking fists at his sides.

"Your treat? Hell yeah I'm in!" his friends rooted in delight.

A wide, genuine smile spread across Dustin's face as he took a breath of relief. He raised his head and widened his eyes when he caught sight of Hana. She gave him a small wave and a bright smile, and he returned the action with the shy curve of his own lips. Dustin was taking things one step at a time, and in the end she knew he would be alright.

* * *

"Just one meeting left, right Jaymes?" Hana rubbed her weary eyes as she leaned her head against the car window. Her eyes fluttered to a close as she tried to enjoy the little rest she could receive before her presentation.

"Just one meeting, Miss Hana," Jaymes confirmed with a nod. He glanced at Hana through his review mirror, and softened at the exhausted state of the younger. "The meeting won't start for another twenty minutes, do you want me to drive in circles around the building so you can rest?"

Hana smiled at his kind suggestion and shook her head as she climbed out of the car, "No thanks, I have to set up for the presentation. President Merile said that there's going to be a businessman from China that'll be present, so I should be there early to greet him as well."

"Just bear with it for a little longer, Miss Hana. You'll be able to see your friends after this meeting is finished," Jaymes stated in an attempt to cheer her up. He got out of the car and locked the doors with his keys.

"Will you be attending as well?" Hana asked with brief surprise. Usually Jaymes would simply drop her off at the front of the building.

"I can't leave you all alone when you're this tired," Jaymes teased.

"I really don't deserve you, Jaymes," Hana chuckled lightly.

"I should say the same, Miss Hana," Jaymes grinned as he held the front door open for her.

"Miss Hana, the meeting will be taking place on the second floor," the secretary immediately greeted the pair with a bow. She snuck a peek at

Jaymes who was standing beside Hana, and flushed a bright red before quickly ducking her head.

"She likes you, you know," Hana smiled as the two climbed onto the elevator. She glanced up at her driver and nudged him with her elbow. "What do you think about her? She's very pretty."

"Is she?" Jaymes responded simply.

"Don't be like that," Hana chuckled as she turned forward. "You're almost about to hit your 30s, Jaymes, don't you think it's about time you found somebody to settle down with?"

"No."

Hana rolled her eyes. She immediately straightened out her face and stiffened her posture when the elevator doors slid open. Jaymes found that to be highly amusing, and stifled a chuckle. The two walked down the hallway until they arrived at the familiar meeting room.

"You think you can survive for another two hours?" Jaymes asked as he glanced down at the girl.

Hana scoffed under her breath, "I've been surviving my whole life, haven't I?"

"On the contrary, I think the boys have made you weak," Jaymes grinned as he pushed open the door to allow her to enter first.

"Ah, Ms. Acacia has arrived," President Merile announced as he greeted the girl at the door. "As punctual as always."

Hana shook his hand. "I thought I should arrive early to greet our foreign guest."

"Always so reliable," President Merile smiled as he clapped the girl on the shoulder. He was joined by another group of businessmen, all holders of important titles ranging from presidents to directors. "Ms. Acacia, this is President Zhou. He has been looking forward to your presentation, as we have all put you in very good words to him."

Hana gave him a small smile of gratitude before she turned to face the foreign stranger with an outstretched hand. "It's nice to meet you, President Zhou." She glanced upwards when her handshake wasn't returned, and stared at the frown that adorned his face.

"Why have you presented me with a young girl? Are you trying to waste my time?" President Zhou muttered angrily in Chinese to the man that stood beside him.

Hana's smile slipped just the slightest and she retracted her hand back to her side.

"I apologize, President Zhou. I will inform the other men that you wish to have the girl's presentation removed," the man responded quietly. He then turned to President Merile to translate the words in a hushed voice.

President Merile's smile slipped as he listened to the words whispered into his ears, and his eyes narrowed at the information. His eyes darted from Hana to the foreigner, as if debating who held a more meaningful position in his company. Hana clenched her jaw once she processed the apologetic look President Merile granted her, and watched as he opened his mouth to agree with the foreigner.

Jaymes stepped forward with narrowed eyes and interrupted in accented Chinese. "You seem to misjudging Miss Hana based on her age, President Zhou. Miss Hana is currently ranked as the top student at her school, and has already received offers of complete scholarships to the top universities around the world. She has been honored with a countless numbers of awards and international business deals, yet you ridicule her intelligence and capabilities because of mere –"

"Jaymes, that's enough," Hana spoke out firmly as she shot him a warning glance. Jaymes immediately pressed his lips together at the command, and bowed his head apologetically. She turned her glare to the men in front of her, sending shivers down each of their spines. Her seven years of Mandarin allowed her to flawlessly respond with, "I am fine with removing my presence from this meeting if that is what you'd prefer to happen. However, I should warn you that the information I was going to present would have been crucial to any future partnership that would have budded between your company and any other in this country."

Both President Merile and Zhou almost immediately realized the mistake they had made once the girl spun on her heels to leave.

"Girl, if you could speak Chinese why didn't you say so in the beginning? If this information is as important as you say it is, by all means, present!" President Zhou spoke in a state of slight panic.

"I'm seen as an insolent child in your eyes, aren't I, President Zhou? Then I will by all means act like one, and will not differentiate my personal concerns with my business matters," Hana stated in a clear and sharp tone.

"Ms. Acacia, please reconsider his miscalculated assumption, President Zhou—" President Merile uttered in an attempt to salvage what he could.

"President Merile," Hana cut in with a hard voice. "I had been meaning to pass a blind eye over the funds you have been sapping from Acacia Corporations under the guise of a "charity" due to the long relationship our companies have had with each other. Clearly your loyalty isn't up to par. You'll receive papers for a contract termination within a few days."

She began to make her way out of the room before stopping momentarily. She glanced over her shoulder and added in, "And a lawsuit," before continuing to make her exit.

"You certainly know how to make an exit," Jaymes humored as the pair made their way downstairs. His attempt to cheer her up was in vain, for Hana's mood was completely spoiled with the turn of events. "At least you will get to see the boys earlier now, Miss Hana."

Hana's mood lightened up. "Let's get going, alright Jaymes?" she sighed in a quiet voice as she climbed into the backseat of the car.

Jaymes nodded obediently as he shut the door behind her before making his way to the driver's seat.

Hana slipped off her shoes and pulled her knees up to her chest before wrapping her arms around them. She released a long and slow sigh as she leaned the side of her cheek against the caps of her knees.

That hadn't been the first time her abilities were underestimated because of her young age. Although she expected to be used to it by now, she simply wasn't.

As a child, Hana never had time to waste on normal juvenile things like playing tag with friends or dressing up dolls. While other kids stalled maturity with video games and water gun fights, her child hood had been the exact opposite. With no petty activities to stunt her mental growth, Hana had matured rapidly during the early years of her adolescence.

She would neither be accepted by the peers of her age because of her mental maturity, nor the adults because of her physical immaturity.

And it sucked, a lot.

The faces of the Noyes drifted into her mind and she unknowingly let her lips curve into a small smile. Maybe that was why she loved them to the extent of sacrificing her own life. Hana had found the place so many people searched for till white stemmed from the roots of their hair.

A place free of the judgments of society – free of stereotypes, of scornful glares of jealously. She found her place of acceptance, her home. A home, a true home, wasn't a place you had come from, but rather a place where you were wanted.

* * *

"What do you think you are doing?" Hana's voice came out tight and strained as she stared at the group before her.

She had arrived at the Noye House with high spirits, determined to desert all the negative energy that had spouted from earlier that day. Once she stepped into the cage, however, all positive thoughts immediately disappeared. Instead of seeing a group of happy faces, she was met with the sight of guards roughly restraining the Noyes.

Kai was sprawled out on the ground, loud growls emitting from his throat as two of the guards held him down. Sean and Aiden were shoved up against the walls with their arms twisted painfully behind their backs. Luca had attempted to shield Chris and had wrapped his arms protectively around the elder's shoulders as a guard gripped each of his arms tightly.

And then there was Haru, face as white as snow and bottom lip tucked into his mouth. He stood with his head hung in shame, tears rolling down his cheeks as Henry shouted profanity at him.

Hana had walked in just in time to hear the shouts of, "You're lucky we're even giving you this chance! Do you know how hard it was to get somebody to take in some stupid retard like you?"

He didn't get to shout anymore insults before he was interrupted by Hana's presence. Her blood ran cold and her body stiffened at the sight of the cruel treatment imposed on the people she held dear.

"I asked what the hell do you think you're doing?!" Hana shouted angrily, her voice climbing to a volume she had never reached before. All motion in the room froze at the echoing voice, shivers running down even the spines of the Noyes from the cold tone.

Henry was the first to snap out of his fright and he glared hard at the girl in front of him. "We're taking this retard to the dock. He knew this would happen if he didn't get rid of his stutter, so it's all on him that he hasn't gotten any smarter."

"Don't you dare insult Haru," Hana growled. She commanded the guards to release the boys. There was clear hesitance in their eyes, for they were unsure as to whether they should listen to her or the son of their boss. The decision was made when she snapped again, however, and they quickly fled the room with their tails between their legs.

Kai climbed to his feet and sprinted to Haru's side once he was released. He wrapped his arms tightly around the quivering smaller, and whispered words of reassurance into his ears. Haru fisted handfuls of Kai's shirt, streams of tears running down his cheeks.

"Come with me," Hana commanded as she stared at Henry. Her cold voice sounded almost unrecognizable to even her own ears.

"W-Why should I?" Henry bit back in a feeble attempt to maintain his dominance.

Hana answered him with a sharp glare and jerked her head towards the exit. She walked out without another word, Henry following reluctantly behind her. He flinched when Hana abruptly spun around to face him.

She took a long breath, calming herself down enough so she wouldn't lash out. "How much?" Hana asked in a calm tone. Truthfully, even she was surprised at how normal her voice sounded when she wanted nothing more than to rip his throat out. "How much are you selling Haru for?"

Henry scoffed with crossed arms. His confidence returned to him now that he knew Hana hadn't brought him somewhere to slaughter him.

"I'll pay you double," she continued. "So don't you dare sell Haru."

"Why the hell do you want him, anyways? The retard is pretty much useless – can't work, hell, can't even speak right!" Henry exclaimed incredulously. His breath was quickly knocked out of him when his back painfully hit the stone wall behind him.

"Don't insult Haru," Hana growled under her breath. The grip she held on his collar tightened and he gulped fearfully as she stared him down.

"W-What do you think you're doing? I thought yo-you were supposed to be a goody two shoes that says no to violence," Henry stammered slightly as he tried to salvage any masculinity he had left.

"I think you've misunderstood something. Did you honestly think that the way I treat the boys is the way I treat everyone? Don't you dare lay another finger on any of them again or I will smash your life to pieces, are we clear?" Hana stated in a low voice as she stared straight into his eyes.

Henry fell silent for a long period of time. Finally, he summoned up the courage to force a smirk onto his face, "You've been treating those Noyes with such kindness, but this is your true character, isn't it? Don't you think you've been too fake with all the things you've done for them? I know all about you, Hana Acacia. I know that you always try to lend a hand to those who are unfit to exist in society. Who do you think you are? Aren't you just a phony pretending to be an angel?"

A victorious smile spread across Henry's lips and he raised his eyes to meet Hana's, expecting to see her orbs swimming with self-doubt and cowardice. He was taken aback, however, to instead see pity and sympathy present in her eyes.

"So pitiful," Hana murmured as she stared straight into his eyes. "So pitiful and pathetic."

"W-What?" Henry exclaimed in a shrill tone, eyes wide with surprise from her ridiculous accusation. "Pathetic? How am I pathetic?!"

"You assumed that because my actions are what you consider as 'too kind', they must have been done with intent other than simple kindness, correct? So it's pitiful that both you and the people you've been exposed to are too selfish and greedy to extend a helping hand to those in need."

"The things I've done should be the natural instincts of all human beings, in which we should all want to help each other out; they're actions that we shouldn't have to think twice about enacting. These things that you've deemed to be "too kind" are things that should be commonly done in an ideal society. Therefore, I don't appreciate being called a fake just because I choose to separate my actions from the tainted social norm," Hana responded with a tight jaw and narrowed eyes.

Henry's jaw gaped slightly open as he soaked in the words the younger girl chided him with.

"You are pitiful, Henry, because you have become so accustomed to the dirtied society we live in that you can't believe that people would actually do things for others just because it's the right thing to do. You are pathetic because you hold all acts of kindness with suspicion, always looking for the ulterior motive," Hana continued, her breaths coming in short huffs. "And I feel sorry for you. I feel sorry for the way you must have lived in order to see everything with such a negative perspective.'"

"The reason why I might extend my kindness a little farther than others might is to make up for all the areas in our world that are lacking; for all the selfish, human trash like yourself," Hana's voice strained as she took one step away from him. "Because our society could do with a little less cruelty and a little more kindness, and these Noyes, no, these *people*, these human beings with beating hearts and blood pulsing through their veins... they're the first ones in line that deserve it."

"That's why I think you're pitiful," Hana concluded, so close to breaking into a batch of tears. Her emotions had gotten the better of her during her well needed rant, "And that's why I think you're pathetic."

Henry stared at her with a tensed jaw, his eye twitching at the sound of being called pathetic. Yet, despite how much her words infuriated him, he couldn't bring himself to argue. He knew she spoke truth in her words, and that simply made him even angrier.

Finally, he could stand it no longer and shoved her backwards to give himself enough space to stomp angrily away.

Hana let out a shaky breath as she ran her fingers through her hair. She leaned against the wall she had previously walked Henry against, and clutched at the cloth in front of her rapidly pounding heart. She didn't know where she had gotten the courage to say such words, but she was glad she did, for it felt as if a large burden had been taken off of her chest. Her lips curved slightly upwards and a soft laughter escaped her mouth.

She could breathe again.

A broken sob snapped her eyes open and she stared in surprise at the six boys standing before her.

"Haru...?" she asked slowly. "Why are you all here?"

Rather than replying, Haru broke into another round of tears as he ran forward to throw his arms around her shoulders. "Th-th-than-thank-nk y-you-you!" he choked out, clinging to her as if his life depended on it.

"Don't scare her," Kai chuckled as he pried the sobbing male off of her. He gave Hana a sincere, grateful smile as he took Haru into his arms.

"We kind of... followed you," Luca admitted as he scratched the back of his neck. "Just to make sure Henry wouldn't attack you or anything..."

"We heard what you said," Aiden spoke up, his eyes gleaming with affection and gratitude.

"Oh," Hana replied simply, suddenly feeling incredibly embarrassed from the stares she received.

"Let's do it," Sean stated suddenly. He was met with cocked heads and raised eyebrows, for they were confused at what he was referring to. He clarified, "The rebellion, let's do it."

Hana's eyes widened in surprise as she processed Sean's sudden words. "Are you... are you sure?"

"Yeah," Aiden slowly spoke up in continuation. "You said we're humans, right? So... so it's time that we're treated that way."

"It won't be easy," Hana warned as she stared at their eager faces. Her heart began to pick up in its beats as her mind processed the words that were being uttered before her.

"We know," Sean smiled as he wrapped his hand around Hana's to give it a comforting squeeze.

"You could die," Hana whispered quietly, her eyes wide with dread.

Her words were met with a long pause of silence.

"We know," Luca whispered as he leaned against Aiden who in turn wrapped a tight arm around the boy's shoulders.

"It might not end as a success," Hana continued with furrowed eyebrows, her eyes fluttering with a series of different emotions – worry, anticipation, nervousness, excitement.

"God Hana, you were the one who was all for it in the beginning, and now you're trying to persuade us out of it?" Aiden chuckled. "Make up your mind!"

"I just... I just want you all to know what you're getting into," Hana responded quietly as her eyes flittered from face to face.

"We know," Sean stated firmly. "We know what we're getting into. We know the sacrifices we're going to have to make, and the consequences that might occur as result. We know it all. But... you've been the one fighting for us all this time."

The corner of his lips twitched upwards as he stared straight into her eyes. "So now it's our turn."

CHAPTER FIVE: TREPIDATION

*trepidation [tre-pə-'dā-shən] n. - a feeling of fear that causes you to hesitate
because you think something bad or unpleasant is going to happen.*

"So... where do we start?"

A quiet pause filled the room as they all exchanged blank expressions.

"Maybe we should just wait until Hana comes?" Aiden suggested as he
scratched the back of his head. "I'm sure she has some good ideas for us."

Luca shook his head, "We can't rely on Hana to come up with
everything; we have to be able to take charge for once!"

"Okay, then what do you have in mind, Luca?" Kai asked with a raised
eyebrow and crossed arms.

Luca's smile slid off of his face and he slumped forward. "Nothing."

Chris suddenly began to write into the ground. The five other heads
bent over eagerly to see what suggestions the eldest had to offer.

We suck.

"You didn't need to tell us that," Luca muttered. "What do you think
Haru? You've been awfully quiet lately."

Haru nearly jumped out of his skin at the sudden acknowledgement
and his eyes darted around the room nervously as he cowered under their
gazes. "I-I-I do-do-don-don't-n't kn-kno-know any-thin-ing."

Kai sighed quietly as he wrapped his arm around the boy's shoulders.
"It's fine, Haru, you can say whatever you think."

Haru looked like he was about to cry.

"Excuse me?" a foreign voice interrupted their conversation and all six
heads turned to the new presence. "I'm Hana's driver, Jaymes."

"Is Hana here too?" Luca asked eagerly as he waited for the familiar
face to swing around the corner.

"Unfortunately I've come alone because I wanted to speak to you all in
private. Miss Hana will be coming at a later time," Jaymes answered as he
glanced around the room.

Aiden cocked his head curiously, "Why would you want to talk to us?"

"I've come to give both a warning and my gratitude," Jaymes answered
simply. "Which would you like first?"

The Noyes exchanged glances with each other.

"I... uh, the warning?" Luca asked with uncertainty.

Jaymes nodded his head, "Then I'll go right into it. Miss Hana... she has a different perspective than most. If at first impression she doesn't label you as what she likes to call beautiful, then you will never find a significant position in her eyes ever again. She believes that if you are beautiful, then everything you do and ever do will continue to be beautiful. You could murder a person and she would still attempt to find some sort of justification. And if you aren't, then everything you ever do will be held at a lower level. I don't blame Miss Hana for thinking in such a way, nor do I hold anything against her. However, it is this mindset that casted her on a path of loneliness since many people don't meet her unknown standards of beauty."

He strengthened the intensity of his gaze, and stared at each of them with hard, cold eyes. "I am telling you all this because I need to know where you stand. In Miss Hana's eyes, you have all been labeled as beautiful, and no matter what you do or say, Miss Hana will always try to find excuses for you. If any of you plan to take advantage of that, I will personally take care of you. This, this is my warning to you all."

A blanket of silence captured the room as they digested the words Jaymes had just exposed to them.

Kai wondered how it felt to possess such a mindset, to be able to force yourself to see the good in a person no matter what they were to do. He wondered if he would want such a trait – if it was a blessing or a curse.

Aiden was curious as to what exactly played as the main factor of beauty in Hana's eyes. He and all the other Noyes shared incredibly different qualities, from their looks to their personalities. What was it that made Hana decide the qualities of beauty?

Sean was scared. He was scared that one day he would disrupt that mindset of Hana's. He was afraid that one day, he might do something so horrible, *so painful* to the girl that she might just strip him of his title – that one day he might no longer be beautiful in Hana's eyes.

"And the thanks?" Luca asked meekly, breaking the silence.

The corners of Jaymes's eyes lifted and he let out a soft chuckle, "I wanted to thank you guys for allowing Miss Hana to abandon her road of solitude. Like I had stated earlier, her rather unique mindset almost automatically places her in a lonely position, for not many are honored enough to be seen as beautiful. It is because Miss Hana has acknowledged you all as pure hearted that she is capable of exchanging words and sharing her laughter with you all."

Jaymes climbed to his feet, "I will now be taking my leave. Miss Hana should be joining you in an hour or so, so I hope you all will spend this time to mull over the words I have left with you."

Aiden swallowed hard as he watched him leave, "He scares me."

The others nodded in agreement as they recalled the intense glare he had gazed at them with.

"He has a good heart, though," Luca sighed as he leaned his head against Aiden's shoulder. "He must care for Hana a lot."

Sean chuckled at his statement, "Anybody who meets her ends up caring for her a lot."

The others couldn't help but nod their heads in agreement.

* * *

Haru bit down hard on his bottom lip as he stared at the glass cup he had stolen from the kitchen. The other Noyes had been called in momentarily to help load boxes from the trucks and Haru was left alone in the cage to be swallowed up in his thoughts. Again.

The harsh words Henry had said flashed through his mind and Haru winced at the bitter pain that coursed through his veins. Haru didn't have a right to be angry with Henry, however, because he was right.

He was stupid. He knew that. Haru knew that he was one of the most stupid people to ever exist in the world and he knew that his existence was a mistake. That's why his parents decided to sell him, after all. He was the useless one, the one his family jumped at the chance to get rid of.

After all, who would want a stupid, stammering Noye like him?

No one.

"Haru? Where are the others?" Hana asked as she walked into the empty cage to see Haru standing alone in the middle.

The boy nearly jumped out of his skin at the sudden voice, and glass cup he had been holding dropped to the floor, shattering on impact.

"Haru! Are you injur—?" Hana asked as she glanced up at the boy. She was taken aback to see tears rapidly springing to his eyes. "Haru…?"

"I-I-I'm so-so-rry! I'm so-so st-tupid-pid a-and-and use-use-less. I-I ca-can-can't- d-do-do any-an-any-thing ri-righ-right! Pl-pleas-please-lease do-don't ha-hat-hate-ate m-me!" Haru sobbed; his heart breaking cries echoed against the walls of the cage.

"Haru, please don't cry!" Hana rushed forward frantically as she tried to wipe away the boy's tears. "You're not stupid at all, so please—!"

"L-Li-Lia-ar!" Haru screamed as he shoved her roughly away. She stumbled backwards in alarm, trying to think of what to do to console the boy that was breaking into pieces before her eyes.

"W-Wh-Why am-am-am I-I-I s-so stu-stup-stupid-pid?!" Haru screamed as he flailed his arms wildly in the air. His eyes darted crazily around the room before zeroing in on the broken glass at his feet. "I-I sh-

sho-shoul-ould j-jus-ust d-di-die!'"

Before Hana could react, Haru dived towards the ground to pick up a piece of the broken glass. "I sh-shou-shoul-ould d-di-die!"

"Haru!" Hana exclaimed in alarm as she shot forward to stop the boy from hurting himself. She grabbed onto his struggling wrists and tried desperately to pry his hands open. Blood began to seep from the broken skin of his palm.

"Please Haru, please stop it!" Hana cried frantically as she tried to get a strong grip on Haru's hands. She winced when the glass shard nicked her arm, but ignored the pain to solve more important matters. Finally, she got the piece to slip from his fingers and tumble onto the ground.

"N-No-No! St-Sto-Stop-op it-it! I-I ne-nee-need th-tha-that!" Haru screamed, his eyes captured by this delirious glint that sent shivers down Hana's spine. Before Haru could grasp a fresh piece of glass, Hana pushed him roughly to the ground, careful to evade the scattered glass. She wrapped her arms around his shoulders to prevent him from thrashing.

"It's alright, Haru. You're alright, everything's alright," Hana whispered in a calm voice as she rubbed his back soothingly. "You're not stupid, do you hear me? You're not stupid. Haru is not stupid, not even close. He's actually one of the cleverest boys I've ever met."

"Y-Y-You're-re a l-liar," Haru muttered in response.

"Have I ever lied to you before, Haru? I only speak the truth and you know that," Hana stated firmly as she continued to soothe the boy in her arms. "Who was the one who improved his speech in such a short amount of time? Haru. Who is the one Kai looks up to? Haru. Do you think Kai would have so much respect for somebody who's stupid? Do you think Kai is patient enough to put up with somebody who's stupid?"

There was a long pause before Haru responded, "N-No."

"That's right, he wouldn't. Yet he spends so much time with you, doesn't he Haru? What does that mean then?" Hana persisted.

"T-Th-That-at I'm-I'm… th-that I'm-I'm n-not st-stupi-pid-id," Haru hiccupped as he fisted the back of Hana's blouse. He cleared his throat and repeated himself, "Th-that I'm n-not stu-stupid."

"That's right, Haru," Hana smiled as she felt his heart begin to calm in its beats. "You aren't."

"I-I… Ha-Hana," Haru sobbed as he pressed his wet eyes into the crook of her neck. "I-I'm s-sorry!"

Hana climbed off of Haru and helped him sit up, "There's nothing to be sorry for, Haru. It's not your fault."

"What the hell happened in here?!" a sudden voice exclaimed.

"What are you yelling about Kai?" Aiden called out as he came running to his side, Luca, Sean, and Chris right on his tail.

"Nothing that can't be handled," Hana answered as she rubbed Haru's back comfortingly.

"I-It wa-was my-my faul-fault," Haru hiccupped as he slowly separated himself from the girl. He stared at his hands, ashamed. "I-I'm so-sorry."

"There's so much blood!" Kai exclaimed as he rushed forward. He took Haru's face into the palms of his hand and stared at him with frantic eyes. "Where are you hurt?"

"He cut his hands," Hana spoke up as she quickly hid her arms behind her back. "Please tend to them, Kai."

"You have a lot of blood on you, are you hurt too Hana?" Luca asked as he rushed forward to inspect the girl.

Haru's eyes widened at the words and his breath hitched up at the thought of injuring her from his stupidity.

"No, that isn't the case," Hana quickly reassured the other. "This is just Haru's blood, I wasn't injured." She turned and gave Haru a smile of reassurance, "Let Kai tend to your wounds right away, okay?"

Haru nodded his head, and followed Kai to the corner where they stashed the first aid kit. He was relieved to know that he hadn't caused the girl any injuries and managed to calm down.

"I'll go call Jaymes to bring more supplies," Hana stated as she climbed to her feet. She quickly walked out of the room before any of them could question her. After sending Jaymes a quick text, she pulled up her sleeves to examine the minor wounds she had received.

Hana registered the sound of footsteps, and quickly pulled down her sleeves. She felt a presence behind her once the footsteps halted, and glanced over her shoulder to see who it was.

"What the hell do you want?" she growled, her eyes immediately narrowing at the sight of Henry.

His eyebrows were furrowed in a never before seen expression of concern, "I… I heard the little one's outburst."

"Happy you caused him that much mental anguish, are you?" Hana snapped as she tossed him a sharp glare.

"No, goddammit! Just let me talk!" Henry exclaimed as he threw his arms up in the air with exasperation.

"What are you trying to do to her?" a cold voice cut across the air and the pair turned their heads to see Sean coming down the hallway. Sean trained his intense glare onto Henry until he was stationed protectively in front of Hana. "Get the hell away."

Henry opened his mouth to protest, but ended up pressing his lips together reluctantly. He glanced at her one last time before leaving, and she stared at him with furrowed eyebrows. Exactly what had he wanted to say to her? Was it really remorse that she had detected in his tone? Could it be that she might have been wrong about Henry? Just the slightest bit?

No, she decided, that was impossible. Hana was never wrong when it came to judging a character.

She was taken away from her thoughts when Sean stepped in front of her. Her eyes raked up his body to meet his gaze and she flinched from the intensity of it. "Are you going to call me an idiot?"

Sean barked, "Are you trying to joke right now?"

"It didn't lighten the mood, so no," Hana responded with a weak smile. "You know I couldn't have revealed my injuries in there."

"I know, but you could have at least whispered it to one of us!" Sean exclaimed with frustration. "How badly hurt are you?"

"It's just shallow flesh wounds," Hana reassured him.

He pulled some bandages out of his pocket and fumbled with the opening. "I managed to sneak some out when Haru wasn't looking."

"Wow, my hero," Hana chuckled quietly.

Sean gave her a pointed look before holding out the palm of his hand, "Arms."

Hana held out her arms obediently, and waited patiently as Sean carefully wrapped the bandages around her injuries.

"Goddammit, why is this so fucking hard?!" Sean exclaimed as he stared at his messy wrapping. He grumbled under his breath and unwrapped them all to start over.

Hana wanted to tell him that it was rather unsanitary to do so after they were already tainted with blood, but kept her lips pressed together.

"This will have to do till later," Sean muttered under his breath as he stared at his messy bandaging. It was better than the first time, but still nowhere near perfection. "Just get someone else to do it; they'll do it a lot better than me."

"Why? I think it looks fine?" Hana cocked her head as she examined her bandaged arms.

"Idiot, are you blind?" Sean scoffed as he rolled his eyes. He still couldn't help the light color that flushed onto his cheeks, however. "C-Call Jaymes already and tell him to come get you."

"I already sent him a message," Hana smiled. "Thank you for your help, Sean. I feel better already!"

"Better my ass," Sean muttered under his breath. He rubbed the back of his neck. "Yeah, well, just… remember to get that treated."

He stared at her with a gentle expression, and spoke in a soft voice,

"Hana? Just… just be careful."

* * *

A week passed, and news of the revolt spread like fire among the other Noyes. Some began to see the lights of hopes in their lives again, while many others disregarded the news with no such optimism. Freedom? Such a word no longer existed in their vocabularies.

Hana was far beyond busy, and no longer had the time to spend her hours talking with the others. The Noyes didn't have too much time to spend being upset, however, for they too were playing their own roles in the rebellion.

"How are we even going to do this?" Kai whispered as he stared at the faces of his fellow Noyes. There was an edge of excitement to his voice, but it was practically hidden under the large amount of nervousness. "There are so many things that we need – how can we get it all?"

"You don't have to worry about that," Hana assured the other. "Just work on spreading the word to the other Noyes around here – mind who you tell – and I'll pull everything else together. I know people who can get us the things that we need."

"But I thought you don't have friends?" Luca asked with a cocked head. He quickly realized the carelessness of his words and clarified, "I mean, not that you're not desirable or anything."

"I don't have friends," Hana agreed. There was a mischievous glint in her eyes and her lips slipped into a slight smirk, "But that doesn't mean I don't have connections."

* * *

"You know how risky this is, Hana?" Adrian, also known as lawyer Hayes, whispered to the girl as they sat together in his office.

Adrian was eight years older than Hana. The two had become acquaintances as children because their fathers used to be good friends. After Adrian's family saw a sudden bankruptcy, however, Chando had broken all ties with his old friend of 15 years.

Hana and Adrian certainly weren't friends, but she knew they had the same ideals in life. In order to survive after bankruptcy, Adrian's younger brother had been sold as a Noye. He died three years later from being physically abused by the master who had purchased him. It was because of this that Adrian became a lawyer.

"I know," Hana replied calmly. "You know it's risky as well, but you're still going to help me."

Adrian raised an eyebrow at the girl's confidence, and leaned back in his leather chair with crossed arms. "How are you so sure, Hana?"

"Isn't this what Caleb would have wanted?" Hana responded curtly.

Adrian's jaw tensed at the sound of his deceased brother's name and he took a deep, shaky breath. "What do you need me to do?"

The corners of Hana's lips curved into a smile and she beamed at the man in front of her. "Just some legal work. I want you to look into the Noye rebellion that happened. Get in touch with some lawyers to see what legal measures are being taken. You don't have to be involved in any dirty work, Adrian, I just need enough information to be assured that this rebellion won't go to waste after it has taken place."

Adrian nodded his head in agreement. He knew a few lawyers who were involved with the case, so his role wouldn't be too hard to complete.

"Thank you, Adrian," Hana stated quietly with a sincere expression on her face. She got up from her seat and bided him goodbye before heading to the door. She was just about to turn the knob when Adrian's voice interrupted her. "Hana?"

"You do know what will happen if you get caught, don't you?" Adrian asked quietly, his voice swimming with insecurity.

Hana's grip on the doorknob tightened and she turned to him with a tense smile. "Don't worry, I won't tell anybody that you were involved."

Adrian sighed and massaged his temples once the girl closed the door behind her. "Idiot," he muttered under his breath as he gazed at the framed photo of him and Caleb on his desk.

Adrian picked up the frame, and gently caressed the glass covered face of his younger sibling with his thumb. "I'll do this for you, Caleb."

* * *

Hana didn't even flinch when a hand suddenly shot out in front of her, preventing her from leaving her classroom. She glanced over at the arm's owner, and raised an eyebrow at the bruised and beaten Dustin that was standing next to her. She eyed the man from head to toe and a small frown slipped onto her face, "What happ—"

"Dustin, I'll wait for you outside, okay?" Nathan called out from down the hallway.

Hana glanced over Dustin's shoulder, and was taken aback to see Nathan in a similar state. Realization dawned upon her and she stared proudly at Dustin, "You've done well."

Dustin flushed at her praise and scratched the back of his neck in embarrassment until he remembered what he had approached the girl to talk about. "Hana, I heard from Adrian."

The smile that had been on Hana's face immediately slipped off and she stiffened at the boy's words. Her eyes glanced from side to side, and after seeing no other students in the hallways she deemed it safe enough to respond, "I thought I told Adrian not to tell a soul?"

"Don't look like that, he only told me and he won't tell anybody else. He knew that I talked to you occasionally, and wanted me to persuade you to change your mind," Dustin explained. His eyes flashed with worry. "Hana, I owe you a lot, and I really do think of you as one of my friends. I know it isn't my place to say anything, but please don't do it."

"If you know it's not your place, then don't over step your boundaries," Hana snapped back in a cold tone. Hana's face softened when she registered the hurt expression that flashed onto Dustin's face, but kept her stern tone, "You fought for what you believed was right, Dustin, so don't try to stop me from doing the same."

"Why?" Dustin called out right as Hana was about to turn the corner.

Hana paused for a few seconds as she thought over his words. She glanced over her shoulder and gave him a small smile, "For the same reason you were willing to get beat up for Nathan."

"I don't understand," Dustin responded with furrowed eyebrows. He jogged down the hallway to catch up with her, "Please, explain it to me."

Hana paused, "What is Nathan to you?"

"Nathan?" Dustin asked with raised eyebrows. He paused for a few seconds before a gentle expression formed on his face, "Nathan is… Nathan is the only person that I can truly act like myself around. He's like a home… if a home could take the form of a person, anyways."

"And why did you finally tell people that he was your brother despite knowing the consequences?" Hana continued patiently.

"I guess… I guess I was tired of Nathan getting hurt by the stupid actions of the people around me. I wanted it to be better for him, even if it did mean that I'd likely get beat up. I wanted him to be happy, and… and I wanted to be happy too," Dustin replied thoughtfully.

Hana gave him a satisfied smile and patted him gently on the shoulder.

"Wait, you haven't said anything. Where are you going?" Dustin called out in protest when Hana turned around to leave.

"Don't you already know the answer? You said it all yourself," Hana responded as she turned the corner, not giving the other a second glance.

CHAPTER SIX: VICISSITUDE

vicissitude [və-ˈsi-sə-ˌtüd] n. - a change of circumstances or fortune, typically one that is unwelcome or unpleasant.

Hana staggered backwards at the sudden weight that clamped onto her body the second she set foot inside the familiar cage.

"Hana! It's been so long!" Aiden whined as he practically swallowed the girl with his tall height.

"You look tired," Sean frowned as he brushed the dark circles underneath Hana's eyes. "You're overworking yourself, aren't you?"

A small smile slipped onto Hana's face and she poked his arm teasingly, "Are you worried for me, Sean?"

"Of course I am, idiot," Sean muttered. "How could I not be?"

His words caught Hana by surprise. She had expected him to strongly deny her teasing accusation, and maybe even flush a light color of red, but definitely not to agree with her.

"Why do you look like that? I'm not that cold hearted, you know," Sean muttered as he gently bumped her with his elbow.

"What is this? What is this I see?" Luca grinned as his eyes darted between Hana and Sean. "Aiden, are my eyes deceiving me or is Sean actually being an affectionate puppy to Hana?"

Aiden rolled his eyes at the description Luca used. "Puppy my ass. He's more like a grumpy mutt." Sean shot him a sharp look and he quickly side stepped behind Luca to use him as a human shield.

Hana rolled her eyes at their childish antics and turned to Kai, "How have the other Noyes reacted to the news you've spread?"

"There are mixed results," Kai answered after a brief silence.

"What do you mean?" Hana asked with a raised eyebrow.

"I mean…" Kai started uneasily. "Most of the Noyes here haven't just been here for a few months, you know. Most of us have been here for years… and after years of cruelty and harsh living conditions, you kind of just… you kind of just stop hoping – for anything. Hana, you've only been exposed to Noyes like us, but most of them… most of them… they can't even smile anymore. "

Silence consumed the room as they all thought over Kai's words. People could only hold on to their hope for so long; especially when you were labeled with the title of a Noye.

"But there have been some sparks of interest!" Luca quickly added in once he caught the dejected look on Hana's face. "It's not a total wash. I didn't expect everybody to jump on board right away – I mean, we didn't. This kind of thing takes time, you know? A lot of time."

"A lot of time is something we don't have," Hana shook her head. She opened her mouth to continue, but was interrupted by a quiet knock. She and the other Noyes turned to the front door to see half of a face staring back at them, the rest of his body mostly hidden behind the door.

"H-Hi," the male spoke quietly, his visible eye darting around the room to gauge their reactions. The others exchanged looks with one another before training their attention onto him.

"Hello to you as well," Hana smiled warmly as she stepped towards the stranger. "What brings you here?"

"I… I wanted to help you," the boy murmured in a voice so soft Hana had to strain her ears to hear.

Hana arched an eyebrow, wondering exactly what the male had come to propose. "Help with what?"

"Your plans," he answered as he slowly stepped into the room to reveal his entire appearance. He was relatively short in height, and had disheveled red hair and hazel colored eyes to match. He glanced bashfully down at the ground as he kicked the dirt at his feet. "I wanted to help you with the rebellion."

Hana, as well as the other Noyes were surprised at the words he spoke. They hadn't expected anybody to actually offer their aid in something as dangerous as a plotting a rebellion.

"Who are you?" Luca asked with an arched eyebrow of suspicion.

"My… my name is Chase," the boy responded bashfully as he rubbed his arm. He glanced up at them with round, hopeful eyes. "I live in the cage next door, and… and I've heard some of your plans."

"You mean you've been eavesdropping?" Kai scoffed.

"Oh get off it," Aiden rolled his eyes as he nudged Kai with his elbow. "The walls are gaping bars. He would hear us even if he didn't want to."

Chase glanced gratefully at Aiden for coming to his defense. "Would… would you mind an extra helping hand?"

"You know what will happen to you if you get caught, right?" Sean asked with narrowed eyebrows. He wanted to be completely sure that the new comer knew exactly what he was getting into.

Chase nodded, "I know, I've heard everything you all have said."

"Maybe we should be a little more discreet," Luca murmured.

"You don't need to worry, we don't have any neighbors until you move a few cages down. It's just me in mine," Chase reassured him.

"Just you? Why haven't we ever noticed you?" Kai asked.

"I... I keep to myself, most of the time," Chase murmured quietly as he fiddled with his thumbs. "I don't... I don't really like interacting with other people."

"Why are you choosing to talk to us now?" Kai asked cautiously.

"I... From what I've heard you are all very good people," Chase smiled shyly. "I want you guys to succeed."

Aiden glanced at Luca at those words, who then glanced at Haru, who glanced at Kai, and so on and so forth until Hana finally trained her gaze on the new male. She smiled warmly, "We'd be happy to have you."

Chase's eyes lit up at her words, and a small squeak of excitement escaped his lips. He flushed a bright red from embarrassment at the sound, and gave them all a shy, thankful smile for accepting him.

Chris patted the ground beside him to signal Chase to sit down. The other male eagerly complied, happy that he had gained some acceptance.

How old are you?

"I... I'm not sure," Chase admitted as he scratched the back of his head. "Maybe 22 or 23? I've lost track of the days."

Chris nodded his head understandingly; many Noyes eventually forget meager details such as dates and hours when stuck in a place for so long.

How long have you been a Noye?

"Only... maybe two or three months, now?" Chase murmured as he scratched his head. "It wasn't very long ago."

"Only two months and you've already lost track of the days?" Aiden laughed. "Man, you must have an even worse memory than me!"

"Ah... it's not really that," Chase murmured with flushed cheeks, "I... I haven't really been keeping track of the days for a long time now."

The cage fell silent at his words, some because of sympathy and others because of confusion.

"Why not?" Aiden asked as he scratched his head. "How do you not keep track of the days? Don't you need to live?"

Chase flushed an even darker red at his words and he clamped his lips together with no sign of continuing.

"Great job, idiot," Luca muttered under his breath as he smacked Aiden on the back of his head. "You really have no social skills."

Aiden pouted at the scolding and mumbled a quiet sorry to Chase before proceeding to sulk in the corner.

"I have to go, but I'll see you all later," Hana stated after a quick glance at her watch. "Don't overwork yourselves."

"Like you're one to talk," Kai scoffed with a smile.

"Stay safe," Sean whispered into her ear. He wrapped one arm around the dip of her waist and held her tightly in his grasp.

"You too," Hana smiled as she gave his upper arm a small squeeze. Her dainty fingers lingered on his bare skin for a few seconds before she pulled away. Hana waved everybody else a goodbye before departing. Sean traced his fingertips against the burning skin she had touched; he was already longing for the next time he would see her face.

* * *

"You seem rather happy, Miss Hana," Jaymes stated as he glanced at the smiling girl from his rear view mirror. "Did something happen?"

"A boy came to us today; he offered to help out with the rebellion," Hana answered. Her eyes gleamed, "I think we have a real shot at this."

A small smile appeared on his own lips. Hana's heart was simply too large.

"Jaymes," Hana spoke up with alarm. "Are those men beating that student? The student with the same uniform as mine?"

Jaymes slowed the car and glanced out the window to see what Hana was talking about. "Would you like me to intervene, Miss Hana?"

"Yes, Jaymes," Hana stated through gritted teeth. "How cowardly of them to gang up on a single person."

Jaymes nodded as he pulled the breaks on the car. He loosened his tie and unbuttoned the cuffs of his suit before climbing out of car.

"Jaymes, wait," Hana spoke up before he could take a step forward.

He glanced back at Hana to see her staring at the victim of the fight. He recognized the expression Hana had on, and knew she was running through her memory to see where she had seen that face before. Jaymes then turned to look at the victim himself and he stared for a few seconds before the light bulb lit up. He remembered that face as one he had beaten up himself, back when Hana had requested for his aid to defend her schoolmate Nathan.

Sure enough, Hana soon whispered under her breath, "He's tainted." She immediately straightened herself up, and stared forward without sparing the group a second glance. "Let's go home, Jaymes. There's work that needs to be done."

Jaymes climbed back into the car without hesitation as he started up the engine once again. It would have taken no more than five minutes for Jaymes to have beaten the amateur fighters to the ground, but he wouldn't disobey Hana's orders.

He glanced with uncertainty at the group of men but drove away nevertheless. He had to correct himself. Miss Hana's heart definitely was rather large, but there was a set standard as to who qualified to receive such kindness.

And unfortunately for him, that child hadn't made the cut.

* * *

Hana frowned when she returned to a half empty cage. "Where are Haru, Kai, and Sean?" she asked.

Luca bit down on his bottom lip, "Haru… got into one of his moods again. Sean and Kai went to try to calm him down."

Hana frowned at the information she was given and her eyes flickered towards the door of the cage. "He's not getting any better, is he?"

Luca quickly denied her words in an attempt to raise her mood, "No, no, he's starting to get better. The progress is slow, but he's getting better. It's just that the words Henry had told him… they weren't exactly lines you could forget overnight."

"Hana."

Hana's head whipped over when a familiar voice called her name. A smile spread across her face at the sight of Sean leaning against the frame of the doorway. A similar smile lit up the Noye's face and he moved forward to engulf her into a hug.

"H-H-Hana?" Haru stammered as he appeared at the front of the cage with Kai beside him.

Hana's ears perked up at the voice and she quickly moved to the door to greet him. Sean frowned for a split second as to how short his reunion was, but smiled contently to himself as he sat down next to Chris.

"It's been hard on you, hasn't it?" Hana whispered quietly as she engulfed the other into a tight hug.

Haru buried his face into her long hair, and sniffled as he gave her a curt nod. Hana glanced up at Kai and offered him a kind smile as a greeting. The other cracked a smile back and patted her on the shoulder. He was happy that Hana was there, for Haru was always much calmer with the presence of the girl.

"Has Henry interfered with anything?" Hana asked Kai in a hushed voice once Haru had released her.

Kai shook his head. "Actually, it was the exact opposite. There were these guards that were trying to pick on Haru," Kai explained, his eyebrows furrowing at the memory, "But Henry told them to knock it off. He even asked Haru if he was alright, afterwards."

Hana frowned at the information she had been relayed. What exactly was Henry trying to play at? She knew people couldn't change that easily overnight, so his sudden display of kindness was suspicious. "Be cautious around him until we know what he is after," Hana warned him.

Kai nodded his head immediately, "You don't have to tell me that."

The pair exchanged another look before joining the other Noyes.

"Before we can continue on as planned, it seems that there's a rather large road block in our path," Hana spoke up.

"Which is?" Aiden asked with a raised eyebrow.

"We need to get our hands on a map of the Noye house," Hana answered. "Unfortunately, the blue prints are kept hidden from the public eye. Even I wouldn't be able to get a glance at such a thing."

"So what are we going to do?" Kai asked.

"We're going to be making our own," Hana smiled mischievously as she withdrew several items from her sack. She handed each of the Noyes a small notebook along with several pencils. "From now on, wherever you go, you must document everything you see in these books. Make estimations as to how far apart buildings are, which hallways lead to which rooms, and so on. This will be a rather rough sketch, but it's the best we can come up with as of now."

The Noyes nodded their heads obediently. It would be complicated to document everything without attracting attention from the other Noyes or guards, but it would still be possible.

"Make sure that you proceed with caution. It's easy to get caught, and if your notebook is confiscated, you'll be punished," Hana stated uneasily. "I've gotten started on my own draft of the area, but there are still a lot of places missing." She pulled out a large paper from her bag, and unfolded the blueprints to show them what she had done so far.

"When did you have the time to look at all of this?" Aiden whispered in amazement as he traced his finger down the familiar hallways.

"I have a good memory," she shrugged. She paused for a few seconds and smugly added, "And Jaymes may or may not have hacked some of the security cameras."

"You are literally my new idol," Aiden murmured in awe.

"There aren't very many cameras, however, so there are still a lot of chunks missing," Hana continued. She wrapped the sketch back up and tucked it safely into her bag.

With a glance down at her watch, Hana figured that it was about time to leave. Her father certainly hadn't been giving her kind looks these past few days for her late returns, knowing that her tardiness was because of the Noyes. As if right on cue, her phone vibrated in her pocket to signal that Jaymes had arrived and was waiting outside. As she climbed to her feet, she felt a light tug on the hem of her dress.

Sean opened his mouth to say something, but hesitantly closed it once more. He let go of the fabric and averted his eyes, "It's nothing, sorry."

Hana nodded, and waved them goodbye as she left the cage. She was about to climb up the staircase to leave the floor until the call of her name and pounding footsteps sounded in her ears.

She was taken aback when a pair of arms engulfed her tightly from behind. Her body tensed for a few seconds, but she relaxed once she processed the familiar scent of – "Sean?"

"When this is all over," Sean stated as he shyly pressed his forehead against the back of Hana's head. "If this ends up being a success and we're all free… even if we're free… can we still stay with you?"

Hana's heart warmed from Sean's question, and the corners of her lips unconsciously curved upwards. "You don't want to leave?"

"No," Sean responded firmly. "I want to be with you."

A few seconds of silence passed and Sean quickly realized how bold his words had been. "I-I mean, I mean only if you want us. I can't really speak for Chris but I'd really like it if I could stay by your side for a long time. I-I mean, I don't really have any advantages but I wouldn't be too much of a pain and I'd try to stay as quiet as possible and I'd do my best to protect you and –," Sean rambled on from embarrassment.

He was cut off when Hana suddenly turned around. She cupped the boy's face with her small palms, "I'd like it if you two were by my side as well." She tilted the boy's face down, and tip-toed to press her lips against the taller's forehead, sealing the unspoken promise with a kiss.

Sean's entire face was bright red by the time she pulled away, but there was still a silly grin stretched across his face.

"Bye, Sean," Hana smiled as she gave the boy another small wave before making her way up the stairs and out of the Noye building.

Hana was met with a grim faced Jaymes and she immediately knew that the news he was about to deliver certainly wasn't positive.

"Your father wishes to see you the second you arrive home," Jaymes informed her as she climbed into the car.

"Is it about the Noyes?" Hana asked cautiously.

Jaymes nodded his head and his grip on the steering wheel tightened. "He's not happy."

Hana exhaled a deep breath, "I haven't assumed that he has been."

"It's serious, Miss Hana. I haven't seen him this furious in quite a while," Jaymes responded with a concerned expression. He furrowed his eyebrows as he recalled the livid state her father had been in when he had demanded for Jaymes to pick her up.

"It was about time," Hana responded calmly. She knew her façade fooled neither one of them, for on the inside, her heart was beating too fast to be normal. The ride home ended much too quickly for her liking and Hana took a deep, steady breath before finally climbing out of the car.

"I'll be right at your side," Jaymes whispered reassuringly. "Stay calm, you know he will take it out on the others if he's angered even more."

"Pretending to keep calm is one of my talents, Jaymes," Hana gave him a dry smile. "You know that."

Jaymes gave her one last look before he pushed open the doors to enter the house. The entire mansion was quiet and Hana squeezed Jaymes's hand a final time for a boost of confidence.

"You're home," Chando announced in a flat voice.

Hana forced a smile onto her face and greeted her father with a nod of acknowledgment, "Yes, just as you've requested, father."

"I assume you understand why I had Jaymes fetch you?" Chando asked with a raised eyebrow. He smiled with satisfaction when Hana answered with a soft yes. "Good, I will discuss this with you later. Good night."

With those as his final words, he departed up the stairs and down the hallway to his master bedroom.

Hana stared blankly, her heart beating twice as fast as it had before.

Jaymes relaxed, "Well that went rather smoot—"

"He's planning something."

"What?" Jaymes asked with raised eyebrows of confusion. "What do you mean he's planning something?"

"He's planning something, I know it," Hana responded. "I recognize that face, that tone of voice – he's planning something."

Jaymes frowned at her words, "What do you think it is?"

"I'm not sure," Hana whispered. "But it's not going to be good."

* * *

Hana decided the next day that it wouldn't be safe to visit the Noye house. Instead, she sent Jaymes to inform them of her absence, and that she would visit them as soon as she got the chance to. She spent the entire day attending meetings and finishing up all the work that had piled up over the last few days, making sure to send her father hourly updates.

"Do you think he's calmed down?" Hana asked uneasily as she stepped out of the car. She glanced up at the seemingly peaceful house before her, and dreaded the thought of her father waiting on the inside.

"I haven't seen him the entire day, but when I had spoken to him over the phone he seemed relatively calm," Jaymes answered as he walked beside her. He patted her reassuringly on the shoulder. "There's nothing you've done today that could have increased the anger of your father."

"You've sent him the project advancements, right?" Hana asked as they slowly ascended the front steps of her home.

"Yes," Jaymes confirmed. "Every one of them. He seemed rather happy with the progress."

Hana nodded her head in relief. "Do you know if he's home?" Hana asked as she removed her shoes after entering the house. "Perhaps I'll offer to meet him out for dinner or something. I think he'd like that."

"From his schedule, it doesn't look like he's left the house at all," Jaymes answered. "He's probably upstairs in his study."

"Will you go see him? Make sure to mention that I'm about to finish the project for President Cayetano right now." She frowned as she listened to the subtle thwacking coming from somewhere in the house. "Before that, could you ask whoever is making that sound to quiet it down a little? I think the gardeners are finally taking down that oak tree in the back."

"Sure thing," Jaymes smiled as he gave her a two fingered salute. He gestured up the stairs and jokingly ordered her to get to work before he left to find the source of the disturbance.

She wasn't all too happy that she hadn't gotten to see the boys today, but it was a sacrifice she was willing to make as long as she could keep them safe. Although she wouldn't like to admit it, the person she feared most in the entire world was actually her father. Her father was a powerful man politically, and it was the reputation he built that allowed her great leverage over other competitors. She sighed as she entered her room.

"Just a little more," she whispered quietly to herself. Just a little more until they could start the first steps of the rebellion. Just a little more until she'd be able to see their warm faces on a daily basis, free from the dirt and grime that caked their skin, free from the timely constraints of her father, free from the cold air that circulated the metal cages.

"Miss Hana, I'm coming in." Jaymes flung the door open.

His eyes were wide with horror and he was slightly out of breath from the sprint he had made to her room.

Hana stared at him with surprise, "What is it, Jaymes?"

"Your father brought them here," Jaymes cried as he wrapped his hand around the girl's wrist to yank her forward.

"What are you talking abo..." Hana's voice trailed off. "Sean? Is that who you mean? Sean and Chris?" Her chest constricted when Jaymes nodded his head, and she immediately tore out of her bedroom.

"Where, Jaymes?!" she demanded as she sprinted down the staircase, nearly tripping over the last few steps. "Where are they?! What is he doing to them?!"

Jaymes fell silent before quietly responding, "The noise."

Hana froze mid step and her head whipped around to stare at Jaymes in horror. "The... noise?" she repeated dryly, her arms falling limply at her sides as she processed the underlying meaning to those words.

"They're in the workhouse in the backyard," he nodded his head, giving her a light push forward to get her moving.

Hana had never sprinted faster in her entire life. She shoved the maids out of her way, not even sparing the time to toss apologetic expressions over her shoulder. The whipping sounds pounded in her ears, growing louder as she neared the workshop her father had created in the backyard many years ago. She nearly ripped the door off of its hinges as she entered, her eyes widening with devastation at the sight before her.

"Touch them again and I'll kill you," Hana let out a growl so low it sounded as if it had come from another person. Her fists curled at the sight of the puddles of blood that dripped onto the ground and her entire body began to tremor.

"Hana," Sean whispered in a hoarse voice, a small smile spreading across his face as he used all of his remaining power to lift his head.

Chris was at his side, his back a raw red from the whip. His arms were twisted awkwardly over his head as a pair of metal cuffs chained his hands to the roof. His once delicate face was covered in dried tears.

"Ah, Hana, you've arrived home, have you?"

Hana slowly turned around to the sound of her father's voice. She stared at him with pure hatred, the only thoughts going through her head consisted of how much she wanted to murder the man on the spot.

"Why?" she asked in a quiet voice, worried that she would break into a rampage if she were to say any more. "Why did you do this?"

"To teach them a lesson," he shrugged nonchalantly. "And to teach you a lesson." He glanced over her shoulder to examine the state of the Noyes, and nodded his head approvingly. "You may go now; you will receive your bonus on your way out." The man who had been in charge of the torture placed the whip down at his side before nodding to Chando. As he walked out, he gave a rough kick to Sean's torso for good measure, smirking pointedly at Hana as he passed.

She made sure to engrave his face into memory.

"It looks like now won't need to waste your time at that dump anymore, now will you?" Chando smiled victoriously with crossed arms.

He nearly snarled his next words, "Take this as a warning, Hana. Visit that place again and you'll find your other *precious* Noyes in a similar state."

Hana's heart clenched tightly in her chest, and a flood of angry words threatened to break down the walls of her restraint. She knew her father well, and the one thing she knew best was that he never made empty threats. She dug her nails into the palms of her hands to let out some of the overflowing anger. Hana waited until she heard the fading footsteps of her father, not wanting to give him the satisfaction of seeing her break down.

"He's gone," Jaymes whispered quietly as he appeared at her side. "I'll call the doctors right away."

That was enough to prompt her to sprint forward to examine the condition of the two. Her mind entered a state of frenzy when she got a look at how much blood had been lost and she dropped to her knees to cup Sean's face gently into the palms of her hands. She couldn't even apologize, for such feeble words could do nothing to relieve his pain.

Hana didn't have to say anything, for Sean understood how sorry she truly was from simply looking at her face.

"Don't cry, please," Sean whispered as he reached out to wipe the tears that Hana unknowingly shed. "Please."

"I'm not crying," Hana responded as she stared into the eyes of the male. He was rather good at withholding his expressions of pain after building up endurance from his experience, but his mask wasn't strong enough to deceive her. "I'm not."

Sean's cracked lips stretched into a small smile, "You…y-you lied. G-Guess you can't say… can't say that you always speak the truth any-anymore."

The only sound that echoed through the four walls of the room was the shattering of Hana's heart.

CHAPTER SEVEN: VICTORY

victory [vik-tore-ee] n. - success in a struggle or endeavor against odds or difficulties

It had been seven days.

Seven days since Chris and Sean had suffered such a harsh and unjust treatment.

Seven days since Hana had visited the Noye house.

Seven days since Hana had lost even the tiniest fragment of respect she had left for the man she called father.

"You need to rest," Sean's voice jolted her out of her thoughts and she turned to see the other attempting to sit up in his bed.

"I should say the same to you," Hana chided softly as she moved to help Sean sit properly.

"I have been resting," Sean scoffed as he gestured to the bed he was restricted to. "Now it's you that needs to take a break."

"There's no time for a break," Hana responded bitterly as she blew a lock of hair from her face.

"Then make time," Sean replied in a stern tone as he reached over to tuck the stray strand behind her ear. He began to wriggle in his bed, scrunching his face at the pain his movements caused him. Hana was about to ask him what he was doing until he finally came to a halt, patting the space he had made beside him.

"Sleep with me," he offered as he lifted the blanket.

She blinked. "You're rather bold, aren't you?"

Sean stared at her blank faced for a few seconds before a bright red flush captured his cheeks. "I don't – You know – I didn't mean it in that way, you know that."

The corner of Hana's lips lifted briefly and she reached forward to ruffle the boy's hair affectionately. She glanced back at the pile of work that rested on her table and let out a reluctant sigh.

Sean grinned victoriously when Hana climbed in beside him, resting her head on the pillow Sean offered. She closed her eyes after receiving a pointed stare from Sean, but fluttered them open just seconds later. "I can't sleep."

Sean chuckled, "You haven't even tried. You must be so physically and mentally exhausted that your body doesn't even remember what relaxation feels like." There was a beat of silence and Sean stared up at the ceiling. "I'm sorry."

"Don't be ridiculous," Hana muttered. She closed her eyes and turned onto her side, ashamed. Even she hadn't told the other such words, for she felt undeserving of them. She deserved every bit of the guilt she felt, and saw it unfit to attempt to relieve her guilt by professing her remorse.

Sean parted his lips to continue, but pressed them together when he saw how uncomfortable Hana was. He stared at the back of her head for a few seconds before a small smile slipped onto his lips. It would be insane of him to say so, but he was happy. He would have hoped that he and Chris would be able to stay with Hana in a state much better than the one they were currently in, of course, but he was still happy nevertheless.

It was selfish of him, he knew, to be happy even when Chris winced from his injuries in his sleep; even when all of the others remained in the cold, dirty cages, anxiously waiting news as to what had happened to him and Chris; even when his presence was nothing but an extra burden on Hana's shoulders – he couldn't help but be happy.

"Can I ask you something?" Hana asked slowly, breaking the silence with her soft voice.

"Of course you can," Sean replied without skipping a beat.

"How long?" Hana asked after a pause.

"I'm sorry?" Sean asked with furrowed eyebrows.

"How long were you here before I came? How long did you have to suffer?" Hana clarified. In all honesty, she didn't want to know. She didn't want the guilt in her heart to grow larger, but she knew she had to ask. She had to know.

"Don't do this to yourself," Sean replied as he shook his head. "Nothing is your fault, so don't—"

"How long, Sean?"

Sean stared down at her for about half a minute before he gave a sigh of surrender. "I... I got a glance at the clock right before we were brought into the backyard..."

"And the time?"

"I... uh..." Sean mumbled. He sighed when Hana called out his name in a sharp tone, and reluctantly confessed, "It was around 4 PM."

Hana inhaled a sharp breath of air at his words; she hadn't come home until around 6 in the evening. "Two hours?" she asked in a strained voice. "You stayed awake, enduring the pain for two hours?"

"Well no, I blacked out occasionally," Sean confessed sheepishly. "But he was still at it when I came to." He winced at the pressure Hana unconsciously pressed against their intertwined hands and mentally cursed himself, "I shouldn't have said that."

"No," Hana responded in a small voice. "I needed to know."

"I won't let him lay a single finger on either you or Chris anymore. I promise," Hana whispered quietly, giving Sean's hand a small squeeze of reassurance. "I'll protect you all."

"Isn't it the job of a Noye to protect his master?" Sean chuckled. His eyes widened in surprise when Hana suddenly cupped her hand around his chin to force him to look at her. She stared straight into his eyes and spoke in a stern tone, "You are not my Noye, Sean, do you understand?"

Sean paused, "Then what am I?"

Now it was Hana's turn to fall silent and she let her fingers fall from Sean's face as she thought. She glanced at him from out of the corner of her eye, and admitted in a quiet voice, "Someone very special to me."

Both he and Hana jerked their heads in opposite directions as flushes of red captured their cheeks. Hana squeezed her eyes shut and allowed the foreign burn to spread through her face. Her heart jumped when Sean cleared his voice.

"You should get to sleep, Hana," Sean mumbled. He reached over with his free hand to press her head gently against his chest. "We've been awake for long enough."

Hana didn't make any efforts to protest and she fluttered her eyes shut. Her soft breaths evened out within minutes, and it was then that Sean dared to train his gaze on the younger's face. His lips lifted into a light smile as he examined the girl's tired, yet relaxed facial features.

"Thank you," Sean whispered quietly, careful not to disrupt Hana of her much needed sleep. He leaned down and pressed a kiss against the top of her head, blushing as he pulled away. He closed his eyes peacefully and leaned his head against the wooden bed frame. It all felt like a dream to be able to sleep peacefully by Hana's side. Although there were tiny nibbles of guilt here and there, he decided to be selfish for the time being and force those thoughts away. For now he would be greedy, and enjoy the very few minutes he had.

* * *

"Do you have to go?" Sean asked in a childish voice, almost whining as he watched Hana prepare to depart for the morning.

"Are you pouting?" Hana asked with a raised eyebrow of amusement.

Sean's face immediately flushed red. He cleared his throat and straightened his back in an attempt to reclaim his masculinity. "N-No."

"Don't make this harder than it needs to be," Hana scolded the elder as if she was talking to a child. She pressed a chaste kiss against his forehead and waved him goodbye. "I'll be back later, be good to Jaymes."

She closed her bedroom door behind her, and halted after taking only a few steps away. Hana glanced hesitantly back at the closed door, and bit down on her bottom lip. Perhaps she should stay home with Sean and Chris rather than attend the meeting. She quickly shook her head and reluctantly traveled down the stairs. If she skipped a meeting as important as the one that was supposed to be held today, her father would certainly see to it that a punishment would be handed out.

"Are you sure you don't want me to go with you, Miss Hana?" Jaymes spoke up hesitantly. Hana had picked up another chauffeur for the day, ordering Jaymes to keep a mindful eye over Sean and Chris.

"I'll be fine, Jaymes," Hana smiled as she stretched up to pat the top of the man's head affectionately. Just as she was about to slip on her shoes to leave, a voice called out her name.

"Hana, your father would like you to come for breakfast," a maid called out. Before Hana could open her mouth to reject, the maid continued with narrowed eyes, "He was very insistent on it."

Hana and Jaymes exchanged glances before she reluctantly headed towards the dining room, Jaymes glued firmly to her side.

"It's been such a long time since I've seen your face, Hana," Chando greeted his daughter with a wide smile as she slipped into her seat.

Hana responded with a simple nod before picking up her utensils to finish her breakfast as quickly as possible.

Chando cleared his throat, trying again to catch the attention of his daughter, but she simply ignored him.

"I am very sorry as to how badly you are taking this, Hana," Chando stated as he stared at his daughter without even the slightest bit of remorse. "I hope you will get over this quickly and realize why I had to do this. It was for your own good, you know."

Hana twitched with nearly every word that came from her father's mouth. Of course, it would be *her fault* that she was reacting negatively to the fact that he had beaten her friends nearly half to death. It was *her fault* that she couldn't understand why he had done such a thing. *Her fault* that she couldn't see why it was for her own good.

"I will do no such thing," Hana responded rather coldly. "I have respected your orders to stay away from the Noye house and I have been finishing all of my work at an impeccable speed. That, however, is the extent as to how much I will obey your wishes."

"You must understand, Hana," Chando exclaimed, slamming his open palm against the wooden table. She didn't even flinch at the loud bang that echoed throughout the room. "Do you know what people have been calling you? They've been calling you a Noye lover! Do you understand how detrimental that is for our reputation?! I refuse to have our family tainted with such a disgusting label!"

There was a pause of silence, and the air rippled with tension.

"Why is that so wrong?" Hana asked in return, her suddenly soft voice contrasting her previously harsh tone. She lifted her gaze to meet her father's and she clenched the cloth of her dress tightly in her fists. "Why is it so wrong to care for those whom are treated like trash by the people we live with? By the people who walk the same halls as us, the people we eat meals with, the people we work with? Why is it so wrong to show compassion to those who need it the most?"

She recognized the expression that flew across her father's face and she knew what words were to come out of his mouth next. It was an expression that Hana had seen multiple times before, but she had always been the bystander to such an occasion, never the recipient. She clenched her fists tightly at her side in anticipation, preparing her heart for the words that were to slip from her father's lips.

"I'm disappointed in you."

Hana blinked.

And that was it.

Those were the words Hana had dreaded to hear for all eighteen years of her life. The words that always pushed her to the limits of her endurance, the words she had nightmares about.

Yet, she felt nothing.

A giggle escaped her lips at how dumb she had been. How could she have feared for such a thing her entire life, something as trivial and meaningless as that? She placed her utensils calmly on the sides of her plate and slid out of her chair to leave the room. The air around her felt so much lighter, and Jaymes followed behind with confusion.

"What are you laughing about?" Chando asked with narrowed eyes. "I just told you that I am disappointed in you."

"You might be disappointed in me," Hana responded, a small, silly grin plastered across her lips. "But I'm not."

Hana didn't even wait for her father's response, as she spun sharply on her heels to skip light heartedly out of the room.

It was then that Hana realized something she wished she had discovered much earlier. Words - they were something that meant nothing unless they were coming from people that meant something.

* * *

"Are you sure about this?" Jaymes asked hesitantly as the car slowed to a stop. He glanced at Hana through the review mirror and was taken aback by how calmly she was sitting there.

"Positive," Hana responded as she gazed out the window. She opened the car door and tentatively set a foot outside, smiling when a rush of cold air welcomed her back.

"What about your father?" Jaymes asked as he stared hesitantly at her.

"What about him?" she carelessly shrugged in return. She turned back to the two boys that remained hesitantly in the car and pursed her lips. "Well, what are you waiting for? I'm sure Luca, Aiden, Chase, Haru, and Kai are looking forward to seeing you both again."

Chris and Sean exchanged glances before filing out of the car one after the other.

"You're just breaking all the rules today, aren't you?" Jaymes huffed under his breath as he ran his fingers through his hair. Nevertheless, he wouldn't disobey her orders.

"I'll complete everything you've asked of me, Hana, and return for you three in a few hours," Jaymes called out before he drove away.

"I never thought I'd willingly return to this hell hole," Sean murmured under his breath.

Chris nodded solemnly beside him, leaning his head backwards to observe the walls of the Noye house that stretched to the sky. He had gazed at this building for so many years, but never from the outside.

"Come on," Hana urged them forward gently.

Sean didn't want to see the others. He knew that was horrible of him to think, but he didn't want to see them. He didn't want to see the grime pressed against their faces when his was clean of any dirty marks. He didn't want to see the bones that protruded from their shirts, when the meals he had been consuming already provided him with a nice layer of flesh. He didn't want to see their faces laced with hope and sadness when he had already achieved his ideal life of luxury.

He didn't want to be consumed with guilt.

Sean wondered if this was how Hana felt every time she visited them. If she felt as if she didn't deserve the luxuries that she had, the luxuries the others could only dream about.

"Hana! Sean! Chris!"

Sean was yanked away from his thoughts when a sudden pair of arms wrapped around his body. He glanced down with surprise to see Luca's face gleaming back up at him. He looked over at the others to see Hana buried behind Aiden's large body, and Haru practically wrapped around Chris. Kai was standing to the side, fidgeting in place to restrain himself from knocking one of them aside to engulf any familiar face into his arms. Chase remained seated in his spot a few feet away, but still had a happy smile stretched across his face.

After a round of tight hugs and tears, courtesy of Luca and Haru, had been exchanged, the group of Noyes settled down in their familiar positions around the room.

"What took you guys so long to come back?! Do you know how worried we were? We thought you two died or something!" Luca cried, still sobbing into Aiden's shoulder.

"T-The tw-two sc-sc-scary men t-took you a-away v-very qu-quickly!" Haru nodded, wiping the tears that stained his cheeks.

"We're fine, Haru," Sean reassured the other with a small smile. He glanced over at Hana, "Hana took really good care of us."

Chris held up the white board Hana had given to him a few days ago. *Did they do anything to hurt you guys?*

Kai shook his head and wrapped his arms tightly around Haru. "Nothing happened, we were all just really worried."

"We thought you weren't going to come back," Aiden admitted. He stared down at his twiddling thumbs. "We thought that… we thought that since you were all free, you would leave us behind."

A tense silence captured the room and everybody waited for another to make the first move, not daring to do so on their own.

"Is that what you think about us, then?" Sean glared at the five offending Noyes. "Is that how lowly you think about Chris and me?"

The five quickly shook their heads at his accusation. "We didn't want to believe it, truly! It was just, a week had passed with no word from any of you, and I guess…" Luca's voice drifted off. "We just thought we were forgotten."

"B-But you g-guy-guys did-didn't for-forget ab-about us, r-right?" Haru asked hopefully.

"Not for a minute," Hana confirmed. "We couldn't send anybody to contact you. There was a bit of a… problem. But that doesn't mean that we haven't been hard at work in trying to make this a success."

"We didn't slack off either!" Luca nodded his head proudly as he held out his notebook. Aiden, Chase, and Kai pulled their own notebooks out of their pockets and offered it to Hana as well. Haru, on the other hand, ducked his head in embarrassment and stared down silently as his feet.

"They… they haven't been calling Haru out to do work, so he hasn't been able to get out very much," Kai explained carefully.

Hana smiled warmly, "Don't worry yourself about such a thing, alright Haru? They're missing out on a wonderful worker."

Haru offered her a weak smile, but didn't say anymore.

"I'll make sure to add them to the larger map tonight," Hana nodded as she tucked the books into her bag. Her eyes gleamed as she smiled up at the Noyes, "Freedom is just a few steps away."

A few hours quickly passed without the others' realization. They had long moved past the talk of the rebellion, and instead enjoyed the simple comfort of one another like they had before.

"You'll be back soon? Promise?" Luca quietly asked with large, pleading eyes when Hana announced that they had to leave. "Soon?"

Hana nodded her head, "Soon, Luca, very soon."

The lot of them seemed satisfied with her response and they sent the group off with reluctant goodbyes and small, sad smiles.

Jaymes was already waiting for them outside and he gave Hana a firm, silent nod to answer her unspoken question. He had completed the task she had asked of him without much trouble.

"He already knows where you've gone," Jaymes murmured quietly once they had all climbed into the car. "Guards from the Noye house must have contacted him and he isn't happy."

"I assumed that they would," Hana responded simply, her heart feeling much lighter than it would have a week ago. She turned to look at Chris when the boy tugged at her sleeve. *Will he hurt you?*

"No," Hana assured the other in a firm tone. "And he won't be hurting you two either."

Chris was slightly dubious, but decided to trust in Hana's words.

The ride home consisted of silence and Hana recalled the decisions she had made the night prior. She wouldn't allow her father to control her life any longer. Now all she could do was hope that everything would play out as planned.

"He won't hurt you, right?" Sean asked again when the four approached the house after climbing out of the car.

"Don't worry," Hana smiled to reassure him. She paused briefly before continuing, "*He* definitely won't hurt me."

"Hana Acacia."

Hana didn't even flinch against the voice and she calmly slid off her shoes before glancing up at her father. "Have you been waiting long?"

"*Hana Acacia*," Chando repeated once again in a hard tone. "You dare to disobey my orders despite my numerous warnings to you?"

"It seems as though I have," Hana answered as she folded her arms.

Chando let out a growl, and his eyes flashed dangerously over at Sean and Chris. "Was the warning I had given you not enough?"

"No, I received it just fine," Hana replied as she stared at the man with an unwavering gaze. "But you've miscalculated something, Father."

Sean gave her hand a small squeeze of support and his action transferred just the right amount of confidence that she needed.

"You need me just as much as I need you. You know better than I do that there are several companies who only have remaining ties with Acacia Corporations because of me," Hana stated in a firm voice.

A dead silence quickly captured the room. The servants who had secretly strained their ears to listen in on the conversation now shamelessly turned to the girl with mouths gaping of disbelief.

"How dare you talk to me like that?!" Chando bellowed, his volume sounding twice as loud due to the silence it contrasted against. "I am your father!"

Hana responded without skipping a beat, "Only by name."

"You! How dare?! You insolent!" Chando spluttered furiously. He stabbed a finger in Sean and Chris's direction and commanded for the security guards to apprehend them.

Hana's eyes narrowed when the guards stepped forward and she darted towards them in a fluid motion.

"Hana!" "Miss Hana!"

Hana's gaze remained unwavering as she tightened her grip on the stalk of the knife that she pressed against her own neck. "Anything you do to them, I'll do to myself in ten folds."

"Hana!" Sean hissed, outraged at what the girl was proposing.

"I wonder how Chando Acacia would look if rumors spread that he was abusing his own daughter?" Hana asked with a cocked head, eyes swimming with courage and defiance.

"Don't pull that bluff with me," Chando scoffed as he rolled his eyes. He nodded at the guards to tighten their grips on the two Noyes.

"Miss Hana, please!" Jaymes cried in protest when a drip of blood rolled down Hana's pale neck.

"You should know me better by now, Father," Hana stated, refusing to wince at the stinging pain. "I'm not one to make empty threats. I believe that's something I learned from you, isn't it?"

Chando's eyes trained on the small trail of blood that spilled from the pierced skin. "What makes you think that injuring yourself will do anything to bring me shame? I can simply claim that you had a psychological outbreak that had nothing to do with me, or that you were ambushed by one of my enemies."

"I don't think you understand just how many people believe my word against yours, just how many people only continue their ties with Acacia

Corporations because of me," Hana responded sharply.

As if on cue, Jaymes pulled a large folder out of his briefcase and flipped to the first page. "Shine Corporations has agreed to pull their 500,000 shares from Acacia Corp. if Hana is to break away from the company. The Jiang family has agreed to eliminate their sponsorship of Acacia Corp's tropical branch if Hana is dismissed. Poon Estate confirmed that they will eliminate the ten year contact they were to sign with Acacia Corp. next month if Hana is removed. The Hayes firm refuses to represent Acacia Corp for any legal disputes if Hana is no longer in place," Jaymes read from the files in hand.

"Do you understand now?" Hana asked as she stared at her red faced father. "The list just continues on, if you'd like to hear. The Tsais, the Sahotas, the Kyees, the Changs, the Greenes– more than half of the companies tied together with Acacia Corporations are only there because of me. I made sure to fulfill my position back when I was being the perfect daughter, and went out of my way to get many of these companies to make contracts with us when they wouldn't have otherwise. The only string connecting them with your company is me. So you understand what this means, correct?"

"If I go down, Acacia Corporations goes down with me," Hana firmly continued. The corner of her lips curved upwards into a smug smirk as she stared at the twitching of her father's veins.

"So, what will it be, father?"

* * *

"That went rather well, wouldn't you agree?" Hana happily clasped her hands together as she stood before the three boys. Their mixed expressions of anger and disbelief completely contrasted her own.

"Are you crazy?!" Sean exclaimed as he grabbed a hold of her chin to tilt her head upwards. He scowled and let out a short grunt when he saw the red line that traced her neck. "You said you wouldn't get hurt!"

Hana opened her mouth to point out that she had actually said that *he* wouldn't hurt her, not that she wouldn't hurt herself, but the angry glint in Sean's eye made her hold her tongue. "It's not too bad. It worked, didn't it?"

"Yeah, but at what cost?" Sean muttered.

"It's just a little cut," Hana protested, wincing when Sean applied rubbing alcohol onto the injury.

"Stay still," Sean scolded as he blew gently on the wound. His eyes flashed with concern, and he glanced over at the girl's face to see any signs of pain. "Does it still sting?"

She shook her head, "It's all better now."

At this point, the attention of the two was completely captivated by one another, and both Chris and Jaymes felt as if they were intruding. After exchanging amused grins, the pair silently slid out of the room to leave the couple on their own. Their departure went unnoticed and the pair continued on as if they hadn't been there in the first place.

"Foolish girl," Sean muttered under his breath as he gently applied a plaster to her skin. "What are you going to do now if that scars?"

"It won't," Hana shrugged in response. She stretched her arms up into the air and fell backwards onto her bed with a soft thump, a wide smile stretched across her face. "We're free."

Sean opened his mouth to continue his scolding, but decided to let it go. It wasn't easy for Hana to stand up to her father the way she had and he was proud that she had summoned enough confidence to do so.

The girl let out another squeal of delight and Sean rolled his eyes affectionately at her childishness. "We're not all free yet, you know."

"Don't be such a spoiler, Sean," Hana whined.

Sean turned to Hana with an arched eyebrow, "Am I hearing correctly? Hana Acacia is actually whining? *The* Hana Acacia?"

He laughed aloud when Hana gave him another nudge, and reached over to ruffle the front of her hair affectionately.

A blanket of silence captured the two and Hana turned on her side to gaze at Sean's side profile, admiring the boy's rugged features.

"It can only get better from here, right Sean?" Hana asked softly.

Sean stared at the girl's face for a few seconds before he reached out to brush a stray strand of hair from her eyes. "I hope so."

* * *

Haru bit down on his bottom lip as he traveled the hallways alone. All of the others had been called out to work, while he was once again, left in the cage by himself. He was tired of being the only one who couldn't bring anything to offer, so he decided that it was time to venture out on his own.

He hated being the one who was left out.

He hated being useless. He hated being stupid. He hated being dumb.

He hated himself.

He knew the others saw him as a burden that they had to carry, even if they were too nice to say so. The others cared for him of course, but they would appreciate him much more if he could actually be of use.

All Haru wanted was to be desired. All he wanted was to be needed.

Haru needed to be doing something, because sometimes, sometimes when he was stuck in that room all by himself, his thoughts took a hold of him; Haru had very ugly thoughts.

Sometimes he would sit in the corner with his knees pulled up to his chest and his face buried in his folded arms as he wallowed in his self-pity. Other times, he would direct his anger at people, even the ones he held dear to him.

He hated himself for thinking so, but he couldn't help but feel bitter towards Chris. Haru loved Chris, he really did, but he felt that it was unfair. It was unfair that Haru was the one everybody picked on for being stupid – at least he could speak, couldn't he? He might stammer rather often, but at least he could articulate his words, right?

Chris wasn't even physically restricted from speaking – he just didn't. Haru didn't exactly know why, for he never had the guts to ask, but what he did know was that the elder had endured events so traumatic that he couldn't formulate his words anymore. Either way, Haru saw it rather clearly – he could speak and Chris couldn't.

So why was he the one chosen to suffer?

It was an ugly thought, he knew. He knew he was a horrible person to question why he was the one treated badly and not the other boy. It was an ugly thought, but it was still there and it wouldn't disappear no matter how much Haru willed it to.

He was just tired of being useless and stupid.

Haru grumbled unintelligibly under his breath as he kicked at the dirt scattered across the ground. He had been so eager to leave the cage that he had forgotten to bring his notepad and pencil along with him.

Even when he was trying to be useful he was stupid.

"W-Why ar-are y-y-you so d-dumb?" Haru questioned himself under his breath as he kicked at a rather large rock. He jumped in alarm when the rock slammed against a door to create the sound of a hollow thud, followed closely by a small creak.

Haru glanced up to see that the rock had hit the door to the private office of the Noye house, causing the unlocked door to open just the slightest bit. It was rather strange that the door was unlocked, for the entrance was often placed under intense security since it contained many of the most important documents.

Important documents.

Haru's eyes widened in realization, and his heart began to double in its beats. If this room really contained important documents, then the map should be somewhere within those four walls.

He could almost hear the praise he would receive from the others if he was to return with something as important as the map to the Noye house.

Haru glanced around to make sure nobody was watching before he silently tip toed over to the slightly opened office. He slipped carefully inside once he confirmed that it was empty. His heart was nearly beating out of his chest, and he glanced wildly around the room to find the place that held the map.

When nothing obvious stuck out to him, he heaved a small sigh, and made his way over to a corner cabinet to begin his search. He knew his time was limited, and that he would suffer punishments if he was caught.

There was a little voice in the back of his head nagging for him to leave while he still had the chance. Haru would have listened to it if it wasn't for the other voice.

The louder voice. The stronger voice.

The voice that told him he could finally gain his acceptance among the others if he were to do something worthy. It was a voice Haru had heard many times before – back when he would be rolled up in the corner of a room. It was the voice that gave Haru bad thoughts, the voice that would always remind Haru of his worthlessness. Now that the voice was finally giving him a chance to redeem himself, Haru wouldn't back down.

He couldn't.

Haru moved from cabinet to cabinet, desperately searching for the single piece of paper that would allow him to redeem himself. A single piece of paper, that was all he needed – and he couldn't even find that.

The chance to enter a room that was normally so carefully locked would never come again and he would never be able to forgive himself if he gave up this opportunity. He would find it even if it cost him his life.

He fumbled through a few pieces of paper before his hands came to a sudden halt. His eyes widened with surprise and he quickly brushed a layer of papers aside to pull out the piece he was looking for.

He found it.

Haru hugged the map to his chest, ignoring the sharp corners that cut into his skin. He had really found it. He let out a cry of victory, a new sense of confidence pulsing through his veins at the success.

"Who's in there?!"

Haru froze.

Two guards entered the room before Haru could even turn his head, drawn by the cry the boy had emitted just seconds prior.

"What do you think you're doing in here?" one of the guards growled as he held up his gun threateningly. "What are you looking for?"

Haru clenched the map tightly in his hands. He wasn't going to let them take it away from him. Not now. Not when he had only tasted the flavor of victory so shortly.

"G-G-Go aw-away," Haru whispered. Perspiration began to build up on his forehead, and his eyes darted from side to side as he tried to come up with a plan to escape.

"Hey, you're that Noye Henry was trying to sell, aren't you?" one of the guards laughed as he approached Haru. He turned to the guard beside him and sneered, "You can put your gun away, Neil. This dumb kid isn't capable of doing anything. You're not supposed to have that out anyways. We're going to get into big trouble if we get caught with that."

Neil laughed mockingly along, and tucked his gun back into its holster. He strolled up to Haru and ripped the paper away from his clenched hand.

"Let's see what the idiot was trying to steal," Neil chuckled as he unfolded the paper and smoothed out the wrinkles. His eyebrows furrowed in and he raised his eyes from the map to Haru. "Take a look at this, Colt, look at what he was trying to steal."

"It-It's m-mine!" Haru cried as he reached forward to grab it.

"You're even stupider than I thought!" Neil sneered as he shoved Haru to the ground with his foot. "Do you think anybody would believe that?"

"Now what were you trying to do with this, huh?" Colt asked as he pulled Haru up by his collar. He held up the map with his other hand and shook it in Haru's face. "What would you want with this map?"

"N-Noth-thing," Haru replied, his eyes trained solely on the paper. He bit down on his bottom lip as he tried to devise a plan to get the map back.

"Hey, you think this has to do with that girl?" Neil asked Colt in a low voice, as if Haru wasn't capable of hearing their exchange.

"You mean that Noye lover girl?" Colt replied thoughtfully as he eyed Haru up and down. "She is pretty close with this brat, isn't she?"

Haru's eyes widened in alarm. He wouldn't get Hana in trouble, he wouldn't! "I-It was-wasn't her! I-I g-got it o-on m-my-my own!"

"Yeah right, like you're smart enough to break into the office to steal this," Neil scoffed as he shoved his fist into Haru's gut. "This is what you get for lying. Now tell me who sent you here."

"N-Nob-body!" Haru wheezed as he clutched his stomach in pain.

"Stop lying to us!" Colt exclaimed as he struck his fist against the back of Haru's head. The blow caused him to hit the ground with a thud and Colt grinned in satisfaction when Haru emitted quiet whimpers of pain.

"I-I'm no-not ly-lying," Haru whispered as he pushed himself onto his hands and knees. He wiped the blood that trailed down his split lip, and spoke again in a stronger voice, "I'm n-not ly-lying."

"Of course you're lying," Neil rolled his eyes. "How the hell would you get in here? Everybody knows you're just some stupid fucking Noye that only fulfills the role of being a waste of space. You can't do anything on your own."

His words caused a flame to ignite within Haru, and with clenched fists, he slowly climbed up to his feet. "Y-You're wrong."

"What? Speak up, I can't hear you," Neil laughed mockingly as he nudged Colt with his elbow.

"Y-You're wr-wrong!" Haru screamed as he ran forward to shove the guard to the ground. "I-I'm not stupid! I-I'm n-not stupid!"

"Get this crazy kid off of me!" Neil exclaimed as he tried to shove Haru off of him. The smaller refused to release the guard's shirt from his hands, however, and he pounded his fists against his chest. Haru's eyes widened in fright when Colt came forward to pull Haru off of his partner.

Desperate for safety, Haru grabbed the stock of the gun from Neil's pants and quickly held it up at the two. "T-Ta-Take it b-back! T-Take i-it back! I-I'm n-not stu-stupid!"

The guards held up their hands in alarm, not having any other weapon to defend themselves. Neil growled as he wiped the blood that ran from his nose.

"Yeah okay, you're not stupid, now give us back the gun!" Colt exclaimed as he tried to reach forward.

"D-Don't!" Haru exclaimed as he pointed the gun at him. "S-Say i-it li-like y-you me-mean i-it!"

"What's going on in here?!"

The door of the office burst open and another pair of guards entered the room. Their eyes widened at the sight of a gun equipped Noye and they immediately froze mid-step.

"What is going on, Neil?!" one of the guards exclaimed as he eyed the gun in Haru's hand cautiously.

"Little shit just brought it out of nowhere! I think he had it smuggled in," Colt whispered, quickly pinning the presence of the gun on Haru.

"L-Liar!" Haru cried as he waved the gun at him. How dare he blatantly lie to Haru's face? "Y-You're ly-lying!"

By then a small crowd had gathered outside the door, curious to see what all the noise was about. The mouths of the Noyes gaped, stunned to see a fellow Noye actually trying to fight against the guards. Those who recognized Haru were even more shocked and a few of them quickly fled to seek out Kai or one of the other boys.

"Look at what this stupid Noye is trying to do," Neil chuckled to the other guards. He turned to Haru and spoke in a louder voice, "Yeah, yeah you're right I'm lying. Now just put the gun down alright?!"

"I-I'm n-not stupid!" Haru cried.

"Nobody said you're stupid, boy, now put the damn gun down!" Colt sighed. "Hurry up and do it before reinforcements come!"

"N-No! I s-sai-said t-take it ba-back!" Haru screamed, his eyes stretched with an almost delirious glint. "S-Say i-it!!"

"Haru," a calm voice sounded above all of the commotion. "Haru, what are you doing?"

Haru's ears perked up at the familiar voice, and his head snapped over to the crowd to search for the face that owned it. "H-Han-Hana!" he cried in relief at the sight of the girl. "T-Tell the-them! Te-tell th-them th-th-that I-I'm n-no-not stup-pid!"

"Haru," Hana broke through the crowd with Sean and Chris at her sides. The trio had come to visit the Noye house, but had been side tracked by the small crowd that had formed down the hallway. The murmured name of "Haru" had met their ears and they had immediately rushed to find the source of the crowd.

Hana stepped forward. Her heart thumped loudly against her chest as she watched Haru wildly brandish the gun. "Haru, you know you're not stupid, so why are you doing this?"

"Th-They sa-said I-I'm st-stupid!" Haru exclaimed as he trained his gun back on the guards. His eyes began to gloss over with tears and his whole body began to quiver.

"Well, are you stupid?" Hana asked as she slowly took another step towards him. She knew that Haru wouldn't hurt her, but she was less certain for the well being of the guards.

"N-No!" Haru exclaimed, outraged that she had even asked him. He wasn't stupid, not anymore; not after he had found the map for them all.

"No what?" Hana urged the boy to continue as she slowly stepped towards him.

There was a beat of silence.

"I-I'm n-not st-stupid-pid," Haru whispered, tears slipping out of the corners of his eyes. He was no longer angry or scared. He was ashamed, ashamed to have allowed Hana to witness another embarrassing situation.

"I know, Haru," Hana replied softly. She reached out and placed a gentle hand on his shoulder.

"I'm n-not stup-pid," Haru repeated himself in louder voice, his hands shaking as he loosened his grip around the stock of the gun.

"You're right," Hana agreed as she slowly pried Haru's trembling fingers off of the weapon.

A loud clattering thud sounded as the gun hit the ground. Haru straightened his back and pressed his arms firmly against his sides as he stared at the small crowd before him.

"I'm not stupid."

"No," Hana smiled as she wrapped her warm hand around his clammy one. "You're not stupid."

The male turned to her with glistening eyes, his quivering bottom lip tucked in between his two rows of teeth.

"I'm sor-sorry," Haru choked out as he quickly engulfed Hana into a tight hug. His body tremored and Hana wrapped her arms around his waist comfortingly. He buried his face into the crook of her neck, "I-I'm s-sorry. I'm sor-ry. I-I'm s-so so-s-so s-sorry."

"It's fine, Haru," Hana whispered as she gently rubbed his lower back. His sobs slowly faded into quiet whimpers. "Everything's fine now. Everything's okay."

A deafening bang shot across the room and Hana's heart stopped when Haru suddenly fell slack against her body. Screams filled the room at the shot, and pounding feet sounded in multiple directions as the Noyes scurried off to safety.

Hana glanced up to see the head of a gun pointed straight at them, not missing the satisfactory smirk spread across Neil's face. "It's about time somebody got rid of that useless scum."

From that point on, everything seemed to move in slow motion.

"Haru?" Hana whispered hoarsely as she stared down at the boy. A seeping warmness began to soak the fabric clenched in her fingers, and the cry of his name got stuck in her throat.

His body began to slide to the floor and she didn't have enough strength to hold him up, so she hit the ground with him.

"Haru? Haru? H-," Hana stared down at the motionless body, and her eyes quickly began to sting with tears. She grabbed his hand and felt for a pulse, her eyes widening when she felt a weak thump beat against her fingers. She ripped her jacket from her shoulders and pressed it against Haru's wound to stop the blood from flowing out. "Haru, come on. Haru, please, please wake up. Please, please, please, don't do this. Please, just – don't, Haru!"

She felt another body drop to his knees beside her and Chris's frail arms reached outwards to shake his friend. His mouth opened and closed as he voiced silent pleas for Haru to wake up.

Haru's eyes slowly blinked open, "I-I'm…"

"Haru! Haru just hold on, okay? Just hold on I'm going to call for help," Hana exclaimed as she fumbled around her pockets for her phone. Her hands shook as she tried to dial for help and she swore loudly when her trembling fingers kept hitting the wrong buttons. "Just hold on for a little bit more. Just for a little and I'll get some help."

"N-No," Haru whispered as his eye lids fluttered open and close.

"We can get you help, we can help you. Please don't give up, Haru, we can help you," Hana pleaded desperately.

"N-N-No," Haru repeated himself in a tone so soft she could barely hear it. He uncurled one of his tight fists, and held up his shaking hand to give Hana the small scrap of paper that had been tucked protectively inside.

Hana quickly took the scrap and flattened out the creases as she tried to decipher what the other had given her. The paper was less than an inch in size, and had three letters printed across it. She choked on her breath once she realized what the tiny piece of paper had originated from.

It was a corner of the map.

She focused her attention back on Haru when he uttered a few choked gasps as he tried to get out his final words.

"I-I-I'm us-u-useful."

The corners of Haru's lips twitched upwards into a small victorious smile before he finally allowed himself to release the small string of life he had been clinging onto.

I'm sorry, it looks like I'm going to be the first to be free.

CHAPTER EIGHT: REPRISAL

Reprisal [ri'prīzəl] n. - Retaliation for an injury with the intent of inflicting at least as much injury in return.

"Hana, get up," Sean murmured as he attempted to haul the girl to her feet. "Please Hana, get up."

He continued to plead with her, but she remained on the floor motionless with tears coursing down her face. Chris sobbed into his arms as he held handfuls of Haru's now blood soaked shirt in his tight fists.

"Haru! Haru what are you-!"

It was this voice that finally got Hana to react and she slowly focused her gaze on the figure that had come running into the room. Kai's head turned furiously from right to left, searching for the familiar face until his eyes finally zeroed in on the lifeless figure next to Hana.

Kai let out a choked gasp and he staggered down to his knees in shock.

Luca let out a sharp shriek when he ran in behind him and Aiden stopped mid-step with a gaping jaw. "Is he...?"

He didn't need them to respond to know the answer.

Loud, muffled sobs immediately filled the room as Luca buried his face into Aiden's chest. Silent streams of tears ran down Aiden's face, but he resisted the urge to cry audibly as he rubbed Luca's back.

The only person that remained still was Kai.

"Kai..." Aiden whispered silently as he stretched out an arm to lay a comforting hand on the other's shoulder.

"Don't touch me," Kai's voice quivered, his entire body beginning to tremble as he stared down at the unnatural shade of white Haru's face was turning. "Please, don't touch me right now."

Aiden obeyed his wishes and immediately retracted his hand.

"Haru is... Haru is..." Kai stammered as he stumbled to his feet to stagger towards the still body. A tear finally broke loose and traveled quickly down his cheek, followed almost immediately by a heavy stream. He fell down to his knees with a heavy thud, his arms hanging lifelessly at his sides.

"H-Hey, Haru," Kai whispered weakly as he reached forward to shake Haru's shoulder. "H-Haru, you need to get up. Ha-Haru, you're m-making everyb-body cry."

Hana stared at the boy in silence with tears pouring down her cheeks.

She felt her heart crack deeper and deeper with each of Kai's words.

"Haru please, Haru get up," Kai sobbed as he clung desperately to the front of Haru's shirt. "Please, Haru, you can't leave me. What am I supposed to do now? What am I supposed to do if I'm all alone? Please, Haru, don't leave. Or just, just take me with you, Haru, I'm begging you."

Sean turned his head away to blink back his own tears, not bearing to see how Kai crumbled to pieces in front of their eyes. In all the years he had known Kai, not once had the other ever shed a tear. It was always Kai consoling the crying Haru, and now it was as if all those years of bottled up emotions were spilling over right on the spot.

"Please take me with you H-Haru, don't le-leave me all alone. I ca-can't sur-vi-vive if I'm all alone, Haru," Kai choked as he pounded his fists weakly against Haru's chest. "Please Ha-Haru you can't die, I don't wa-want to be al-al-on-one. We promised we'd b-be together for-forever. We promised we'd b-be free!"

Hana couldn't bear the sight any longer and she reached forward to press a comforting hand against Kai's back. She wanted him to know that he was wrong, that he wasn't all alone. He wasn't alone because the rest of them would remain by his side forever.

"I said don't touch me!" Kai nearly screamed as he spun around to shove her to the ground. His eyes were glazed with sadness, anger, and pain, and he couldn't bear to think that somebody actually thought they could comfort him. What a joke. What a painful, humorless, joke.

Hana ignored the sharp pain that jolted up the palms of her hands that broke her fall. Her bottom lip trembled as she stared down at the ground.

"It's your fault you know," Kai whispered in a cold voice.

Hana's eyes lifted off the floor to meet Kai's dark ones.

"It's your fault he died," Kai growled as he took a step forward. He appeared twice as dangerous with Haru's blood smudged over his skin and clothing. "It's your fault any of this shit happened. It's your fault he died! It's your fault!"

Hana froze once she processed his words, not even realizing that Kai had begun to charge forward to attack her from rage. He was whipped to the side, and pinned to the wall by Sean's frightening strength.

"Don't you *dare* blame this on Hana," Sean growled in a low tone. He knew that Kai was out of it, and that he would most certainly regret his words and actions once he was to get a hold of himself. "You know as well as I do that this is not her fault. Don't you dare try to point fingers."

"Then whose fault is it, Sean?!" Kai screamed, his eyes gleamed a hint of madness as he stared at Hana from over Sean's shoulders. "Who was the one who tried to get us to do this damned rebellion?!"

Kai managed to break free from Sean's grip and he charged at Hana once again before Sean could block him off. She simply stared at him as he came forward, not even attempting to shield herself. What right did she have? Her eyes widened in surprise when she was suddenly blocked by a figure and Chris let out a soft grunt when Kai's clenched knuckles met roughly with his back.

"That's enough, Kai!" Luca shouted angrily as he ripped Kai off of Chris. "Do you think that Haru would be happy with this?! With you hurting Hana?! With you hurting Chris?! Save him some face, would you?! Don't you dare make it so he... so he died f-for nothing!"

Luca's bottom lip trembled as he stared off to Haru's body that remained still against the cold floor. "Don't you dare, Kai. We're all hurting and we know that you're hurting the most, but show some decency for god's sake!"

Kai sat there with his head hung in shame as he listened to the words Luca had to say. His body began to shake as he broke out into another round of sobs. Luca stared at him with uncertainty, but slowly inched forward to place a gentle hand onto Kai's shoulder. When the other didn't protest, Luca quickly engulfed Kai into a tight hug, breaking out into a fresh batch of tears himself.

"He's gone, Haru's gone. Luca, he's gone and he's never coming back," Kai stammered as Luca rocked him back and forth. "I didn't even get to say goodbye to him. I did- I didn't-"

"Are you okay?" Sean asked quietly as he helped Chris to his feet.

Chris nodded his head, but glanced down at Hana in worry. Her face was stretched into the familiar stoic expression she had abandoned long ago, and tears continued to roll down her pale cheeks.

"I'll take care of her," Sean whispered as he placed a warm, gentle hand on top of Chris's head. He glanced over at Luca and jerked his head in his direction. "Go to him, Chris, you don't have to act brave."

Chris's bottom lip quivered and he broke into another round of sobs when his eyes unconsciously strayed over to Haru's lifeless body. He nearly flung himself onto the sobbing pair and Luca immediately welcomed him by wrapping an arm tightly around his shoulders.

"Look at me, Hana," Sean stated quietly as he tilted up her face. He gently wiped away her tears, "Don't listen to Kai, okay? Don't listen to what he said, he's not in his right mind."

Hana offered no words in response and Sean bit down on his bottom lip as his gaze traveled from her to the others of the room. Tears stained the faces of each and every one of them, and even Sean himself had to gulp down hard to prevent similar features from appearing on his own face. He had to be strong. Even when it hurt, he had to be strong enough for the rest of them.

* * *

Hana leaned her back against the window sill, her eyes closed as she listened to the heavy rain pattering against the other side of the cold glass.

Even the sky was crying for Haru that night.

She knew Sean was right. Kai would regret the words he had mindlessly spouted earlier that evening, and would without a doubt apologize once she returned tomorrow morning.

She knew that ultimately, it wasn't her fault. Hana wasn't the type to always see oneself as the cause for everybody's suffering, but that didn't mean it hurt any less. The pain still continued to feed on her heart.

Even though she knew that she wasn't the one to be blamed, she still would never forgive herself.

"Stop thinking, will you?"

Sean sighed when the smaller ignored him. He stepped forward with outstretched arms to engulf her into a comforting hug.

"Please leave, Sean," Hana whispered quietly, causing Sean to freeze mid-step. She shrunk away from his arms, forcing herself flat against the cold glass to avoid his warmth.

"No," he replied in a firm voice as he stared at Hana with narrowed eyes. "No, I won't leave." Still, he dropped his arms to his side to avoid making her even more uncomfortable.

Hana remained silent before finally muttering under her breath, "Do as you wish."

Scan offered her a small smile and sat down to lean his back against the base of the seat Hana was resting on. The back of his head leaned against the side of her left knee and he closed his eyes when Hana began to run her fingers gently through his hair. A silence captured the room; the only sound made was the hard pattering of rain against the roof and walls.

"Can I ask you something, Sean?" Hana asked in a voice so soft Sean had to strain his ears to hear.

"Hm?"

"How... how can you be so collected when I know that you're hurting inside? How do you stop yourself from crying?" Hana whispered, her voice cracking midway through her sentence. A few tears slipped down her cheeks and she quickly wiped them away before Sean could notice.

Sean remained silent for a few seconds, before he tipped his head back just far enough so he could meet eyes with Hana.

His lips lifted into a small, sad smile, and he raised his hand to wipe the corner of Hana's eyes.

"Because you're crying," he whispered. "Because you and everybody else are crying, so I can't cry too. I have to be calm enough to protect you and the others when you guys aren't capable of doing it yourself."

"Because if I cry," Sean continued in a small voice. His eyes swam with tears. "Then who else is out there to protect us?"

* * *

Hana's eyes darted up gratefully when she felt a large, warm hand engulf her smaller, shivering one. Sean gave her a small smile when their eyes met and he gently squeezed her hand reassuringly. He glanced at Chris who was curled up into a small trembling ball beside him, and reached out an arm to pull him closer.

Chris's eyes flashed with gratitude and he snuggled into Sean's side, enjoying the warmth the boy projected. He glanced up when a hand much smaller than his own slipped into his grip. Hana had reached across Sean's lap with her free hand to offer her comfort as well.

It was hard on all of them.

"We're here," Jaymes called out in a soft voice as the car slowed to a stop. He glanced at the solemn trio. "I'll be back in two hours."

The group of three turned their heads to gaze out the window; the Noye building appeared twice as somber as it did before.

"Thank you, Jaymes," Hana smiled weakly, Jaymes gave her a comforting pat on her shoulder as she climbed out of the car.

The three of them waved goodbye to Jaymes before they began to head into the building with heavy hearts and stoic faces.

Sean stopped when he suddenly felt the warmth of the small girl missing from his side. He glanced back to see Hana frozen in place. She hung her head as she clenched each side of her dress tightly in her fists.

"Hana?" he called out gently as he walked back towards her.

"What if he's still angry with me?" Hana whimpered, flinching when Sean laid a warm hand on the top of her head.

"He's not," Sean reassured her. He wrapped his arm around her shoulders to urge her forward. "Come on, Chris's waiting for us."

Hana timidly nodded her head and the two passed the iron gate to join Chris on the other side.

"Chris, wait for—" Sean's eyes widened in horror. He quickly smacked his hand to Hana's eyes, flinching when it met a little too roughly with her face.

"Sean?" Hana asked in alarm, her voice tinged with a bit of panic.

Sean was relieved that she hadn't seen what laid before them just yet. He quickly spun her around to face the opposite direction. "What's wrong?"

"Don't look, Hana," Sean pleaded as his hands clenched her shoulders, his fingers digging a little too deeply into her skin. "Please promise me you won't turn around."

There was a beat of silence and Hana nodded her head, "Okay."

"Chris come here," Sean pulled him back and engulfed the smaller into a tight hug. "Chris don't look, don't look any more."

Chris let out a few sobs as he held tightly onto Sean. Sean ignored the dampening of his shirt, and stared up in horror at the sight of Haru's lifeless body hanging off a wooden post. A thick rope was knotted around his neck as it hung him from above, swaying gently when the wind hit parts of Haru's body.

Sean choked back a sob, not wanting to alarm Hana and tempt her to turn around. She must have already known that something was wrong with the quiet sobs Chris emitted. His eyes darted around the empty courtyard and he was relieved to see that nobody else was in sight.

They were the first ones to discover the warning; the warning of what was to come if you were to step out of line.

The warning that came in the form of Haru.

"Come on Chris," Sean whispered quietly as he gently pulled him over to Hana. He had to get the two of them out of there quickly before someone came out. He wouldn't be able to shield their eyes if anybody else was to make a ruckus.

A scream shot across the air and Sean swore under his breath. A group of Noyes had come out to the courtyard and discovered the body that was hanging lifelessly in the air.

"S-Sean?" Hana called out in a shaking voice, terrified of what she would see if she turned.

"Please, don't turn around," Sean pleaded once Hana began to shift in place. "Don't turn around, please, Hana."

He didn't understand. He had been standing right next to Hana yesterday when she had given out shaking orders to transfer Haru to a safe place. How could they have failed their job to such a degree?

A loud murmur quickly filled the air and Sean broke out into a cold sweat. He froze when he heard a familiar cry of "HARU!" slice across the air and he looked up to see Kai shoving his way through the crowd with Chase, Luca, and Aiden following closely behind him.

Hana automatically spun around at the cry of Haru's name, and her lips parted in horror at the ragged sight of his body. She ignored Sean's pleads to stay still and shot forward.

A handful of guards came out to suppress the mob.

Hana was shoved roughly aside when she attempted to free Haru of his restraints and Kai suffered a similar fate shortly after.

"Don't you know who that is? That's Hana Acacia!" one of the guards hissed. The other guards immediately fell still at the information, not wanting to give her any reason to hold them with disdain.

Kai was about to charge blindly forward once more, but was held back by Hana's outstretched arm. He turned to scream angrily at the girl, but pressed his lips together once he glanced at her face.

He wasn't the only one who was hurting.

He clenched his teeth to seal his screams, and stepped aside to allow her to handle the situation. His blunt nails sunk into the palms of his hands as he stared up at Haru's body, and tears prickled his eyes at the sight.

"What is going on here?" Hana let out a low growl as she seized a guard's collar to pull him roughly forward. "Who ordered Haru's body to be treated this way? Do you have no respect for those who have passed?" Her words were said in an almost silent volume, but each syllable was dripping with acidity. "*Who?*"

The guards exchanged nervous glances with each other, not knowing what they should say or do.

"Are you deaf?" Hana hissed. Her eyes flashed dangerously and she pulled the guard closer to glare straight into his eyes. "*Who?*"

"It was your father."

Hana's eyes darted towards the new presence and she released her grip. Her eyes narrowed dangerously at Henry. "What did you say?"

"Your father called mine to return the body after he found out that you had your people take that Noye," Henry explained as he slowly stepped forward. He held up his hands in surrender, a signal that he didn't intend to fight. "Your father said it would set a good example to the other Noyes." He gestured to the wooden post. "He had this set up overnight."

Hana's blood ran cold with his words. She knew her father well enough to know that this was exactly something he would try to pull.

"Take down Haru's body," Hana whispered, her whole body trembling with anger as she stared at Henry. Her head whipped over to the pack of guards that stood beside her and she spoke in a venomous voice. "*Take down his body now.*"

"Miss Hana, we can't do that. It was your father that—"

"You heard her, take him down."

Hana's eyes darted over to Henry in surprise, but she refused to let any emotion seep onto her face.

"B-But Sir! We can—"

"Have you forgotten who the actual owner of this place is? I said take it down," Henry barked as he stormed forward. The guards cowered under his gaze and they quickly moved to get Haru's body down from its post.

"Sean, call Jaymes," Hana ordered as she handed the taller male her cell phone. She turned to Henry with narrowed eyes and gestured him forward, "You come with me."

"It's fine, Sean," Hana reassured the other when his eyebrows furrowed in protest. "I'll be fine."

"What is he, your body guard?" Henry asked dryly once the two stepped away.

"Are you joking with me right now?" Hana snapped.

Henry's eyes flickered up to her tense face and he licked his dry lips nervously. "S-Sorry, I was just trying to loosen the mood."

Hana didn't respond and he felt himself break into a cold sweat under her intense glare.

"What are you trying to pull?" Hana finally asked.

Henry's eyebrows furrowed, "What do you mean?"

"What are you trying to get by pretending to be the good guy? What do you want from me?" Hana continued with narrowed eyes.

"I just wanted to help. I might be a bad guy, Hana, but I know when wrong is wrong," Henry defended. His eyes flickered to the area where they were trying to get Haru's body down. "And this was just wrong."

"Don't pull that bullshit with me," Hana growled as she shoved Henry against the wall. "You can do whatever you want with me, but don't you dare harm the other boys. Pull something like this again and I will personally see the destruction of both you and this whole damn place."

"I'm being honest," Henry exclaimed defensively as he pushed her off of him. "I don't have an ulterior motive!"

"Didn't I already establish that I'm not in the mood for jokes?" Hana spat in anger.

"I'm not joking!" Henry shouted. This time it was his turn to push Hana backwards. "Why won't you give me a chance to prove myself?! You're right, I am pitiful! I'm pitiful and pathetic, and I'm tired of living this way! I'm tired of suspecting everything, tired of having to look for the loop holes of everything that's done!" His eyes drooped in sorrow as he lifted his gaze to meet hers. "Just give me a chance to prove myself."

Before Hana could respond, Henry was whipped away from her and onto the ground with an audible thud.

"Are you alright, Miss Hana?" Jaymes asked as he stood protectively in front of the girl. He glared down at Henry and was about to attack until Hana stopped him with a small tug on his shirt. "Let's go, Jaymes."

"Are you okay?" Sean asked quietly as he pulled her away from Jaymes to engulf her into his arms.

Hana stared at the small body Kai clung to. He desperately fought anybody who tried to pull him away from Haru. She glanced over her shoulder at Henry who remained lying on the ground where Jaymes had left him. She watched as Luca, Aiden, and Chase tried to get Kai to release Haru's body in vain. She gazed at Chris, who was on his knees sobbing heavily into the palms of his hands.

"No," Hana finally responded in a voice so silent that it was swallowed by the loud commotion around them. "I'm not okay."

* * *

The first thing Hana noticed when she returned to the cage was the absence of Kai. She and Sean had been gone for a majority of the day making sure that Haru's body would receive the proper treatment it deserved. Night had fallen by the time they returned and the cages were dimly lit by the cheap light bulbs that hung above.

"You two are back," Aiden acknowledged their presence with a nod, rubbing a hand soothingly against Luca's back.

"Where's Kai?" Hana asked as she glanced around the room.

"He stormed off," Aiden responded bitterly.

"And you didn't go after him?" Hana stared blankly.

"No, he was being an asshole," Aiden growled under his breath.

Hana immediately opened her mouth to scold the taller, but reluctantly pressed her lips together. Scolding him wouldn't solve anything, and it would only result in an even darker atmosphere.

"I'll go out and look for him," Hana sighed as she wrapped her scarf tighter around her neck before exiting the cage. She hoped the other wasn't out looking for trouble, for she didn't know what he was capable of doing in a state as delirious as he currently was.

She treaded the hallways quickly, opting to stay silent rather than call out Kai's name. She knew the other would rather spend his time moping alone, but she couldn't take the risk that he was out causing mischief. She wouldn't lose another one of them. She refused to.

After searching the hallways she decided to try her luck outside. The dim sky provided her with barely any light, so she made sure to be twice as cautious. She folded her arms together to project warmth against the nipping cold. There weren't any Noyes outside, for they all had retreated for shelter against the chilly night.

Her ears perked up at the sound of a running liquid as she neared the guard house and she searched for the source. Her eyes caught onto a familiar tuff of messy hair and she let out a sigh of relief now that she had discovered Kai's whereabouts.

"Kai, it's cold out here, please come back insi – Kai what the hell do you think you're doing?" Hana hissed in disbelief at the sight of the empty gasoline bottles that were littered around Kai's feet.

"I'm giving those bastards what they deserve," Kai growled under his breath as he continued to splatter gasoline on the walls.

"Kai, stop this!" Hana cried in a silent voice, not wanting to alarm anybody of their presence.

"No!" Kai threw the now empty can down at her feet. "They deserve this. They deserve more than this for what they did to Haru!"

"What if you get caught? They'll kill you, Kai," Hana pleaded.

"Then let them kill me!" Kai shouted angrily, tears beginning to sting his eyes. He turned around to prevent her from witnessing the sight, and stared hard at the gasoline splattered walls. "Let them kill me."

Hana mentally swore at his stubbornness. She clasped her hand around Kai's wrist and pulled him forward to face her.

"What are you doing?" Kai's eyes flashed dangerously as he glared at her fingers. "You better let go, Hana, I'm not in a good mood."

"Is this what you think Haru wants you to do?" Hana stated firmly, her eyes narrowed at his stupidity. "Do you think he's proud of what you're doing right now?"

Kai scoffed loudly and yanked his arm out of her grip. He hissed, "Yeah? And how the hell do you know what Haru would want?"

Hana slipped her hand into the pocket of her dress. She pulled out a tiny piece of paper and placed it into Kai's hand.

"What the hell is this?" Kai scoffed as he threw it to the ground.

Hana stared down at the paper. "It's a piece of the map. It's small, useless, and it looks like trash, but it's what Haru put his life into protecting. It's what let Haru leave the world with a smile on his face. Haru was willing to discard his life in order to protect the dream that we all created together; the dream that you're throwing away."

"Haru...?" Kai spoke quietly. His eyes darted down to the paper that was about to catch the wind and he quickly snatched it up into his hand. He pressed down on its wrinkles, and desperately tried to smooth it out as nicely as possible. "Sorry Haru, I'm sorry," he murmured as he tried in vain to brush away the gasoline that had stained the parchment.

A few minutes passed in silence, and after trying to clean the tiny piece of paper as well as he could, Kai slowly lifted his head.

"Let's go back."

"Promise me you won't do anything like this again," Hana responded as she stood rooted in her spot. "Promise me."

"I promise," Kai mumbled under his breath as he peeked at her from beneath the fringe of his hair. "So let's just go back, alright?"

The corners of Hana's lips twitched into a small smile and she let go of the boy's wrist, "Everybody is worried about you."

"I doubt it," Kai muttered bitterly under his breath. "They're probably happy that I'm gone."

Hana's eyes narrowed and she rewrapped her fingers around his arm to pull him back, "Why would you say that?"

Kai casted his eyes to the ground. "Because I've been a jerk to them. I've been biting off their heads ever since –" Kai paused mid-sentence.

"Put more faith into them, would you?" Hana sighed as she gave him a reassuring pat on the shoulder. "They love you more than that."

"I've been a jerk to you too," Kai admitted shamefully. "I... I shouldn't have said the things I did, Hana. I just—"

He stopped midway when Hana pressed a finger to his lips, her eyes narrowed as they darted from side to side. Her ears perked up at the sound of slowly crunching leaves, signaling that somebody was approaching them but didn't want to be noticed.

"Guards are here," Hana murmured quietly. She pulled up her dress and tried to clean the stench of gasoline off his skin. She quietly picked up a stray bottle of gasoline, and poured the contents all over her dress, causing Kai to drop his jaw in surprise and confusion. "Push me and run."

"W-What?" Kai stammered, confused on what she was planning.

"Push me to the ground and run," Hana hissed in a low voice, her eyes catching a movement in the shadows. "Run around the guard house and back to the cages. On three, okay Kai?"

"H-Hana I can't—"

"One, two – make sure you push me hard – three." Once Hana reached three, she let out a blood curling scream. Kai hesitated for a split second before deciding to obey her wishes, and pushed her down before sprinting around the corner and out of sight.

Hana winced when the palms of her hands hit the hard ground to break her fall. The sacrifice was worth making, however, because no more than a few seconds after Kai had disappeared did a small group of guards come running out of the bushes from their hiding spot.

"Miss, what happened?! Where'd he go?!" one of the guards demanded as his head shot from side to side. "Did you see who it was?!"

Hana swallowed down her pride in order to play the "weak little girl" card. She bit down hard on her bottom lip to force tears to her eyes.

"I-It wa-was too dark," Hana sobbed as one of the guards helped her to her feet. She lifted up her gasoline drenched dress and whimpered pitifully. "I called out to ask what he was doing and then he poured gasoline all over me and pulled out a match! H-He was ab-about to light it, but then y-you guys came out. He ran th-that way!" She stretched out a finger in the direction opposite of where Kai had run.

Three of the five guards quickly darted to the direction Hana had pointed to, while the remaining two decided to stay and help. They immediately recognized the girl's face, for she had been a rather popular figure in the Noye House.

"Miss, are you okay? Are you injured?" one of the guards asked as he inspected her for any wounds.

"Just some scuffed palms," Hana shook her head. She stared meaningfully in the direction she had made the guards run and let out a loud sigh. "Do you think they will catch him?"

The guard nodded, "We won't lose him, Miss! We'll make sure of it!"

Hana's ears perked up at the sudden call of her name and she furrowed her eyebrows when she saw Henry making his way over to them.

"Hana, are you okay?" Henry asked with wide eyes as he inspected the frazzled state of the girl. He pulled out a handkerchief and attempted to clean the dirt off Hana's dress, but she quickly pulled away.

"I'm fine," Hana responded coldly, biting down on her tongue to prevent her from saying any more.

Henry was disappointed with Hana's hostile reaction, but he didn't let it show. "We'll catch the person who did this to you, okay?"

Before Hana could respond, Henry turned to the remaining guards, "Use the speakers to make an announcement that all the Noyes must return to their cages immediately, and have the guards blockade all the entrances. Get the attendance list and we'll go inspect all the Noyes to see if any of them are acting suspiciously."

Hana mentally cursed at Henry when he ran away to gather the guards. She chewed on her bottom lip, desperately trying to come up with a solution. She broke into a sprint, and headed back towards the cages.

"Is Kai back?!" Hana exclaimed frantically as she skidded into the cages. The other Noyes stared at her with gaping mouths, surprised to see her in such a disheveled state.

"What happened to you?" Sean demanded.

"I'll tell you later, where's Kai?!" Hana exclaimed as she scanned the room to look for the familiar face. She began to panic when she didn't see him and she spun quickly around to search for the other.

"I'm here, I'm here," Kai gasped as he leaned over to catch his breath.

"What's happening? Why are there so many guards?"

"They're trying to find a suspect," Hana answered as she frantically racked her brain to come up with some way to avert attention from Kai.

Sean quickly grasped the situation at hand and he yanked a spare change of clothes and threw them at Kai. "Change quickly!"

Kai caught the clothing and immediately tore his soiled shirt over his head. Sean didn't fail to spin Hana around once Kai's bare skin was revealed and she would have laughed if the situation wasn't as it was.

"Luca, the first aid kit!" Hana ordered as she pointed to the box that was stashed under the table. Luca was quick to obey her commands, and he handed the kit over to her in a flash. "Kai, come here quickly."

Kai hopped over to her as he finished pulling his second leg into the respective hole of his pants.

"Sit in front of me and pretend you're tending to my wounds," Hana explained as she shoved the first aid kit into his hands. "If they suspect you of smelling like gasoline, simply answer that my stench rubbed off on you, you understand?"

Kai remained silent for a few seconds as he stared at the girl in awe, but snapped out of his trance when she hissed, "Do you understand?"

Kai nodded his head and took her hands into his own; there wasn't a point in pretending to fix her wounds. He stared guiltily at the scuffed palms, and quietly pulled a bottle of ointment from the kit.

"You really like getting us in trouble, don't you Kai?" Aiden snapped bitterly as he glared at the other. His gaze softened when he saw the sorrowful and guilty expression stretched across Kai's face and he let out a small sigh. He reached forward and began picking out the leaves that had settled into Kai's hair. "You're going to give yourself away."

"Thank you," Kai murmured quietly as he applied ointment to Hana's wounds. "And I'm sorry."

"Don't be an idiot," Luca responded as he placed a warm hand on Kai's arm. "We all understand."

Kai lifted his head and parted his lips to express his gratitude, but was interrupted by the sound of loud footsteps.

"You're already here, Hana?" Henry asked with brief surprise as he stepped into the cage.

"As you can see," Hana responded, not even sparing the man a glance.

"I… yeah…" Henry murmured as he casted his eyes down to the ground. He cleared his throat once he remembered his job and loudly announced, "Are Luca Grey, Aiden Park, Kai Ainsley, and Haru— Are the three of them here?"

They all flinched at the reminder of Haru's absence and Hana let out a small growl. "Clearly you can see that all three of them are present. Chase Berlitz of the cage next door is here as well, so don't waste your time."

Henry fell silent at the girl's harsh tone and he opened his mouth to say something in return, but decided against it. Instead, he spun around to retreat from the cage with the guards trailing closely behind him.

Hana waited until the group was a few cages down before letting out a breath of relief, "That was close."

"What were they looking for?" Chase asked curiously.

"Me," Kai admitted shamefully. "I did something bad."

Luca rolled his eyes and smacked the boy lightly on the back of his head, "We inferred that much, idiot."

Kai glanced up at him with tears swimming in his eyes. He quickly swiped at them with the back of his hand, "Luca…"

"Don't you dare cry or it's going to make me start crying too," Luca warned despite the fact that his eyes were already beginning to gloss over.

"Are you okay?" Sean asked as he pulled Hana up to her feet. He frowned at the sight of her injured palms. He tried to clean Hana's dress with his hands, but was swatted away. "Don't do that, Sean, you're going to get yourself dirty."

"I don't care," Sean shrugged as he stepped forward to help the girl once again.

Hana sighed and shook her head. They would all need to get a proper cleaning once they returned home anyways. A chime from her phone informed her that Jaymes had arrived to pick them up and the group of three waved the other Noyes a goodbye before heading to the exit.

Hana stopped abruptly when a hand suddenly wrapped around her wrist and she turned back to stare at Kai in confusion.

"I… I want to thank you. I wanted to thank you for saving me," Kai whispered in a soft voice as he stared at the girl with a gentle expression. He pulled Hana in for a tight hug, and his voice cracked as he continued.

"… and I wanted to thank you for saving Haru."

CHAPTER NINE: AUDACIOUS

audacious [aw-dae-shus] adj. - to be recklessly bold or daring

The seven people sat somberly in the cage, a curtain of tension draped around each and every one of them. The seat beside Kai lay empty, for nobody dared to take the spot that belonged to Haru.

Hana sat with the side of her face pressed against Sean's chest, listening to the slow beats of his heart to calm down her nerves. The taller soothingly ran his fingers through her hair in a gentle motion.

"Okay, let's get to work!" Luca jumped to his feet with a fake smile plastered across his face. "There's no time to be lazy!"

"Stop it, Luca," Aiden responded simply. "Don't push yourself."

Luca's fake smile fell and he plopped back down. "Sorry."

"Don't apologize," Aiden replied as he wrapped his arm around the other's shoulders. "Thank you for trying."

"Luca's right," Kai spoke suddenly. He stared at the empty spot beside him. "We can't let this time go to waste."

"We don't have a map," Aiden said flatly. "We can't do anything."

"Yes we can," Kai responded with a hard glare. "We can do something, anything, as long as we're not just sitting on our asses doing nothing."

"What do you suggest?" Luca asked quietly.

"Whatever it is, we can help."

All seven heads snapped upwards at the sudden voice. A pair of Noyes stood at the cage entrance with determined expressions on their faces.

"Archer? Ethan? What are you guys doing here?" Aiden asked with furrowed eyebrows. He recognized the pair of Noyes, for he and Archer often exchanged words when they were working.

"We're going to help you," Archer's deep voice responded as he walked further into the room, tugging Ethan who was hiding behind him. "We're going to help you with this rebellion or whatever."

"Why would you do that?" Kai asked with narrowed eyes.

"Don't think that we're happy in this hell hole, Kai," Archer replied. "We want to get out of this place just as much as you all do. And... and it was wrong what they did to Haru. They've pulled a lot of horrible shit before, but that was just crossing the line."

"What makes you think we can trust you?" Kai asked, his tone now just the slightest bit softer from the remorse Archer showed towards Haru.

"We can't prove anything to you," Archer responded flatly. "You're just going to have to trust us. You're going to need all the hands you can get, and it just so happens that we have a few extra pairs to offer."

"Who else is there?" Aiden asked with a raised eyebrow.

"The rest of my boys," Archer answered. "Logan, Skyler, and Nash. That's five extra hands you can't afford to reject."

"Nash?" Kai immediately rejected. "No way, that guy's a rat."

"He's a brother," Archer responded. "It's either all or none of us."

Kai opened his mouth to reject, but was interrupted by the sharp call of his name. Hana stared hard at him and he let out a small growl.

"Fine," Kai muttered reluctantly. "You're in."

"I thought that would be the case. I'll go let the other guys know," Archer nodded his head as the two left the room.

"We can't trust Nash," Kai stated once the pair had left. "That kid's a rat. He's always selling out the other Noyes to get extra perks."

"I don't trust him either, but we need the others," Aiden sighed. "We'll watch ourselves around Nash, but we can't pass them up."

Kai opened his mouth to protest, but pressed his lips reluctantly together. He knew Aiden was right.

"Hana, can I talk to you?"

The seven heads snapped upwards once again; this time with more hostility. They tensed at the appearance of the familiar other; had he heard their exchange?

"No, you can't," Sean growled with narrowed eyes.

"Sean," Hana warned in a soft voice. "What do you need, Henry?"

"I just want to talk to you," Henry replied quietly. He could feel Sean's glare bore into his skin. "In private."

"You can say it here," Sean replied. "In front of all of us."

"Sean," Hana called out again, a little firmer than before.

Henry's eyes drifted from Hana's face to Sean's angered expression. He observed the protective hand Sean had resting on Hana's shoulder - not gripping her too tightly, but firm enough to express his dissent. He watched as Hana pressed the tips of her fingers against Sean's hand, persuading the boy to release his grip almost immediately. Hana gave Henry a small nod to tell him that she would follow him.

"What's going on between the two of you?" he asked when the pair made their way into the hallway. "You and that Noye, I mean, Sean."

He noticed how Hana stiffened just the slightest and he arched his eyebrow higher into his hair line.

"I don't believe that's any of your business," Hana responded in the stoic tone he was all too familiar with. "Tell me what you needed to say."

"He obviously harbors feelings for you," Henry continued with crossed arms. "And you have feelings for him in return, don't you?"

"If this was the nonsense you wanted to tell me, then I'm leaving," Hana replied with narrowed eyes.

"It won't work out between the two of you, you know that right?"

Hana tensed.

"Those kind of relationships never work out," Henry shrugged. "Being in love with a Noye won't get you anywhere except shunned."

"Thank you for your concern," she replied in a flat voice.

"Are you really willing to risk everything for him?" Henry asked in a raised voice. "I'm trying to help you, Hana. Being in love with a Noye is the worst thing you can do to your social status. Why are you doing this to yourself? How could you fall in love with somebody so... so filthy?"

Hana froze at the words. "Don't you dare insult Sean," she growled as she stepped threateningly towards the male. "It's none of your damn business what I do, and whether or not I have feelings for him is none of your concern. Don't pretend that you're trying to help me when you don't even know what it means to truly help somebody."

Hana let out another angry huff, and shoved him against the shoulder with the palm of her hand just for good measure. She spun around and stalked angrily away, silently fuming to herself.

"Hana."

Hana glanced up in surprise to see Sean staring down at her. She caught the light pink that tinged his cheeks and she realized that Sean must have heard what she had said.

"I... I just wanted to make sure he wasn't trying to pull anything," Sean mumbled as he awkwardly rubbed the back of his neck.

"O-Oh..." Hana swallowed as she trained her gaze on the ground, not daring to meet the other's eyes. "Let's get back to the others, alright?"

"Hana," Sean called her name again, holding on to her upper arm when she tried to move forward. "Hana, I want to know."

"Know what?" Hana asked as she glanced over her shoulder. Her heart skipped a beat at how he stared at her and she bit down on her bottom lip. She had a feeling she knew what he wanted to say.

"I want to know how you feel about me," Sean stared firmly. He didn't know where the courage had come from, but the words had escaped his lips and there was no going back. He had to follow through till the end.

"I... I know you know that I have... that I have feelings for you," Sean blurted out, flushing furiously once the words had been said. "And I... I want to know if you feel anything towards me. Just... just even the slightest bit."

Hana's face softened, "Sean, I don't think this is the right time to do this. Not with Haru, not with the rebellion, and I—"

"I know, Hana," Sean cut her off. "I know this is so inappropriate and that Haru is probably damning me to the pits of hell, but I need to know. I need to know if this is all just some stupid fantasy of mine, or if... or if this..." He couldn't bring himself to continue.

"I... Sean, I don't... I don't know if—" Hana stammered uncertainly, not knowing exactly what she should say to the other. She knew there would be consequences for either answer she chose.

Sean held up a hand to cut her off. "It's okay. You don't have to continue." He let out a soft, humorless chuckle and ran his fingers through his hair. "I was just being stupid, sorry."

"Sean, I like you."

Sean's heart stuttered in its beats and his head darted upwards in alarm. "W-What did you say?" Sean gaped with an open mouth.

"I said that I like you, but Sean, this doesn—"

"No, don't say anything else," Sean quickly pressed a finger against her lips. "Don't go on about how this won't work and about all the bad stuff that will happen. Don't say anything, just... just let me enjoy this."

Hana opened her mouth to protest, but was taken by surprise when Sean suddenly engulfed her into a tight hug. "Sean...?"

"Thank you," Sean breathed quietly into her hair. His heart was nearly beating out of his chest at their close proximity. He feared that she would be able to feel his thumping heart, but still refused to release her from his grip.

She liked him.

She liked *him*.

"Thank you, thank you," Sean whispered over and over again like a mantra, more to himself than to the girl clasped in his arms. "Thank you."

* * *

"Sean, let's talk," Hana stated as she stood in front of the male who was lounged across the bed reading a book. He glanced up at her and averted his gaze, knowing exactly what she wanted to talk about.

"I'm kind of busy right now," Sean mumbled as he flipped to his side. "Try again later."

Hana rolled her eyes at Sean's immature behavior. "Sean, come on."

"No," Sean responded, refusing to obey the girl's wishes.

Hana huffed and climbed onto the bed. "Sean, don't be such a child."

"No, I'll be a child all I want," Sean replied with crossed arms.

"You can't make me do anything."

Hana blew her hair away from her face, and sat on the bed with folded legs. "If you're not going to face me, then I'm just going to talk like this." She sighed when Sean didn't respond, and poked him with her foot.

"I want to talk to you about what happened yesterday," Hana began slowly, gauging Sean's reaction from her only view of his back.

"I don't want to hear what you have to say," Sean finally replied after a short period of silence. "I'm not listening."

He didn't have to hear her words to know what she wanted to tell him. She was just going to tell him how a relationship between the two wouldn't work. How dangerous it would be in the eyes of society, and how hard a life they would have to lead. He didn't want to hear it when he already knew himself.

"Hana, could I talk to you? It's about the…," Jaymes called out as he popped his head into the room. He arched an eyebrow at the couple that was situated on the bed. "Am I interrupting something? I better not be interrupting something."

Hana glanced at Sean and let out a quiet sigh. "No, it's alright Jaymes." She uncrossed her legs and slid off the bed. "It's not like we're doing any talking here, anyways."

Sean winced at the harshness of Hana's tone, but refused to budge. The sound of her footsteps faded away and the door closed shut to signal that she was gone. Despite her absence, Sean continued to remain in that uncomfortable position.

He registered the click of the door reopening, and held his breath as light footsteps approached him. He felt the bed dip beside him and a hand reached out to gently shake his upper arm. Realizing that it wasn't Hana, he glanced over his shoulder to see Chris with his board. *What's wrong?*

"I told her that I liked her," Sean admitted as he stared up at the ceiling, his hands tucked behind his head. "I shouldn't have done that, huh?" Sean continued flatly as he observed the elder's expression.

Chris stared at him uneasily before hesitantly nodding his head.

"But why?" Sean huffed as he jolted up in his seat. He crossed his legs and folded his arms. "Why is it so wrong?"

The corners of Sean's lips drooped, and his eyes stared at him with desperation. Chris stretched out an arm and patted Sean's head sympathetically, knowing, yet not knowing, what pain the younger must have been suffering emotionally. He pulled Sean in for a tight hug, silently reminding the younger that he would always be there for him.

"Chris," Sean spoke softly, clinging to the front of Chris's shirt like a child would to his mother. "Why are people so cruel? If it doesn't affect them, why can't they just let others be happy?"

Chris didn't know what to tell him.

* * *

"President Acacia would like to see you."

The slight thud of Chris's white board hitting the bed sounded. His now empty hands began to shake as his eyes darted to Sean who looked like a deer caught in headlights.

"What does he want with Sean?" Jaymes asked with narrowed eyes. Hana had left for school no more than an hour ago, and already her father was seeking out one of the two boys.

"I don't believe that is any of your business," the security guard responded. "Come Noye, he doesn't like to be kept waiting."

Normally Sean would have growled at the way the man called for him, but now he was too frightened to do so. What did Hana's father want with him? He knew what the man was capable of, for he had never failed to show off his power in the cruelest of ways.

"I'm going with him," Jaymes growled with folded arms.

"No, you have to stay with Chris," Sean shook his head.

Jaymes turned to him with an incredulous expression plastered across his face. "Sean, I'm not going to—"

"Please," Sean pleaded as he wrapped his fingers around Jaymes's wrist. "Stay with Chris." His gaze traveled to the other who was already beginning to shake in his seat. He forced a smile onto his face and gave Chris a small wave, "I'm going to go talk with Hana's father for a little, okay Chris? I'll be right back."

"Follow me," the guard ordered as he left the room.

Sean reluctantly turned to follow, but stopped when a hand grabbed his upper arm. He glanced back to see Jaymes staring at him uneasily.

"Try not to get hurt," Jaymes offered after a pause of silence. "Because Miss Hana will kill both of us if you do."

"I'll keep that in mind," Sean responded dryly.

Sean could feel his palms begin to sweat as he climbed up the spiral staircase to the third floor of the house. His heart was nearly beating out of his chest by the time they arrived and Sean wiped his hands against his jeans as the guard knocked on the door.

A voice on the other side called for them to enter. He took a slow, deep breath before stepping inside. The room was brightly light, for the curtains were all pulled open to reveal the bright sun of the afternoon.

"Noye," Chando bellowed. "Aren't you going to greet me?"

Sean's eyes widened in alarm and he quickly lowered his head into a 90 degree bow. "I apologize for my rudeness, sir, I m-mean Pre- President." Sean winced at his mistake. His upper body remained completely parallel to the floor until Chando finally spoke up. "That's enough, boy, come sit here."

"I… Please excuse me," Sean mumbled as he nervously took the seat.

"I think you know why I've called you here today, boy," Chando spoke as he took a bite out of the sandwich he had been in the middle of eating.

"I... n-not really, Sir- President Acacia," Sean responded nervously, training his gaze on the crumbs that littered the top of his desk.

"Will you not look at me when I speak to you?" Chando snapped.

Sean's head immediately darted up and he swallowed hard as he stared at Chando, "Forgive my rudeness, President."

"That's better," Chando nodded as he drummed his fingers against the polished desk. "I called you here because I have an offer, Noye."

Chando picked out a piece of bread from between his teeth and rummaged around his desk with his free hand. He pulled out a briefcase from one of the drawers and slid it over to Sean.

Sean didn't even need to look inside to know what it consisted of.

"250,000 dollars," Chando stated as he tapped his hand against the briefcase. "I will give you 250,000 dollars to run away with that other Noye. 250,000 to restart your lives far away from my daughter."

Sean's mouth went dry. Was he honestly offering him *money*? He was offering him money to stay away from Hana? Half of Sean was kind of grateful. The man could have easily forced the two to stay away, but instead Chando had offered him monetary compensation.

Chando must have known what he was thinking, "You should be grateful that I am offering such an amount to somebody as lowly as you."

The other half just wanted to punch him in the face.

"I… I don't believe I can take this, President," Sean replied as he slid the case back to Chando. He gripped the handles of his chair and began to push himself out of the seat, "If that's all you have to say, then—"

"You will sit until I tell you to leave!" Chando ordered in a loud voice.

Sean clenched hard on his teeth and slowly sank back into the chair.

"I thought you would be stupid and decline," Chando stated as he pulled the briefcase back to tuck into his drawer. "You should have just taken it, but now you have to turn me into the bad guy, don't you, Noye?"

He let out a drawn out sigh as if it pained him to say what he does next. "I will hurt you, Noye, if you don't listen to me. I will hurt Hana if you don't obey my wishes. You might think I'm bluffing when I say I'd hurt my own daughter, but you should know well enough that I don't bluff."

There was a pregnant silence as Sean thought over his words.

"I believe you will do everything you say, President," Sean finally nodded in response. His voice hardened, "But my answer is still no. I don't mean any disrespect, but I doubt you will be able to hurt Hana. You and I both know that she is capable of doing amazing things, things that will surpass anything you will ever be capable of doing."

A small voice in the back of Sean's head was telling him to shut the hell up and beg for forgiveness while he still could, but he decided to ignore it for now.

"As for myself... Life for me would be far worse not being by Hana's side than it would be being beat every day," Sean murmured.

A warning bell went off in his head and he immediately continued with, "That's the job of a Noye. Since the second we are bought, we must dedicate our lives to our owners and not allow our emotions to take any role in our actions."

Chando stared at him and gritted his teeth in annoyance. Just how stubborn did the Noye plan to be? Realizing that his second approach wouldn't work, he decided to go for his final one.

"Don't try to fool me, Noye, I know you and my daughter have a relationship that borders being romantic. If you think I will stand by and allow such an atrocity to happen, you sure as hell thought wrong! If you really cared for her with your so called love, then you will leave her," Chando growled as he stared sharply into Sean's eyes. "Do you know what would happen if she chooses to be with you?"

Sean held his breath.

"Nothing," Chando spat. "Actually worse than nothing because she'll lose everything. She'll lose everything and then she will become nothing. She will become meaningless, because there is no place in this world for *Noyes* to associate themselves with people of higher class. You will *ruin* her, do you understand? You will destroy her life. She will never be able to build her career back up; she will never be able to lead a normal life, and that will be all *your* fault."

Sean's mouth went dry and he clenched his fists so tightly he could feel his nails piercing his skin. He remained silent for a few minutes.

Chando leaned back in his chair with a victorious smirk, knowing that his final round of attack must have gotten into Sean's head. If this Noye loved his daughter as much as he thinks he does, then how would he be capable of bearing the responsibilities and guilt of destroying her future?

"You're wrong," Sean whispered quietly.

Chando's eyes flashed in alarm, "What did you say?"

"I said you're wrong," Sean repeated himself in a firmer tone. "Hana is stronger than that, you would know if you paid more attention to her. She wouldn't let this destroy her; she'd only allow it to make her stronger. She… she's not a coward. She's not a coward like the rest of us."

He swallowed hard and glanced up at Chando with hard eyes. "And I won't leave her. You said it yourself, right? Noyes are the scum of the earth and you can't get any lower than that. You thought I would leave her for her own good, but what if I don't care? What if I'm selfish enough to let her own good break into pieces as long as it means that I can stay by her side?"

"I'm a selfish man," Sean stated as he stood up in his seat, the legs of his chair scraping against the wooden floor as he pushed it back. "I'm the most selfish, lowest scum on the face of the earth. I am a Noye. I am poor, I am stupid, and I won't be able to provide any benefits for your daughter, but I won't leave. Even if you have to kill me and drag my body away, I still won't leave."

He bowed a stiff 90 degrees, "I apologize for my rudeness today, President. I don't want my measly existence to take up any more of your time, so I will leave you alone now." Sean was out of the room before the President could even open his mouth to respond.

Sean let out a shaky breath as he leaned his back against the cold, wooden door. Half of him was proud of standing up to a man as intimidating as Chando, but the other half was damning himself to the pits of hell. He knew his words wouldn't go without consequence and he was an idiot to have let them escape.

Sean meant every single word he had said, however. He wasn't willing to let Hana go without a fight and he was willing to sacrifice everything he had if it meant that he could remain by her side.

He clenched down on his jaw and felt his heart drop at his next thought; he just didn't know if Hana was willing to do the same.

CHAPTER TEN: PREPARATION

Preparation [pre-pə-rā-shen] n. - A preliminary measure that serves to make ready for an event or occasion.

Chando's head snapped up when his office door suddenly flung open. He opened his mouth to angrily shout at the perpetrator, but paused once Hana entered the room.

He knew that she had finally summoned the courage to approach him, for he hadn't gotten even a glimpse of her ever since he suggested to Michael to use that dead Noye as a warning.

Although his face remained neutral, he was mentally smirking triumphantly. He knew his daughter well enough to understand that she was hiding her true emotions beneath her stoic mask, and that it was he who had come out victoriously. Perhaps now she would take more care to mind his words.

"To what do I owe your presence to, Hana?" Chando smirked. "It's certainly been quite a while since you've come to meet me."

"I saw the performance you organized a few days ago," Hana stated as she swiftly closed the door behind her. The image of Haru flew into her head and she gritted her teeth. "I can't say I appreciated it."

"I thought I needed to show you just how serious I am about what I say," Chando shrugged as he leaned back in his leather chair. His eyes widened slightly in surprise when Hana's lips lifted into a small smile.

"Funny you'd say that," Hana responded with a cocked head. She held out a folder and placed it onto his desk. "I was thinking the same thing."

"What is this?" Chando asked with an arched eyebrow as he flipped to the front page of the folder's contents.

"I guess you could call it a proposal," Hana replied as she observed her father's expression. "If you haven't realized already, the page you're looking at consists of all the shareholders who currently have a significant proportion of Acacia Corporation ownership."

"And?" Chando scoffed. "If you can't see, Hana, it states rather clearly that I have the largest percentile ownership."

"Oh I see that very clearly," Hana responded. She pointed to her own name that was printed right below her father's. "But don't forget that I hold a rather large percentile as well."

"14%?" Chando barked in laughter. "Are you trying to threaten me with your 14% when you know full well that I possess 32%?"

"Yes and no," Hana answered. "You see father, although both you and I possess the largest quantity of shares in this corporation, the remaining 54% is distributed amongst a large number of shareholders, both regionally and internationally."

"And?" Chando asked with an arched eyebrow.

"And," Hana smiled in response. She leaned forward and tapped the folder with her finger. "You might want to flip to the next page."

Chando grumbled quietly to himself as he flipped to the next page of the folder. His eyes scanned the bolded letters at the top, and it took him a few seconds to process exactly what the words meant. Hana watched in amusement as his eyes widened in a mix of anger and surprise. "What the hell are you trying to pull?"

"I'm not trying to pull anything," Hana responded with folded arms. "I'm not pulling dirty tricks behind peoples' backs like you do, father. I'm giving you a clear warning about what is to come these next few days."

"And what is that?" Chando snarled.

"You can read, can't you?" Hana shrugged her shoulders. "It says proposal to dismiss Chando Acacia from office."

Chando let out a low, bitter laugh as he trained his gaze on Hana. "You don't think people are actually going to vote for this, do you? There isn't a clause! I'm not ill or elderly – nobody will vote me out."

"I guess we'll find out, won't we?" Hana smiled knowingly as she coolly turned around to walk out of his office. She paused on her way out, "You might want to flip to the next few pages, father."

"You did well," Jaymes greeted her with a smile once she completely exited her father's office.

"My heart is beating so fast I think it's going to come out," Hana confessed as she pressed her hand against her chest. She eyed the suitcases Jaymes was holding in his hand, and a small smile slipped onto her face. "So you already know, do you?"

"I'm hurt that you actually think you can hide something from me," Jaymes scoffed as he began to pull the empty luggages up the stairs.

"What's that?" Sean asked as he stared at the suitcases the pair brought in. Chris joined him with raised eyebrows of curiosity.

"We're moving," Jaymes stated as he gestured to the suitcases. "I thought that was apparent enough."

Sean's eyes widened in surprise. "…Why?"

"I told you to trust me, didn't I?" Hana simply asked as she began to pull an empty suitcase into her closet.

"Hana, I don't understand," Sean murmured as he followed her into the closet. "Why are we moving?"

"Because I want to show you," Hana responded simply.

"Show me what?" Sean asked, his eyebrows furrowing even further from confusion.

Hana paused for a few seconds before turning to him with a small, shy smile spread across her face, "That… t-that…"

"That?" Sean urged.

"That I'm willing to fight for you too… for us," Hana mumbled under her breath, a light red blush capturing her cheeks. She quickly turned her head in embarrassment, allowing her long hair to shield her florid skin.

Sean sat there silently for a few seconds as he processed the meaning behind Hana's words. A smile stretched across his cheeks and he stared at the girl with affection and pride swimming through his eyes. "Hana."

He quickly pulled her forward with a jerk. Hana's eyes widened in surprise when she felt Sean's lips press briefly against her own and she tilted her head up to look into his mischievous eyes.

"I'll go help outside now," Sean grinned as he childishly saluted the girl before exiting the closet.

Hana sat there motionless for a few minutes, and a tinge of red captured her face as she replayed the kiss over again in her head.

"Need some help?" Jaymes asked as he walked inside with a knowing look in his eyes. "My little Hana is growing up so fast," he cooed.

Hana shot him a dirty look out of the corner of her eye, causing him to chuckle good naturedly. Silence engulfed the pair as they worked to pack clothes into the large suitcase that laid before them.

"Jaymes…" Hana called out softly as she continued to fold her clothes. She glanced at him from the corner of her eyes, "You're free, you know."

"I know," Jaymes nodded, not offering any more words of response.

"You don't have to stay with me any longer," Hana continued as she stared down at her hands. "You're not under any contract anymore."

"I know," Jaymes repeated himself with a shrug.

There was a beat of silence. "Are you going to stay?" Hana finally summoned the courage to ask. She glanced at him hopefully.

Jaymes turned to her with a pair of raised eyebrows, "I'm sorry, but it's going to take a lot more than this to get rid of me."

* * *

"I think it's time we test out what we have with a little experiment," Hana announced as she gestured to the bits and pieces of the Noye house layout they had scribbled across various pieces of paper.

"What kind of experiment?" Aiden asked with an arched eyebrow.

Hana smiled mischievously as she pulled an object from her bag.

"What's that?" Aiden asked curiously as he reached forward to prod the black cube.

"Let her finish before you ask questions," Luca snapped as he slapped Aiden on the back of his head.

"It's a bomb," Hana quietly informed them as she set it in front of her. "Just a small one that won't do much damage."

"What are we going to do with that?" Aiden asked with a cocked head. He flinched when Luca raised his fist threateningly, and quieted down.

"We're going to sneak this into one of the storage line pipes and set it off," Hana explained.

"How are we— Ouch! Jesus, okay! I'll shut up!" Aiden grumbled when Luca had roughly yanked a tuff of his hair.

"Tomorrow when you guys are at work, I'll sneak—"

"Over my dead body," Sean interrupted before she was even capable of finishing. "You aren't sneaking around anywhere by yourself."

"He's right, I'll do it," Aiden nodded his head as he swiped the bomb from her hands. "I work near the storages so it'll be easier for me to do it."

"Are you out of your damn mind? You'd get caught in a heartbeat!" Luca hissed as he snatched away the explosive.

"Luca's right, just let me do it," Kai agreed as he plucked the bomb out of Luca's open palm. "It's okay if I get caught, I don't... I don't have a partner to worry about leaving like you guys do."

"No way in hell," Sean glared as he yanked the bomb out of Kai's hands.

"I'll do it."

All heads turned to Chase who had been sitting quietly in the corner of the cage. He meekly rose his hand and crawled forward to carefully take the bomb from Sean. "I'll do it."

"Are you... are you sure?" Aiden asked slowly and hesitantly.

Chase bit down on his bottom lip. What did he expect? Of course nobody would speak in his defense. He didn't possess a close friend or lover like they all did. If he were to get caught, sure they would be sad, but they wouldn't be as heartbroken as they would be if they lost one of their own. He didn't have any complaints, however. He was used to this; this was how Chase had lived his entire life.

"Yeah," Chase nodded his head. "I'm sure."

"Chase..." Hana called out softly as she stared at him.

"Don't worry, I'm sure I want to do this. Positive," Chase smiled. "Can you tell me what you want me to do, exactly?"

Hana hesitantly nodded her head. She moved closer to him and explained everything in precise detail.

The day quickly concluded and soon it was time for Hana and the two others to travel home – to their new home.

The house was relatively small in size, but it would still grant them an appropriate amount of space. The house possessed four bedrooms, one for each of them, two bathrooms, a small study, a kitchen, and a living room. It was quite a contrast to the mansion they had previously lived in.

"Do you guys like it?" Hana asked as she turned to face the other three. "I'm sorry I chose it without asking you all. I've already had a bed and desk moved into each room, but everything else is free for you to choose."

She bit down uneasily on her bottom lip. "Well?"

A pair of arms wrapped around her waist and she glanced up to see Chris beaming down at her. He stepped back and quickly scribbled something across his white board. *It's perfect.*

Hana smiled happily and took his hand to bring him inside. "Aren't the two of you coming?" Hana called over her shoulder.

The two men exchanged glances and small smiles before picking up the luggage to bring into the house.

"You can all pick which room you want," Hana nodded her head as she gestured to the four closed doors. "Clean up and get to bed, okay?" Hana called out before heading into her own bedroom to wash up for bed.

The decision to select a house to live in had come rather suddenly, but Hana honestly couldn't have been happier. Sean and Chris now had the freedom to roam wherever they desired. Just as she was about to climb into bed, a light rap sounded on her door, and a stream of light entered her dark bedroom. "Sean?"

Sean stood silently for a few seconds with florid cheeks. He inhaled a deep breath of air to calm his nerves and then quickly asked in a single breath, "Can I come sleep with you?"

"This is a singles bed," Hana replied with an arched eyebrow. She chuckled at the frown that spread across Sean's lips and scooted over to make room for him. A wide grin stretched across his face and he quickly closed the door behind him. There wasn't much room to spare, but the two managed to fit comfortably under the blanket.

Just as they were about to fall asleep, they registered the quiet click of the door knob turning, and looked up to see Chris sheepishly tip-toeing into the bedroom. He stilled when he spotted Sean already lying in bed with Hana, and quickly dove under the covers without even bothering to ask for permission.

"It's a singles bed, Chris," Sean protested as Chris squeezed in between the pair. It was an extremely tight fit, but they managed to all find a comfortable position.

An abrupt bang sounded through the room and the three heads looked up when a sudden flood of light entered the bedroom.

"I find it utterly insulting that you all had a sleepover without me," Jaymes stated with furrowed eyebrows and crossed arms. A grin quickly spread across his face as he moved towards the trio.

"It's a singles!" Hana and Sean exclaimed as Chris threw a pillow at the male to prevent him from advancing.

Jaymes barked in response, "It's either all of us or none of us!"

* * *

"Are you nervous?"

"Not really," Chase shrugged as he fingered the small bomb that was lying in his pocket. "Worst case scenario is that it doesn't work."

"Are you kidding me?!" Luca exclaimed incredulously. "Worst case scenario is that you get caught!"

Chase remained silent for a few seconds before shrugging off his words, "That's no big deal."

"What happens if he gets caught?" Logan asked curiously. He, Archer, Ethan, Nash, and Skyler had joined the other Noyes that morning and had just been filled in on what was going to happen.

"Isn't it obvious?" Nash scoffed as he slid his thumb across his throat. "You saw what they did to that other Noye."

"Don't say that Nash, Chase will be fine," Ethan scolded the other. He glanced at Hana and blushed when she smiled gratefully at him.

"Well, it's time to go to work," Aiden cleared his throat as he clapped a hand onto Chase's shoulder. He added under his breath, "Don't listen to that asshole, you'll do just fine."

"You can do it," Logan pitched in with a raised fist of triumph.

"Good luck," Kai nodded his head as Chase passed.

Chris tugged on Chase's sleeve and held up his board. *Stay safe.*

The corner of Chase's lip twitched upwards and he nodded his head gratefully. "I will."

"He probably won't make it back alive," Nash scoffed as soon as Aiden and Chase were out of earshot.

"Hey, don't say that," Skyler scolded the male. "You don't know that."

"Like hell I do," Nash snorted as he waved Skyler off. "Authorities have a bird's eye on us at all times. I bet they're watching us right now and know every little thing you guys are scheming."

"I'm starting to get real sick and tired of you," Kai snapped.

Nash climbed up to his feet. "The feeling is mutual, bastard."

"What did you just call me?" Kai growled as he shoved Nash roughly.

"Don't touch him," Skyler shot up to stand in between Nash and Kai. "He might have a dirty mouth, but he's one of us."

He turned around and scolded Nash, "And you, you need to shut up if you don't have anything useful to say. We all voted to decide whether or not we would help them and you agreed to go with the decision."

"That was before I knew how dangerous this was," Nash protested.

"Because you're not smart enough to assume that there would be danger in staging a Noye rebellion?" Sean scoffed. "What the hell did you expect?"

"I'll tell you what I didn't expect!" Nash shouted as he stretched a finger in Hana's direction. "I didn't expect our leader to be some prissy rich girl who's probably never dirtied a finger her entire life!"

"Didn't I tell you to shut your mouth?" Logan growled as he shot Nash a threatening glare.

"I'm just saying what we're all thinking!" Nash defended as he crossed his arms. "How are we supposed to trust some rich girl who's never had to suffer the same things we did? Are we supposed to believe that she's going to risk her time, money, and life for something she doesn't benefit from? Do you actually think—"

"Are you not going to shut up?" Hana interjected with annoyance. "Or should I just interrupt you now?" All eyes turned to the girl, surprised that she had spoken up.

"If you want to leave then leave," Hana continued. "Nobody is stopping you. If you don't believe in me, then you don't believe in me. I'm not going to try to persuade you to trust me; that's not what I'm here to do. You're just wasting time that nobody has by whining, so if you're not going to do or say anything productive then get out."

Sean grinned at Hana's words, proud that she had stood up for herself. He was initially surprised that the girl had spoken up in such a manner, but it just made him adore Hana all so much more.

There was a beat of silence before Nash let out a loud scoff, "I was just stating my opinion, no need to get all nasty."

"I'll show you nasty if you let out another word," Kai growled under his breath. He grinned when Hana made no move to reprimand him, and flicked him off with his middle finger before turning to the other boys.

"What do you need us to do Ha-Han...I-uh, yeah," Ethan stammered nervously as he trained his eyes on the ground.

"You don't need to be afraid of us, Ethan," Hana smiled reassuringly.

"Yeah, because that's what he is," Kai scoffed. "Afraid."

"You might as well drop the crush now, kid, we already have one puppy chasing her tail," Luca jerked his thumb at Sean.

Sean nodded his head with crossed arms, proud that the others had come to his defense.

Ethan's cheeks flushed a bright red and he quickly clamored to his feet in embarrassment. "I-uh... I didn't mean to. I just... s-sor-sorry!" he exclaimed. "I didn't know she was yours!"

"It's alright kid," Sean nodded his head as he disheveled the younger's hair. "I'm flattered that you chose to like her."

"Idiots," Hana sighed. She clapped her hands loudly together to catch their attention, and pointed down at an area of the map. "Do any of you know the guards' routine schedule?"

Ethan's hand shot up in the air. "I can find out, I work in the office," he explained eagerly, hoping to make up for his earlier mistake.

"You're pretty useful after all, aren't you?" Sean nodded his head approvingly. Ethan gleamed brightly at the praise, quickly forgetting the small affection he had developed for Hana earlier.

"Looks like he's Sean's fan now," Luca chuckled under his breath as he wrapped his arm around Hana's shoulders. "You might want to watch out, Hana, it looks like you have competition."

The exchange within the cage was interrupted by sudden footsteps and they all glanced up with alarm.

"Chase? What's wrong?" Hana asked with furrowed eyebrows at the appearance of the male. She caught the bomb that he carefully tossed to her, and stared up in confusion when he shook his head.

"It won't work. The pipes are too small, and they have a downward slope with a damp interior. Anything we put inside would just slide to the bottom and into the sewer system," Chase explained.

Sighs of disappointment echoed across the room, and Hana nodded her head. "Thank you for trying, Chase, you should get back to work before they notice you're gone."

"We really do need a map, don't we?" Kai sighed as he ruffled the front of his hair with frustration. "The one we made just doesn't have enough detail. Who knows what might happen if we base everything off this crap."

"We have to make do with what we have," Luca sighed. "We can't get our hands on a map, so we'll have to try to perfect this one as best as possible."

"But that's all we've been doing," Kai protested as he threw his hands up in the air. "For weeks that's all we've been doing and it still isn't good enough." He licked his dry lips and darted his eyes around the room. "Maybe we should try to take it, you know, the real one?"

"Are you out of your damn mind?" Luca hissed. "Do you not remember what happened to… what happened?"

Kai let out a bitter chuckle, "You really think I'd forget?"

"Stop fighting, you guys," Sean sighed. "We're just going to have to do what we can with what we have. One failure doesn't mean anything, we can always try again."

"Looks like somebody is growing up, isn't he?" Luca teased as he patted the younger's head.

"I don't know what you're talking about," Sean scoffed as he swatted the offending male's hand away. "I was always like this. It was just you and Aiden that acted like children."

"Hey!" Luca laughed as he pulled Sean into a headlock.

"Are you guys going to continue wasting our time?" Kai growled as he shot the pair a sharp glare. "We don't have time for you to fool around, if that wasn't apparent enough. I'd appreciate it if you would stop acting like stupid children and focus on what's in front of us."

Sean narrowed his eyes at his friend's harsh remarks, "You know Kai, you've been act—"

"No, you're right, sorry," Luca quickly interrupted. He pinched Sean's side and smiled up at Kai. "We'll pay better attention."

Kai simply shot them another look before staring down at the bits and pieces of their hand drawn map. He pointed at one area that lacked in details, and picked it up to slide into his pocket. "I'll go note down some more points."

"Kai?" Hana called out quietly after a short beat of silence.

Kai glanced over his shoulder to look at her, his eyebrows already furrowed in with frustration. "What?"

The girl offered him no words, and simply granted him a warm smile.

Kai lightened slightly at the sight and he returned it with a quick twitch of his own lips before turning sharply around to leave the cage.

"Why didn't you let me finish?" Sean muttered. He rubbed the bit of skin that Luca had pinched before continuing bitterly, "He should know he's been acting like an ass."

"You know what he's going through, Sean," Luca sighed sympathetically. "He's still hurting."

"But that's the thing, he needs to learn how to manage himself, because he'll never stop hurting," Sean muttered in response. "None of us will ever stop hurting."

CHAPTER ELEVEN: INTREPID

Intrepid [in-ˈtre-pəd] adj. - characterized by resolute fearlessness, fortitude, and endurance

"I'll send you a message once I've spoken to Adrian and inform you of the current status of the explosives, alright Miss Hana?" Jaymes called out as Hana, Sean, and Chris stepped out from the car.

Hana nodded her head, fumbling through the contents of her purse to check for her phone. A frown dawned her lips when she realized that it was missing, and huffed a sigh of annoyance. "I think it fell out when somebody here carelessly tossed my things onto the table yesterday," Hana responded, not failing to shoot Sean a dirty look. The boy in question innocently turned away, suddenly incredibly interested in the black smudge on Chris's whiteboard.

"It's fine, I'll go back and get it," Jaymes nodded his head as he held up an O.K. sign with his fingers.

"Thanks Jaymes," Hana smiled gratefully.

"Okay time to go in!" Sean announced loudly as he wrapped his arm around Hana's shoulders. He tossed a lazy wave behind him as he marched Hana into the building.

"He really is such a child, isn't he?" Jaymes scoffed.

Chris nodded in agreement and scribbled across his whiteboard. *He thinks you're going to steal her away from him.*

Jaymes chuckled as he ran his fingers coolly through his hair. "I don't blame him," he laughed as he sent Chris a wink. "You better go catch up with them, Chris."

Chris nodded his head and waved goodbye to Jaymes. He quickly tucked his board under his armpit and sprinted to catch up with the pair.

"Hi Sean!" Ethan quickly stumbled to his feet to greet the other. He dug into his pocket and pulled out a small loaf of bread that was already beginning to crumble. "Did you already eat? I saved you some bread."

Hana and Chris exchanged a small smile before settling themselves beside Aiden and Luca who were quietly arguing between themselves.

"It's alright," Sean chuckled. "You should eat it."

Ethan's face fell at his words and he stared down at the small piece of bread. He mumbled quietly under his breath, "But I saved it for you."

"And I'm really grateful for it, but are you telling me that you aren't hungry at all?" Sean asked with a raised eyebrow.

Ethan eagerly nodded his head and held the bread up higher to Sean, "Not hungry at all!"

Sean scoffed, but before he could continue, he was interrupted by Hana's raised voice, "What do you mean you don't know where Kai is?"

"Why should I care about that asshole?" Aiden shrugged before folding his arms. "He could go die in a hole for all I care."

"Aiden Park!" Hana scolded with a furious expression. "How could you say that about Kai?"

Aiden felt guilty about his words, but he refused to take them back, "He deserves it! The bastard was yelling about how we were all useless to the rebellion and how Haru would be disappointed in us. Who the hell is he to say those kind of things?"

"And so you just let him go? Do you not remember the last problem he created when he left angrily by himself?" Hana glowered.

Aiden bit down on his bottom lip. "He isn't a child! It's his own fault if he decides to go make trouble."

"Do you even hear yourself?" Hana responded in a softer tone, disappointment etched onto her face. "Do you hear what you're saying?"

"I... I..." Aiden stammered, now completely ashamed for the way he had been acting. "I—"

He was suddenly interrupted by the cracking of the speaker overhead. "We are on lockdown, I repeat, we are on lockdown. All Noyes report to your cages immediately. Report to your cages immediately."

The words of the announcement slowly sunk into their minds, and similar horror struck expressions sprung to their faces.

"You don't think he..." Chase trailed off, not daring to continue what he had been thinking.

"You guys stay here, I'll go out and look for him," Hana stated as she quickly shot to her feet.

"There's no way in hell you're going alone," Sean responded immediately as jumped up to follow.

"What has he done? What did this idiot, oh my god," Aiden mumbled to himself as he pulled at his hair. "Stupid! Stupid, stupid, stupid!"

"Do you think... do you think he went to go steal the map?" Luca whispered as he licked his dry lips. His eyes widened in horrid realization. "Is that why he was going on and on about – oh my god he's gone to get it. He's gone to get it and now he's caught and he's going to get himself killed and Kai's going to die. Kai's going to die and—"

"Will you shut up? I'm not going to die."

They all spun around to see Kai standing at the entrance.

"Kai Ainsley!" Hana exclaimed as she clutched her chest in relief.

"Where the hell have you been?!" Aiden demanded as he sprung to his feet. "You – I can't – you're so stupid!"

Kai scoffed, "Don't you even star- Aiden? Hey, are you okay?"

"I was so..." Aiden didn't even need to finish his words for Kai to understand how worried he must have been.

"I'm alright," Kai responded quietly, feeling slightly guilty at their frazzled appearances. "I'm not -" He was interrupted once again when Aiden suddenly jumped in place.

"You need to hide, Kai!" Aiden exclaimed in realization. His head darted around the room to find a proper place to stash Kai. He wrapped his hand around Kai's wrist and yanked him from his spot. "Hurry before they come to look for you!"

"What the – hell are you – stop it!" Kai exclaimed, stopping Aiden from shoving him forward any longer. "Why the hell do I need to hide?"

"Because you did something bad and now they're after you!" Aiden cried with exasperation. "Now pull yourself together and hide!"

"Look, I don't-"

The speaker overhead crackled to life once more, "You may now report back to work and continue as you were. The gas leak has been discovered and fixed. I repeat, you may now report back to work and continue as you were."

A blanket of silence captured the room and all were eyes trained on Kai who stood with crossed arms and raised eyebrows.

"You mean... you mean that wasn't for you?" Aiden asked.

"No," Kai answered as he ran his fingers through his hair.

"So you didn't do anything bad then?" Luca sighed with relief. He glowered and wagged a finger at him, "You piece of shit, you took ten years of my life!"

There was a pause of silence before Kai mumbled, "I didn't say that."

Before anybody could ask questions, Kai slid an object out of his pocket. "I took this from your bag yesterday, Hana, sorry."

Hana recognized the device Kai was holding up as her cell phone, and she cocked her head curiously. Kai carefully handed it over to her and she glanced down at the photo that lit up the screen. It took her a few seconds to process the content, but finally she recognized the pathways, the pipes, the cages, and all of the other areas they all had spent weeks gathering information on. This version, however, was in great, and accurate detail. The spots they had left blank were now filled in to the greatest extent – all that was missing was the small corner Haru had managed to tear off.

"Kai..." Hana murmured speechlessly as she slowly tore her gaze off of the picture to look up at Kai. "How did you..."

Kai grinned, "Now the rebellion has really begun."

"You're crazy, aren't you?" Luca asked as he stared down at the photo with disbelief. "You're crazy, absolutely crazy."

"How the hell did you do this?" Aiden asked incredulously; he didn't know whether he should be impressed that Kai had managed to capture a picture of the map, or furious that he had even tried.

"If I tell you, you'd get mad," Kai answered simply. "So I'm not going to say a word."

"Kai, seriously what did you do?" Sean asked with narrowed eyes and crossed arms. He was actually incredibly impressed that Kai achieved such a success, but refused to give the other any bit of satisfaction. Kai could have died for what he had done and Sean wasn't about to congratulate him for getting lucky.

There was a long pause as Kai contemplated on whether or not he should confess his actions.

"Kai," Luca called out in a warning tone. He held his hand up threateningly, not afraid to smack the boy upside his head.

"I may have knocked the guards out or something like that," Kai admitted under his breath. "And then I stole the key to the room."

"You did what?!" Aiden exclaimed incredulously. "Oh god, you're dead. They're going to come looking for you and take you and kill you."

"Relax, they didn't even see me," Kai waved his hand dismissively. "And I didn't punch him or something like that; I just mixed a few chemicals around and smashed it in his face. I returned the key too."

A small smile spread across his face as he recalled the memory, "It was kind of funny to be honest; he just fidgeted around for a few seconds before going limp." The smile quickly disappeared once Luca shot him a deathly glare.

"That's even worse!" Aiden cried as he threw his arms up into the air. "How did you know what you were doing? You could have killed them!"

Kai rolled his eyes at Aiden's nagging, and shrugged him off. "You know I work in the chemical storage after all. There was this one time one of the newbies knocked over a few bottles and the combination knocked him out for a few hours. I just mixed them together in a little bottle, soaked it in a bit of cloth, and shoved it against the guy's face."

"You're either a genius or an idiot," Sean sighed.

"An idiot is my pick," Aiden muttered under his breath.

"Why can't you guys just be appreciative?" Kai sighed. "We wouldn't be able to make it anywhere without this, so you're all welcome."

"Kai."

Kai flinched against Hana's hard tone and he glanced meekly at her.

Hana continued to stare blankly at him for a few more seconds before softening her expression, "Thank you."

A wide grin quickly spread across Kai's face and he held a thumb up, "No problem!"

"But if you ever try something like this again, we won't have to wait for the guards to kill you because I'll do it myself," Hana continued. "Are we clear?"

Kai gave her a two fingered salute, "Yes Ma'am!"

"I'll look this over tonight, and organize areas as to where we should plant the bombs," Hana nodded as she carefully tucked her phone into her pocket. "There's going to be a browsing event in a few days, so security around certain places will decrease."

"If it's a browsing event, doesn't the security tighten up?" Aiden asked with a confused expression.

Hana shook her head, "Most of the Noye house security is stationed in the main hall where all the guests will be attending, which means security in other places will be lightened. You all will be split up into pairs and assigned a specific area. Unfortunately, I won't be able to directly help you because I'm one of the guests attending the event. Still, I will keep my eyes and ears open for anything that might be happening. I'll organize everything tonight and provide the details tomorrow."

"This is going to be dangerous, and although it isn't likely that you'll be caught, it still remains as a possibility. If you don't want to take the risk, tell me now and I'll remove you from the planning," Hana continued, training her eyes mainly on Nash.

"You don't even need to tell us that," Kai smirked as he folded his arms. He glanced at the latest additions of the group. "Well?"

Nash opened his mouth to protest, but closed it after being shot a sharp glare from Archer. He nodded his head, "We're in."

"Looks like things are finally starting to get interesting around here," Kai smirked as he cracked his knuckles. He slid his hand into his pocket, and clenched his fingers around the small scrap of paper Haru had sacrificed his life protecting. "It's about damn time."

* * *

"Why can't I be with Luca?" Aiden whined childishly. "No offense to you Chris, but I can protect Luca better than anybody else can!"

"I don't need your protection, giant," Luca rolled his eyes as he elbowed his way out of Aiden's grip. He wrapped his arm around Chris's shoulders and grinned, "I'm perfectly fine with my partner!"

Chris smiled gratefully up at Luca, causing the latter male to reach out and happily stretch the elder's cheeks for "looking so damn cute!"

"No complaints, Aiden," Hana shrugged as she handed him and Chase the area they were assigned to. "I split you up into these pairs for a reason. You and Chase go best together because you work in the same area and therefore know the surroundings a lot better. Chris and Luca both work in the guard house often, so they're the best pair for that place."

"But they are both two little shrimps," Sean added in, holding his hands up defensively when both Chris and Luca shot him dirty looks.

"The guard house is the safest place there is," Hana explained. "It should be completely abandoned because nobody wants to be caught or suspected of slacking off during such a big event."

"A friend of mine, Adrian – don't look at me like that Kai, he can be trusted, will bring the explosives in the morning. He's disguised the boxes as food crates and you have all been assigned to transport them in," Hana continued. "They vary in sizes, so I'll go over where each specific bomb is supposed to be planted."

"We have access to the security cameras and there are very few installed, so you won't have to worry too much about being caught on film. I'll meet briefly with you all in the morning to hand out ear pieces so we can easily communicate with each other. Adrian will be monitoring the screens," Hana explained. "You only have one job, so be careful. You get in, plant the bomb, get out – easier said than done."

A shy hand slowly rose from the crowd of heads. "I wanted to ask earlier, but what is a browsing event?" Ethan asked as he scratched his head. He was a relatively new Noye, and didn't know much about this society's customs.

A dark expression took over Hana's face and she clenched down on her teeth in silence.

Ethan was taken aback by her sudden change and he quickly waved his hands, "You don't need to tell me, I was just curi—"

"It's an event sponsored by a different Noye house every year. They take their best Noyes, or Chonyos as they call them, that they've been training for years and put them up for auction," Hana explained quietly.

"What's so special about them?" Aiden asked with a cocked head. He had heard of the browsing event held at their Noye house every few years, but had little idea as to what was done there. Many Noyes had kept their label for years, but very few knew anything outside of what the Noye house wanted them to know.

There was a brief silence before Hana slowly continued, "Chonyos are females. Haven't you ever wondered why only males are titled as Noyes?

These females are usually taken at seven or so years old, and are kept in isolation until they are around sixteen. During their captivity, they're…"

"They're trained," Luca continued as he placed a hand on Hana's upper arm. He had learned the details after eavesdropping on the guards. "To relieve any desire of their future master. What makes them so special is that they're young, beautiful, and most importantly, virgins."

The room went silent as the occupants absorbed Luca's words.

"Can't we… can't we save them too?" Ethan asked as he turned to Hana with a hopeful expression. "We can free them too, can't we?"

Hana dropped her gaze to the ground and quietly responded, "There is an extent to what we can and can't do."

"Chonyos aren't kept in the Noye house," Luca explained as he gestured to the cages. "They grow up in a place a lot bigger than this. They sleep in beds and eat meals and have classes, but if I got to choose, I'd pick our life without a doubt. They're whipped both mentally and physically into condition; they're starved to be skinny, trained to be obedient, it's… it's really horrible."

"Life is cruel," Chase murmured quietly under his breath.

They all remained silent, knowing well that his words were all too true.

* * *

Several days passed and the browsing event had finally arrived. The four of them were seated in the car as Jaymes drove them first to the residential building before he and Hana would leave to the main Noye House. Hana was nearly sweating through her new dress as she sat in the car.

"Maybe we should scrap this plan and come up with something else. I don't think it's a good idea to have you all risk your lives like that," Hana murmured to herself as she fidgeted in her seat.

"We only have one job, Hana, you said so yourself," Sean grinned "Get in, plant the bomb, and get out."

"I also said easier said than done," Hana snapped.

"Besides, we already knew that we would have to risk our lives to make this a success from the very beginning," Sean added as he rewrapped his hand around hers like nothing happened.

Hana let out a huff of air as she drummed the fingers of her other hand against her lap. She looked up when a hand wrapped around her fidgeting one, and met eyes with Chris. *We'll be fine.*

"You don't know that," Hana frowned.

Chris's eyes crinkled into crescents as he erased his words to replace it with new ones. *If anything happens we'll sacrifice Nash first and run.*

"Chris!" Hana exclaimed with disbelief. "Don't joke about that!"

Chris grinned at Hana. *I'm just saying what we're all thinking.*

"He's got a point," Sean agreed with a nod.

"You two are terrible," Hana sighed. Her heart thumped against her chest, and a flood of horrible possible events kept entering her mind. She was yanked out of her thoughts when she felt a pair of soft lips press against her temple.

"We're here," Jaymes announced as he pulled the car up to the entrance. "The browsing event starts in half an hour, so you have some time to stay down with the others until it begins."

"Come on, let's go see if the others are as nervous as Hana," Sean grinned mischievously as he tugged on Chris. They practically ran to the cages with Hana following slowly behind them.

"How are you all completely calm about this?" Hana asked as she stared at Kai and Aiden who were carelessly arm wrestling each other.

"What is there to be worried about?" Luca shrugged, crying out in protest when Aiden lost.

"You are all ridiculous," Hana sighed as she shook her head. "Alright, come here so I can help you attach your ear pieces."

After attaching their ear pieces – Aiden with a bit more difficulty than others – they all split up into pairs and prepared to depart to their areas.

"Adrian is watching the surveillance cameras so he'll let you know if somebody is approaching. Still, keep your eyes and ears wide open," Hana warned as she glanced down at her watch. She chewed on her bottom lip once she realized it was time to go, and quickly pulled Luca, who was closest to her, in for a hug.

"Be safe," Hana whispered as she wrapped her arms around Sean when it was his turn. "Make sure you watch out for yourself and Kai. Don't get caught or I'll kill you."

Sean watched as she walked away after exchanging quick words of encouragement with the others.

"Come on, are you ready to stop staring at Hana? She's already gone," Kai sighed as he wrapped his arm around Sean's shoulders.

"Isn't she cute?" Sean smiled lightly.

Kai rolled his eyes, "Yeah, of course she is, now let's get going."

Sean's eyes narrowed and he pulled away from Kai with a frown on his face, "What did you say? Have you been checking her out?"

"You are an idiot," Kai groaned as he spun Sean around to shove him forward. "Now hurry the hell up."

"Because that's not cool with me, Kai," Sean continued.

"Sean, just shut up."

"And you might be my friend but –"

"I am going to shove my fist up your ass if you don't shut up right now."

* * *

"Hello President Flynn, Director Kirk, it's very nice to see you again," Hana smiled brightly. "I heard Mrs. Flynn gave birth not too long ago. I hope your baby girl grows up into a lovely woman."

"It would be great if she became just half the woman you are, Miss Hana," President Flynn laughed in response. He paused and leaned in to whisper, "I hear you and your father are going through a temporary feud?"

"Oh it isn't temporary," Hana responded with a gentle laugh. "I think my father is losing his touch in his control and it would be such a waste to see a company as great as Acacia Corp self-destruct. It's really painful to fight against my father, but I have to be selfless and place my family ties aside to do what is best for the people."

"Yes, such dedication. I will be voting in your favor when the time comes," President Flynn agreed, with Director Kirk nodding along.

"Will your father be here today?" Director Kirk asked.

"I have to admit that I'm not sure. He has refused to contact me," Hana sighed dramatically. "It's heartbreaking."

"How childish of him," President Flynn frowned as he clapped the girl gently on the shoulder. "Everything will be fine in time."

"Thank you, I appreciate it very much," Hana smiled before the small group split up to mingle with others. Her face dropped the second they turned their backs, "Was this always so tiring?"

"Maybe you're just losing your touch," Jaymes chuckled. Hana shot him a pointed look, and he laughed once more. "Shouldn't you check up on your boys?"

Her eyes lit up at the suggestion and she fumbled with the small device that was in her ear. "How is it going, Adrian?"

She winced at the static that sounded through her ear piece before a voice finally crackled through. "All is well; Sean and Kai are working the quickest and have already managed to install one."

"And the others?" Hana asked.

"Fine as well. Chris and Luca almost ran into some trouble, but it went smoothly," Adrian answered. "Calm down, Hana. It'll be fine."

"The fact that you guys are so calm is what's making me nervous," Hana muttered under her breath. "The unexpected always happens."

"Well since you expect it, it shouldn't be happening now, should it?" Adrian laughed cheerfully in return.

"I will hit you, I swear to god I will," Hana grumbled as she folded her arms to sulk against the wall.

"Are you pouting?" Adrian asked with amusement.

"No," Hana muttered.

"Don't lie, I can clearly see you through the camera," Adrian laughed.

Hana's eyes narrowed before wandering around the room, finally discovering the camera that was faced in her direction. Adrian laughed again when Hana stalked to the side to avoid being caught on film.

"Could you guys, I don't know, stop talking?" a sudden voice intercepted their conversation. "I don't know why, but we can hear everything you guys are saying and Sean looks like he's about to strangle somebody."

"Kai? That's strange, your transmit signals shouldn't be blending with others. I'll see if I can get that fixed," Adrian replied.

"No, leave it," Sean's voice grumbled. "I want to know what you have to say, pretty boy."

"Don't you think the jealousy act is getting a little old?" Kai asked. There was a brief thump and a short yelp before he continued with, "Okay, fine, fine."

Hana chuckled quietly to herself, finding Sean's jealousy cute rather than irritating. "Alright, I'm going back to the party so you can all argue amongst yourselves."

"Heads up, Hana, your father just walked in," Adrian informed her.

Hana froze for a split second before relaxing her body. She pressed her lips into a smile, and walked back into the center of the room to rejoin the guests. She caught sight of her father almost immediately. Chando had planned to avoid the girl, but Hana would allow no such thing.

"Hello father," Hana greeted as she forced a pleasant smile onto her face. She spoke rather loudly, purposely attracting the attention of the attendees. "It's nice to see you again."

Chando scoffed, obviously showing no attempt to return the polite mannerisms – exactly the thing Hana had been hoping for. "You have some nerve."

"I can see that you still haven't forgiven me," Hana sighed as she slowly reached forward to place a hand on her father's chest, knowing well that he would allow no such thing.

"Don't touch me," Chando snapped as he slapped her arm away with an audible smack. The noise echoed even louder against the hollow walls, and all eyes blatantly trained themselves on the father daughter pair.

"Do not lay your hands on Miss Hana," Jaymes growled as he took a threatening step forward.

Hana turned to her father, "I hope one day you will realize why I had to do this, father." Her eyes flashed, "It was for your own good, you know."

Chando's eyes flashed in recognition as he recalled the similar words he had said to her himself.

"Now, President Acacia, you can't treat your daughter like this," President Park smiled awkwardly as he stepped forward to defend Hana.

"No matter what, blood is thicker than water," President Raie agreed.

Chando let out a low growl as he noticed the gazes that were trained on him. He scoffed, "It looks like you have all these people wrapped around your little finger, haven't you?"

He stepped closer to Hana. Chando sneered in a volume inaudible to foreign ears, "I didn't know you could be this despicable, Hana."

"I think you've forgotten who raised me, father," Hana responded quietly without skipping a beat.

Chando curled his upper lip into a small snarl before spinning sharply on his feet to disappear into the crowd of people.

"I was hesitant to vote against Chando at first, but he really has lost it."

"How disgraceful, he should be ashamed of his actions."

Hana forced down the victorious smile that was threatening to spread across her lips, and accepted the sympathy of the other presidents. After all, every piteous expression was another vote in her favor.

"I have to applaud your acting skills, Hana," Adrian's amused voice entered her ears. "The ending line was the perfect touch."

"It's starting," Jaymes nodded as the lights around the room began to dim. A single spot light lit up the center stage, attracting the eyes and attention of the audience.

"Come on, let's go," Hana murmured as she tugged at Jaymes's wrist. He was hesitant, but obeyed her wishes.

"They'll notice if you leave, you know," Jaymes spoke up once they had left the voices and applause behind them.

"They won't," Hana shook her head as she rested her back against the wall, feeling the nice breeze of the wind hit her skin. "All their attention will be focused on those poor girls."

"It's not your fault, Hana," Jaymes stated firmly as he placed a hand on her shoulder. "It's not your responsibility, so you shouldn't feel at guilt."

"I... yeah," Hana gave in, knowing there was no point in arguing with Jaymes. The Chonyos were a whole new level of social injustice, and it was one that was out of her control. She knew better than to bite off more than she could chew.

"This is really disgusting," Adrian's low voice entered her ears.

"I'm sorry you have to watch, Adrian," Hana sighed as she closed her eyes. "I never made it through one whole show myself whenever my father used to bring me to these."

"Our world is disgusting, isn't it?" Adrian murmured sadly as he watched the repulsive actions of reality through the monitor screens.

"No," Hana's eyes fluttered open. "Just the people living in it."

"The showcase presentation is finally over, Hana," Adrian informed her. "You might want to return before the browsing actually begins or they'll notice your disappearance."

The browsing was the worst part. The main hall would be split into different areas, each one putting a very poorly clothed Chonyo up for display. Men would be allowed to poke and prod the girls, to touch them in places that should never be shown to the public, to speak to them in a manner fouler than if they were the dirt beneath their shoes, before placing their offer. The offers would all be totaled up, and the girls would be sold to the highest bidder.

It was all disgusting, absolutely revolting.

"Will you be making a bid of your own, Miss Hana?" President Brewer chuckled as he came to Hana's side. His eyes zeroed in on one of the Chonyos and he licked his lips as if she was prey to be devoured.

"I don't believe so," Hana responded, hiding her clenched fists behind her back. Her eyes narrowed down at the wedding ring on his chubby finger and she forced a smile up at him. "Mrs. Brewer is quite a saint to allow you to make a bid. You're certainly talented in finding the best women out there, President Brewer."

"Oh, she doesn't know about this. The thing I buy today will be placed in the vacation house, so the two will never meet," President Brewer laughed loudly. "What she doesn't know won't hurt her," He laughed once again before waddling off into the direction he had been eyeing.

"Loosen your fists, Miss Hana, or your nails will pierce your skin," Jaymes spoke up as he gently pried her fists open. "Just bear with it. We'll be able to leave soon."

"Hey Adrian, I think we have a problem," Kai's voice crackled through the speaker. "Sean sort of... he's sort of bleeding. He cut himself on some broken glass, except it's a really big cut and he's, I... he's kind of bleeding, like a lot."

"He's over exaggerating, I'm fine," Sean's soft voice sounded.

"Sean I don't think this is over exaggerating, I don't think... holy shit, holy shit Sean what do I do?"

"Calm down Kai, being frantic won't do anything to help Sean's injury. First, get some cloth, clean cloth, and press it against his wound to stop the bleeding," Adrian instructed.

"We already did but he's bleeding through it," Kai exclaimed.

"Where are you? I'll go down right now," Hana nodded her head as she began to head towards the exit.

"You can't Hana, all eyes are on you right now," Adrian argued. "Send Jaymes. Tell him to bring Sean to me and I'll take care of him."

"But I…" Hana sighed reluctantly. She turned to the male who was standing curiously as her side, "Jaymes, go find Sean and Kai in the chemical storage and take Sean to Adrian. Quickly, go."

Jaymes gave her a firm nod before departing to fulfill her wishes.

"Hana, some people are headed towards you," Adrian spoke up suddenly. "Be calm and don't give yourself away."

"I don't think you understand, Adrian," Hana murmured as she took a deep breath. A bright smile immediately spread across her face as she made eye contact with the group of Presidents. "Pretending is one of my best qualities."

After twenty minutes or so, she felt a presence creep back to her side. A gentle tap on her hip reassured her of who it was. She glanced at Jaymes from the corner of her eye, "How is he?"

"He's fine," Jaymes nodded. "Adrian fixed it up with a couple of stitches. Everybody finished successfully, by the way."

Instant relief flooded over Hana's chest and she let out the breath of air she had been holding. "That's good."

"The event should be ending soon, Miss Hana," Jaymes informed her after glancing down at his watch. "Would you like to depart early?"

Hana bit down on her lip and eyed the crowd that remained as large as it had before. It would look bad if she was the first to leave, but she didn't want to remain there for even a second longer.

"Let's go," Hana nodded firmly.

Jaymes glanced down at her with surprise – never before had Hana allowed her feelings to get in front of her business. His lips slipped into a small smile and he nodded his head without questioning her command. She was growing up now.

"You go to the car, Miss Hana. I'll get Chris," Jaymes nodded as he gave her a gentle nudge towards the exit.

Hana's whole body instantly relaxed the second she stepped out into the fresh air. She closed her eyes, peacefully enjoying the warm rays of the sun and the soft breeze of the wind. She cringed when a sudden yelp interrupted her brief moment of bliss, and her eyes remained closed. She contemplated for a few seconds – just for a few seconds – to not do anything. To remain completely still and ignore the cries that reminded her of the society she lived in.

She let out a slow breath and parted her eyes, turning her head to the source of the noise. A frown slipped onto her face as she observed a man dragging away a Chonyo, the girl putting up a fierce fight of refusal.

Hana stood there in surprise for a few seconds; it was certainly rare to see a Chonyo who still possessed the will to fight – the will to live. She winced when the Chonyo was struck down, her face hitting the concrete ground below her to leave a fresh wound; the bright red blood contrasted against her snowy pale cheeks.

"Is that really necessary?" Hana spoke up suddenly, her voice interrupting the shouts of the pair. Both heads turned to look at her, each of them reflecting a different emotion across their face. "She might be called a Chonyo, but she's a human just like the rest of us."

"Don't joke around," the man spat angrily, not sparing another glance at Hana as he focused his gaze back onto his purchase. "Now get up you useless bitch!"

Hana clenched down hard on her teeth, and a hand clasped firmly onto her shoulder. She glanced back to see Jaymes staring at her with hard eyes. He shook his head once, "Let it go, there's nothing you can do."

Hana glanced at the girl once more, this time meeting eye contact. The Chonyo shook her head briefly and gave Hana a small, saddened smile. She climbed to her feet and brushed off the dirt that clung to her dress.

"Come on," Jaymes steered her away from the sight and toward their car he had parked nearby. Chris slipped his hand silently into Hana's and Hana knew that even if Chris could speak he would have nothing to say.

CHAPTER TWELVE: CHANGE

change [chānj] n. - the alteration of something or someone to result in an outcome different from its initial form or state

"It's just a small cut, it's not like I'm going to die," Sean muttered under his breath. He propped up his face with his hand and stared at Hana who was focused on his injury.

"You say that, yet you would huff childishly and sulk if I gave you no attention," Hana responded pointedly.

Sean's cheeks flushed and he shot a dirty look at Chris who was silently giggling beside them. "Why are you so happy, huh?" he grumbled as he picked up a stray cotton ball to throw in Chris's direction.

Chris's grin spread even wider at the sound of Sean's unhappiness and he patted him cheerfully on the back before holding up his white board. *I'm going to find Jaymes.*

"Chris and Jaymes have been getting pretty close, haven't they?" Hana mused quietly to herself, smiling at the thought of the unusual friendship.

"Yeah, that's probably why he has been so much of a brat lately," Sean scoffed under his breath. He continued gazing at Hana who was completely unaware of the attention that was trained on her.

"All done!" Hana smiled proudly as she gently patted the fresh bandage. She glanced up and met Sean's eyes for a split second before he darted them away.

"Like a child," she commented, laughing when he cried out in protest.

Hana gleamed up at him and he resisted the urge to pinch the younger's cheeks. Instead, he brushed away a stray strand of her hair and gently tucked it behind her ear. "You've changed a lot."

A brief, peaceful silence settled between them as they both thought over Sean's words.

"We've both changed," Hana smiled and Sean nodded in agreement. She eyed him and added teasingly, "It feels like it was just yesterday that you treated me as if I was going to kill your first born child."

Sean scrunched his face at the memory, and ran his fingers through Hana's hair as a late apology for his rude behavior.

"And it was like just yesterday that you always had a stoic expression on your face and spoke like you had a stick up your ass," Sean smiled as he patted Hana's hair. He easily avoided the fist that went flinging in his direction and he wrapped his fingers around her outstretched wrist to pull her into a hug.

"I'm glad we changed," Sean breathed into her hair, smiling when she nodded her head in agreement.

"And it was like just yesterday that you guys would keep to yourselves and talk from a distance," Jaymes pitched in as he popped up beside them to pull the couple apart. "I miss those days."

"Has anybody ever mention how annoying you are?" Sean glared as he smacked Jaymes's arm away from him.

"No," Jaymes responded without skipping a beat. "Come on Miss Hana, they are all probably waiting for you at the Noye House."

Hana nodded her head as she walked towards the door with a thoughtful expression on her face, "I didn't get to see them after the browsing event yesterday. I wonder how they are faring now."

* * *

"I'm not sure what you were expecting," Sean started slowly with a gaping mouth, "But I don't think this was it."

"Hana! Sean! Chris!" Luca cried out happily as he ran towards them.

"What the hell happened here?" Sean asked with narrowed eyebrows. He pulled Hana aside to avoid the Noye that almost went running into her, and stared at the amount of Noyes swarming in and out of the cage. "Why are there so many people?"

"They're here to help," Luca laughed as held up his arms to gesture to the new aid. "Word about our… little operation spread, and it looks like Noyes are starting to get curious." He reached forward and clasped Hana's hands into his own, "You've restored hope."

Hana stood there in silence for a few seconds as she processed the words Luca had just said. The corners of her lips lifted into a small smile and she reached forward to ruffle the front of Luca's already messy hair, "No, you all did."

Before Luca could respond, she clapped her hands loudly together and announced, "There are too many people here. Please send only one member from each cage housing. They will relay all the information back to you all."

Although her words weren't spoken with much volume, they were immediately obeyed by the surrounding Noyes. The crowd diminished until only a good 15 people were left, all staring at Hana eagerly to find out what they were to do next. While Hana spoke to them, the rest of the boys watched on with proud smiles stretched across their faces.

"This might actually work after all, won't it?" Aiden murmured with bright eyes as he gently squeezed Luca's shoulder.

"Of course it's going to!" Luca nodded. "Look at all the support!"

"Too much support, if you ask me," Nash scoffed with narrowed eyes. He gestured to the small crowd in front of Hana, "With this many people, people are bound to talk, you know. Just let one little loose mouth go and the whole staff of guards will find out about this little plan."

"I guess we'll just have to keep this loose mouth under control, won't we?" Kai snarled as he stepped towards him with a dark glare.

Nash held up his hands and chuckled bitterly, "Don't worry about me. I may be a lot of things but I'm no betrayer."

"I have my doubts," Kai growled in return.

"Don't fight, you guys," Luca piped up as he gazed at Hana who was talking to the crowd that surrounded her. "From the looks of it, I think we have a pretty good chance of pulling this thing off."

* * *

"Please Dustin!" Hana pleaded as she trailed after him in the hallways, ignoring the looks of surprise from bystanders.

"No! I said no and I mean no!" Dustin barked.

"Dustin, please. You're one of the only few people I can trust. You know I wouldn't be asking you for such a big favor if I didn't think this was completely necessary," Hana persisted as she cut in front of him.

"Hana, I'm grateful for that but this is just… this is just pushing it too far. What if we get caught with them? I'm not going to let Nathan get hurt when I've just patched together our friendship," Dustin shook his head.

"Why would I get hurt?" Nathan piped up as he appeared behind the pair. "What are you two talking about?"

"It's nothing important," Dustin responded as he waved Nathan off. "Hana is just trying to persuade me to do something ridiculous."

"Are you talking about the whole Noye thing?' Nathan asked with a cocked head. "Because I already told her it was fine."

"You what?!" Dustin exclaimed incredulously, spinning around to gawk at his half-brother. "Do you know what you just agreed to?!"

"Well yeah," Nathan nodded thoughtfully. "I mean, all we're going to be doing is keeping a few Noy—"

"Do you want to get killed?!" Dustin exclaimed, immediately slapping his hand against Nathan's mouth. He lowered his voice to a hiss, "We're in public, Nathan. You can't just say stuff like that and not expect anybody to be listening in."

He glared at the people who were attempting to eavesdrop on their conversation, and heaved a sigh of annoyance. He wrapped his hands around both Hana and Nathan's wrists and dragged them into an empty classroom. After securely locking the door behind him, he spun around to face the pair with his hands pressed against his hips.

"It's two against one, Dustin," Nathan shrugged with Hana nodding her head enthusiastically beside him.

Dustin opened his mouth to retort, but paused for a few seconds. He let out a loud groan once he set his eyes on their pleading expressions, and threw his arms up into the air with exasperation, "Fine."

"Yes!" Nathan grinned, turning to give Hana a high five.

"But we'll only take a few!" Dustin exclaimed with an outstretched finger. "Only three, you hear that Hana?"

"Did you say 15?" Hana cocked her head. She turned to Nathan, "He said 15, right?"

"I think he did," Nathan nodded his head in agreement.

"You guys are terrible," Dustin snarled in annoyance.

"We know," Hana and Nathan piped up simultaneously.

"Jaymes and the boys are waiting for me outside, so I'll see you two later," Hana smiled. "Thank you, I promise I'll repay this favor."

"Wait," Dustin called out.

Hana stopped mid step and glanced over her shoulder, "Hm?"

"I... I heard about what's going on with your family's business. I just... I wanted to know if you were doing alright," Dustin murmured as he rubbed the back of his neck. "If you need any help you can just ask me for it, you know that."

"I just did," Hana responded with a cocked head.

"I mean help with yourself, you know," Dustin clarified.

Hana remained silent for a few seconds before she smiled at him. "Thanks, Dustin. I really appreciate it."

"You've changed a lot, haven't you?" Dustin grinned.

Hana let out a small laugh, "Everybody seems to keep saying that."

She held up her hand and waved them goodbye. "I'll see you two later. I don't want to keep them waiting any longer."

"What took you so long? You were literally gone for like two hours," Sean huffed as soon as Hana climbed into the back seat of the car.

"We've been waiting for ten minutes, Sean," Jaymes deadpanned, rolling his eyes at his childish behavior. "If this is what love does to you then I obviously never want to experience it."

Chris held up his white board. *Did Dustin agree?*

"It took some persuading, but he did," Hana nodded her head in satisfaction. "What about you? I don't think Adrian would give you too much trouble."

"He agreed right away," Sean nodded his head. "He even offered to open up his storage house as well. It's not very homely, but it could easily fit a good 50 of them until official legislation is released."

"Of course, leave it to Adrian," Hana smiled.

"Still, I don't think that's enough. Where else can we let them stay?" Jaymes asked. "We can't keep any of them under anything owned by the Acacia family, for I'm pretty sure that's the first place officials will look."

"We'll figure something out," Sean added lightly as he gently took Hana's hand into his.

"No lovey dovey stuff in my car," Jaymes called out as he shot the pair a dirty look through his review mirror. "Chris, you're on patrol!"

Chris's hand flung to his head to salute him before he leaned over to pull Sean and Hana apart.

"Hey!" Sean exclaimed, shooting Chris a look of betrayal.

Chris shrugged with a guiltless expression. *I'm just doing my job.*

* * *

"There are a total of 8 escape routes," Hana stated as she pinpointed the locations on the map with her finger. "3 are open on this side of the Noye grounds, but 5 more will be opened after the first detonation."

"And what happens after we escape?" Logan asked.

"There will be people waiting to take you back to safety. You can trust these people, don't worry," Hana reassured them after getting pointed looks from some of the Noyes. "They'll take you in until words comes out as to what will be done with the rebelling Noyes. Please do your best to be kind to these people, for they are risking their lives for your safety."

"But…" Hana paused as a solemn expression took over her face. "They cannot take all of you. Many of you will have to fend for yourselves…"

Sean pressed a comforting hand to Hana's shoulder to signal that he would continue, "Hana has tried her best to guarantee everybody a spot to safety, but even her best cannot solve the greatest of problems. If you find yourself as one of the unlucky ones, quickly find shelter. Don't trust people too easily if they are to offer you help, but don't anger them into reporting you either. To avoid getting split apart from your friends, make plans earlier as to where you are to gather."

"And when will this be happening?" a Noye spoke up in a hushed tone.

There was a pregnant silence, "You'll know when it does," Sean responded simply.

"The guards are coming back, everybody go back to your cages," Kai called out in a hushed whisper as he sprinted down the hallway. He had been keeping watch at the cage entrance. The Noyes scattered apart like bugs, quickly heading back to their respective cages.

"Do you really have no idea as to when—" Luca stopped mid-sentence when Hana pressed a hand to his mouth. She shook her head, nodding over to Henry who had just turned the corner.

He paused in front of their cage and open and closed his mouth several times to speak.

"You look dumb," Hana stated bluntly after a few seconds passed by. She crossed her arms, "What do you want?"

"To talk," Henry answered. His eyes darted around the room and he flinched under the dark glares of the other occupants. "Alone, please."

"What about?" Hana asked cautiously.

"Your... your plans," Henry responded after a moment of pause.

Hana tensed for a split second before immediately relaxing her body. She couldn't give anything away; not only hers, but everybody's life depended on it.

"What nonsense are you trying to spout now?" Hana scoffed. She nodded her head towards the exit. "Let's go."

The pair traveled not too far away from the cages, but far enough to be out of earshot from snooping ears. "If you're trying to accuse me of something, I'm not going to stand for it."

"I know something's happening, Hana," Henry responded immediately with narrowed eyes. "I know you're brewing something together with those other Noyes of yours. The guards have been telling me. Noyes are being caught sneaking through the halls around the cage of your... *friends*."

"And why would that have something to do with me?" Hana asked with a cocked eyebrow.

"Why would it not? I've been running this place since the moment I could walk, and nothing like this has ever happened until you started showing your face around here. I've been nice while it lasted, Hana, but I'm not going to—"

"This is what you call nice?" Hana chortled. "Then I would like to see how you look when you're mean."

Henry's eyes flashed dangerously and he let out a low growl, "I should warn you not to mess with me, Hana. Anyways, I just wanted to give you a warning. If you try anything, and I mean *anything*, I will make you go through hell."

"I'll look forward to it," Hana responded dryly. She watched as Henry spun sharply on his heels, stomping angrily down the hall and out of sight.

She let out a sigh before returning to the cages, informing Sean and Chris that it was now time to go.

"You have to be careful from now on, Hana. You can't afford to get caught," Sean frowned as they headed towards the car.

"Like I hadn't known that already," Hana chuckled. She greeted Jaymes with a smile before climbing inside.

"You think… you think we'll have to start it soon?" Sean spoke up quietly after a brief lull in the conversation.

"I don't know," Hana responded honestly. "I don't… I don't think we're ready for it yet, to be honest. We've prepared for this so much, and over such a long period of time. We've discussed every escape route, every back up plan, every course of action, and we couldn't be any more physically prepared than we are now… but…"

Her unspoken words were continued in each of their minds – they weren't mentally prepared. They weren't prepared to lose a loved one, to lose one of their own. They weren't prepared to see the deaths that would happen left and right. They weren't prepared for the days and weeks of fear and worry that would immediately follow.

This was something they could never be prepared for.

The only thing more frightening than death itself were the moments that led up to it.

* * *

"Hana, do you have extra shampoo?" Sean called out as he knocked on her door. He sighed when he was met with no response, "I'm coming in."

He smiled lightly when he saw Hana already asleep on her bed. He paused, however, when he noticed dried tears etched onto her face.

Hana's eyes groggily opened to look up at Sean. "Se…Sean?" she called out, her voice coming out in a rasp whisper.

"Why were you crying?" Sean asked immediately, giving her no time to think up an excuse.

Hana stared at him for a few seconds before her eyes slowly widened in realization. She quickly pushed him away and pulled the covers over her head, "Go away."

"Hana," Sean called out firmly, pulling the covers away from her.

Hana quickly slapped her hands over her eyes, flinching lightly when her palms met a little too roughly with her cheeks. "Sean, please don't."

Sean's heart wrenched at the sound of Hana's broken voice and he sat down beside her. He reached forward and gently pried her hands away from her face.

"Hana," Sean repeated her name in a gentle voice as he pulled her forward into a hug. "You don't need to tell me what it's about if you don't want to, but just... just don't cry all by yourself."

He smiled with satisfaction when she nodded her head, and gently began running his fingers through her hair, humming in what he hoped was a comforting manner.

"I had a bad dream," Hana spoke up in a small voice. "That I died."

Sean tensed. "You know it won't happen right? You won't die," Sean stated firmly as he tightened his grip around her small body.

"Sean," Hana spoke up suddenly, pulling away from his hold to look him in the eyes. "What if I do?"

"Hana, please," Sean responded desperately. "It won't happen."

"No, hear me out," Hana shook her head as she held a firm grip on his arms. "Sean if I die you have to take care of them."

"Hana you aren't going to die so please just don't—"

"Sean, please," Hana stated firmly. She cupped his face into the palms of her hands and forced him to look at her. "If I die, promise me you won't give up. Promise me you'll stay strong and take care over everybody else."

"I... I promise," Sean responded dryly.

Hana smiled and pecked him on the forehead. "You promised."

Another silence captured the pair, a comfortable, intimate silence as the two continued their locked gazes. Sean reached over and tucked a stray strand of hair behind Hana's ear, smiling lightly when his fingertips grazed her soft skin.

Sean stared at the girl's face for a few seconds, and gulped heavily as a thought crossed his mind. He finally summoned up the courage and slowly began decreasing the space between the two of them, his heart nearly jumping out of his chest. "C-Can I...?"

Hana froze. She knew exactly what Sean was trying to ask. Her tongue darted out to lick her suddenly dry lips and Sean's eyes followed every movement.

"I... I really, really like you," Sean whispered quietly as he looked into her eyes before pressing his lips against Hana's.

It was a rather blunt contrast; Sean's chapped, dry lips molding against Hana's soft ones, yet the fit seemed rather perfect. He cupped Hana's face gently with the palm of his hand, as if it would break if he were to treat it any rougher. Hana pressed closer to him, wrapping her arms tightly around Sean's neck to eliminate any gap of air between the two. He cupped the back of her head with his other hand and slowly began to lower her onto the bed, refusing to part their lips as he hovered above her. He balanced his weight on his arms, resisting the urge to pull away for a breath of air. It was perfect.

After what seemed like hours, the pair finally parted, each with a light blush dressed across their cheeks.

Hana was the first to interrupt the silence. "Let's go to sleep, okay?" Hana lightly suggested, her face still colored a soft shade of red.

"Y-Yeah, okay," Sean mumbled under his breath as he quickly climbed off of her. "Goodnight Hana," he murmured as he spun on his heels to escape to his bedroom.

He stopped mid-step when he felt a tug at his shirt and he turned to glance over his shoulder at Hana.

"I really, really like you too."

Sean felt blood immediately fill up his cheeks at the words and he swallowed hard, "S-Sure."

Hana laughed at his failed attempt to sound indifferent and she reached over to flick him gently against the forehead, "And I'll try my best not to die."

CHAPTER THIRTEEN: SACRIFICE

sacrifice [sakrə fis] n. - an act of giving up something valued for the sake of something else regarded as more important or worthy.

"We need you to come with us."

Hana's entire body tensed as she slowly turned to face the intruders. She recognized the pair of official badges pinned to the collars of the two men and she forced a smile onto her face, "What seems to be the problem, gentlemen?"

She held out her hand to stop Sean from advancing, shooting him a sharp warning glare out of the corner of her eyes.

"You're being detained for treason, Miss Hana," one of the men spoke up in a gruff voice. "Please come with us."

"Under what grounds?" Hana asked calmly. She knew exactly what she was being suspected for, and inwardly swore for not being more careful about the whole thing. Somebody must have told and she had a hunch as to who the rat was.

"You'll find out when you come with us," he responded simply. "Now please follow us or else we will have to use force."

"That won't be necessary," Hana smiled. She turned to look at the other boys, smiling reassuringly at the horrified expression that crossed their faces. "I'll be back soon, okay guys?"

"H-Hana," Luca stammered, his eyes quickly filling with tears.

"Tell Jaymes what happened immediately," Hana whispered into Sean's ear as she pulled him in for a hug. "Tell him to tell Adrian."

Sean let out a low growl when Hana was yanked away from him, but stood his ground when she shot him a sharp look.

A tense silence took over once the footsteps of the three faded away; everybody was at a loss as to what they were supposed to do.

"What are they going to do to her?" Luca choked quietly, falling to the ground as his legs lost their strength.

"Oh shit, oh shit, this was our fault!" Aiden cried fearfully.

"No, this wasn't our fault. I know exactly whose fault it is," Kai let out a low growl as his hands curled into tight fists.

Sean's head shot up immediately once he processed Kai's words and the pair of them tore out of the cage with lighting speed.

"Hey guys what's up—"

"You goddamn rat!" Sean shouted as he slammed Nash against the wall.

"What do you think you're doing?!" Archer shouted as he shot forward to rip Sean off of Nash. He was shoved aside by Kai, who glowered at him with barred teeth.

"You ratted us out, didn't you?! You squealed!" Sean exclaimed as he slammed Nash repeatedly against the wall.

"Get off of him!" Skyler exclaimed as he and Logan worked together to pull the raging Sean off of Nash.

"What the hell is your problem?!" Skyler demanded.

"No, what the hell is his problem?! He snitched on us to the guards! They just came to take Hana away!" Sean raged as he thrashed against their restraints.

All eyes turned to Nash who now seemed extremely nervous against the questioning eyes.

"Is it true?" Ethan spoke up softly, his eyes darting back and forth from Sean to Nash. "Did you really tell?"

Nash opened his mouth to protest, but decided against it in the last second. "What did you expect me to do?! They would have gotten us killed! I didn't tell them everything, I only said that that prissy rich girl was trying to get us to rebel but none of the Noyes would stand for it."

"You bastard!" Sean shouted as he tore forward once more. This time neither Skyler nor Logan did anything to stop him. Sean slammed his fist against Nash's face, not even the slightest bit satisfied with the audible crack that sounded. Blood gushed out of his nose and coated Sean's fist.

He pulled his arm back for another punch, but stopped when he felt a tug on his sleeve. Chris stared firmly at him and shook his head. *There's no time for this. We have to call Jaymes.*

Sean grunted in defiance, but reluctantly retracted his arm.

"How could you have done this?" Archer asked with a strained voice as he stared down at Nash, not even bothering to help him up.

"I-I did th-this for u-us!" Nash cried as he tried climbing up to his feet.

"No," Archer replied with a disgusted expression, "You did this for yourself."

"Come on Kai, we have to go save Hana," Sean nodded to Kai who took a step towards Nash.

"Just let me get in one punch," Kai replied as he snapped his clenched fist forward to pummel Nash's lower stomach. He pulled back with a refreshed smile, satisfied by the loud yelp of pain Nash emitted. "Okay now I'm done, let's go."

"Wait," Archer called out. His face was filled with shame as he lowered his head. "I… I'm so sorry."

"Yeah," Sean responded in a dry voice. "So am I."

"I've already called Jaymes to come," Chase informed the trio when they returned to the cage. "Hana left her bag in the corner, so her phone was still here." He eyed the blood that coated Sean's hands, and stared firmly into his eyes, "Did you get him good?"

"Not as much as I would have liked," Sean admitted as he nodded to Chris to take Hana's bag, not wanting to dirty it with blood.

Sean glanced down when he felt a tug at his sleeve, and frowned at the words Chris had scribbled across his board. *You don't think they'll hurt her, do you?*

"Don't worry," Sean reassured him. "They can't lay a single hand on somebody as important as Hana. We'll get her back. We'll bring her back quickly, safely, and unharmed."

* * *

Hana bit down on her bottom lip to contain the scream she wanted to let out. She would never give those bastards the satisfaction of her pain.

"I hope you all know," Hana stated calmly, wiping the blood off the corner of her lip. "That you're all going to be sued the minute, no, the second I step out of this place." Her eyes flashed darkly at the men in front of her and she let out a low growl when one of them stepped forward. "What? Haven't had enough fun beating around a teenage girl?"

"We're just doing our job," the man growled in return, daring to take another step forward.

"Come closer and I'll upgrade it to a death penalty," Hana snarled. "I think you guys are underestimating how powerful I am."

The man hesitated to move forward and he exchanged glances with the other occupants of the room.

"Let me guess," Hana scoffed as she eyed each of the men's poor clothing. "You guys are either low life thugs or random poverty stricken people who was offered a quick way to get lots of cash, am I right? Do something as easy as beat up a little girl and you'll get a good sum of money for it. Stupid, aren't you? Didn't you suspect anything? Do you really think the money you get from this will be worth the long term? Why do you think you were hired to do a small, dirty job when these people easily could have done it themselves? There's obviously a catch, don't you think?"

There was a lengthy pause of silence in the room as they processed her words. "Wh-What do you mean?" one of the men finally dared to ask.

"You all apparently don't ask for any details, don't you? Stupid," Hana scowled as she ran her hand through her hair. "They hired you because they're too scared to do it themselves. You all are clearly unaware of who I am, which is why you are willing to freely impose harm on to me without any fear for future consequences."

"My name is Hana Acacia, heir to Acacia Corporations," Hana stated firmly. Her gaze narrowed and her voice went cold, "And you're all going to go through hell once I get out of here."

"Acacia Corporations?" a hushed whisper went through the room. "That sounds familiar."

"You idiot! It's that big electronics company!"

Similar fear stricken faces slowly turned towards her, striking absolutely no pity with Hana.

"Now that you know, you should leave before you make matters any worse," Hana snapped. "And tell your employer that he is going to hell."

The small group of men immediately fled the room, making sure to lock the door tightly behind them.

Hana let out a loud sigh as she leaned her back against the cold wall. She massaged her aching jaw, flinching when her fingers came in contact with the dark bruises she knew would quickly form. She mentally cursed herself; how could she have foolishly followed the men without asking any questions?

The badges that dawned their suits were undoubtedly real, but they must have been hired to lure Hana away from the others. Once she set foot out of the Noye house, she had been blindfolded and gagged before being thrown into a car. She knew exactly who was behind this: that bastard Henry, his dirty father, and most likely her own. Hana glanced around the small room she had been thrown into shortly after the car ride, and bit down on her bottom lip in search of an escape.

The sound of footsteps met her ears, and her head shot over to the door as it slowly opened, revealing one of the men she was itching to kill. She growled and clenched her fists at the sight of Henry.

"I'm sorry it had to come to this, Hana," Henry spoke softly as he stepped into the room, closing the door behind him.

"Don't give me that bullshit," Hana scoffed as she pushed her hair out of her face.

He frowned once he saw her bruised cheeks, "Please, you have to understand why we have to keep you here."

"No I don't, so leave," Hana replied coldly, her heart retaining not even the slightest drop of sympathy for Henry. "You won't get away with this for much longer."

"This is my life, Hana! This is my family's life! This is my family's business! If you ruin this, how are we supposed to survive? We couldn't, Hana. I couldn't let you take away the only thing that was letting us survive," Henry tried to explain. "Why couldn't you just listen to me? I warned you! Why couldn't you just let everything be as it was?!"

"That's great," Hana responded in a dry voice. "Then continuing surviving, Henry. Continue surviving by stepping on others."

"You would do this if you were in my shoes, Hana," Henry choked as he stepped towards her. "You would do this too if it was the only way you could survive!"

"No," Hana growled, her eyes flashing with hatred. "I wouldn't. I wouldn't degrade myself to be as disgusting as you are."

Hana's face snapped to the side, her cheek burning with pain from the slap Henry had just delivered. She clenched down on her teeth to prevent herself from crying out, and turned to glower at Henry.

"You want disgusting?" Henry asked with a clenched jaw. "Then I'll show you something you'll really be disgusted with."

With those as his final words, he stomped out of the room. The door slammed behind him with a loud bang, allowing Hana to finally release the breath of air she had been holding.

She dropped down to the ground, gently rubbing her aching face. The room had dropped several degrees and she pulled her knees to her chest to gather as much warmth as she could.

"I have to get out of here," Hana murmured under her breath as she rested her head against the tops of her knees. Her heavy eye lids slowly drooped to a close; the rest she had postponed for over 24 hours finally claimed her as victim. "I have to get out."

* * *

"It's been two days," Luca whispered quietly as he tucked his face into the crook of his arm. "Two days since Hana was taken."

"You think I don't know that already?" Sean snapped.

"Don't talk to him like that, he's just worried!" Aiden growled as he wrapped a protective arm around Luca's shoulders. "We're all worried, Sean, not just you, so could you stop acting like such a dick?"

He and Sean stared hard into each other's eyes until Sean finally let out a small sigh. "Yeah, I know, sorry," Sean muttered as he ran his fingers through his coarse hair. "I just... I can't..."

He concluded his words with a loud shout of distress, slamming his fist against the wall.

"Hurting yourself isn't going to save her," Kai piped up. Sean's head turned to the boy who was leaning against the cage door with crossed arms and cold eyes. "Take it from me."

Sean turned and pressed his back against the wall, slowly sliding down into a helpless heap. He clenched tight handfuls of his hair with his fists, "What am I supposed to do, Kai? How can I save her?"

"Pull yourself together," Kai growled as he yanked Sean up by the collar of his shirt. He shoved him against the wall, ignoring the cry of protest from Luca. "You pull yourself together, Sean."

"I know, I know," Sean murmured as he stared down at his feet. "I know I have to pull it together! I know! I just don't know what to do, Kai. I'm so pathetic, aren't I? If Hana was in my shoes she would have already come up with ten different ways to save me, but I just can't!"

"Sean, you need to calm down right now!" Kai glared as he slammed Sean against the wall again. "If you don't calm down you'll never be able to save Hana, do you understand me?! Nothing good will come from you losing control of yourself! Hana is probably sitting somewhere alone and afraid, and all you can do is whine about how you don't know what to do?! Bullshit! You'll never be able to save Hana if you're like this! You'll never be able to save Haru!"

Sean froze at the sound of Haru's name that accidently slipped from Kai's lips. Kai seemed to realize his mistake, for he released Sean's collar with trembling hands. Sean slowly stared up into Kai's pain filled eyes and he nodded his head silently, "Yeah, I got it."

Kai let out a shaky breath to calm himself down.

"She's being kept here, Hana, here at the Noye house," Kai folded his arms. "Don't say anything before I'm done," Kai quickly added in once Sean's eyes widened with surprise. "I'm not going to tell you where she is until I'm finished talking so you better keep quiet."

"Kai! She could be--!" Sean exclaimed, this time taking Kai's collar into his grasp.

"Sean," Kai stated firmly with hard eyes. "I don't care what she could be. What I do care about is you not letting your emotions get the better of yourself because you'll only make the problem worse."

Kai was so sure that Sean was about to punch him in the face from how the other glared at him, but to his relief and surprise, Sean simply nodded his head. "Make it quick," he spoke in a strained voice.

"I overheard Henry telling a guard not to give Hana any food until she confesses that she's been plotting to act against the Noye House," Kai explained in a hushed voice. "I don't know much of what they have been doing, but I know what they plan to do."

There was a pause of silence, and anticipation built as they all trained their eyes on Kai to listen carefully for what he was going to say next.

Kai's eyes flashed, and the corner of his lip curved upwards into a small smirk, "And I know exactly how we're going to stop them."

* * *

Hana stared up at the ceiling, wondering how many days had passed since she was captured. She let out a sigh as she pressed her cracked lips against her cold arms, thinking about what the others must have been doing.

"Probably going crazy at this point," she chuckled quietly to herself.

Her stomach strained in protest at the action and she let out another sigh. She didn't know it was possible to literally feel the strength slowly seep from one's body, but now she did.

The bruises she had received from the beating a few days prior had begun to shift into nasty shades of yellow and green. She was actually kind of happy that the others weren't here to witness her in such a state. She bit down on the inside of her mouth, thinking about how enraged Sean would be when he came to rescue her.

She didn't know how he would, or when he would, but she still held onto the belief that he would. It was a bit irritating, to be quite honest, for her to accept the position of being a damsel in distress, but at this point she couldn't care less.

Hana just wanted to go home. She wanted to go home to the small cozy house they had just moved into, and snuggle on the bed with Sean and read stories with Chris and joke around with Luca and Aiden. She wanted to work with Jaymes and argue with Kai and tease Chase and –

Her thoughts were suddenly jerked away from her as a large explosion shook the room. Her eyes widened in alarm and she registered the sounds of shouting guards and pounding footsteps outside the door of her jail. The dust that caked the walls fell down like rain and she held in her breath to prevent herself from inhaling the dirt.

What the hell was causing the ruckus? Hana froze in realization, and her hand slowly dropped to her side. They wouldn't.

She stared at the door in horrifying anticipation, silently pleading to the gods that what she assumed was happening wasn't actually happening. They weren't ready for it, none of them were ready for it and she'd be damned if they risked everything just to save her.

A loud thud banged against the door and she took a step back as a precautionary measure.

"Hana?! Hana are you in there?!"

Hana recognized that voice all too well, and her insides began to quiver in fear. She dropped to her feet and wrapped her arms around her knees, hoping, pleading, that this was all just a dream.

The door to her room burst open and she squeezed her eyes shut. She felt a pair of warm arms pull her in, and the familiar scent of Sean wafted around her like a protective shield.

"Hana, you're here," Sean whispered as he squeezed her tightly in his arms. He feared that she would disappear from his sight if he let her go.

"Se… Sean," Hana whimpered as she slowly responded to the hug. She clenched handfuls of the back of Sean's shirt into her small fists.

"You're here, you're here," Sean breathed in relief as he pressed kisses all over Hana's face. His hands patted her body to see if she had any serious wounds and he let out another breath of relief when none were found. "You're here and you're okay. I was so worried, I thought... I thought that you might have... but you're okay."

"Y-Yeah," Hana chuckled as she wrapped her arms around Sean's neck to pull him in for another hug. It was only now that she realized how much she had really missed him. "I'm okay, I'm okay."

A hard tremor shook the room and Hana was pulled back into reality.

"You shouldn't have come," Hana whispered as she slowly pulled away from Sean.

"What are you talking about?" Sean demanded as he stared into the girl's weary eyes. He felt a sudden anger spread through his chest as his fingers brushed against the girl's fading bruises. "I'm going to get you out of here, okay? It's going crazy out there so we have to be quick."

"Sean, you shouldn't have done this. We're not ready for this, Sean, so many people are going to die," Hana's voice shook as she held onto his shirt. "It wasn't worth it. You can't do this just to save me."

Sean stared at her with momentary confusion until he finally realized what she meant. He let out a soft chuckle and pressed a gentle kiss to her forehead. "Hana, trust me," Sean replied as he cupped the girl's face gently with the palms of his hands.

"Everybody's going to die and it's going to be all my fault," Hana whispered, her entire body beginning to quiver in fear.

"Hana, listen to me," Sean stated firmly. He pressed his lips gently against hers, and stared straight into her eyes as he pulled away. "Trust me, okay? Just trust me."

"But Sean I- O-okay," Hana nodded her head slowly.

"Good, now we have to get out of here," Sean stated as he pulled her to her feet. "Can you walk?"

Hana nodded her head. "Where are the others? Where are Chris and

Luca? Aiden, Kai, and Chase? Are they safe?"

"I don't know," Sean honestly replied. He wrapped an arm around her waist after noticing her weak steps. "We all agreed to meet up at the end of the 5th hall, so let's head there now."

The sights that met Hana's eyes the second they stepped out of the room were ones that she knew would haunt her for days. The rebellion had started not more than ten minutes ago, yet so much destruction had already hit the area around. Buildings were on fire. The screams, shouts and pounding footsteps were deafening to her ears and she would have remained frozen if it wasn't for Sean who tugged her along.

She now realized that it was the dead of night, but the sky was lit up by the fire that licked the air. Another bomb exploded and Sean caught her before she could topple over.

"Are you sure you can walk?" Sean asked as he glanced down at her with worry. "Do you want me to carry you?"

Hana shook her head and urged him to continue forward. They moved faster; the adrenaline that was pumping through her body gave her a surge of strength. She realized now that something was missing. "Where are the guards?"

"Most of them are still in the guard house," Sean answered as he wrapped his arm protectively around her head to shield her from any flying debris. "It's 3 AM right now, so most of them were sleeping when the first bomb went off." He let out a dark chuckle, "They didn't even know what was coming to them."

"What about Jaymes? And Adrian? What about everybody who was supposed to help the Noyes?" Hana asked as she stumbled after him.

"They're all here, Hana," Sean reassured her. "I told you to trust me, didn't I? Now watch your step or you're going to fall."

Sean continued to lead her through the destruction and fallen bodies. She blindly followed after him, not allowing herself to look very far. She knew she would remember every detail of it. Every dead body that littered the ground would remain engraved into her memory forever.

Hana cringed every time she heard a shot being fired, knowing fully well that it was most likely a Noye at the receiving end.

The hot blaze of the fire licked at her skin, and her lungs were probably filled to the brim with smoke by now.

She watched as a watch tower toppled over into a building; a number of screams shortly followed afterwards.

Would it be worth it? In end, would it all be worth it?

Hana froze once she caught sight of a lone figure standing in front of the guard house. She blinked and rubbed her eyes, not believing who she saw.

"Hana what are you doing? We have to go!" Sean exclaimed as he tried to pull her from her spot.

"Chris…" Hana whispered, recognizing the small white board that laid at the figure's feet. She pulled away from Sean and burst into a sprint towards the male, "Chris!"

Chris's head slowly turned towards her and he gave her a small, sad smile. His eyes were glazed over with a layer of tears, but he refused to let them fall. He slowly parted his lips, and spoke in a soft, gentle voice that contrasted the chaos that was happening around them. "Hana."

Hana froze mid-step, her eyes widening in shock as she processed the word and the unfamiliar voice that said it, "… Chris?"

"Hana! Chris! What are you doing?!" Sean exclaimed as he caught up with the pair. "Chris, let's go!"

Chris slowly turned towards the younger male, his tears now threatening to spill over.

"Sean," Chris nodded slowly, feeling the familiar word roll off his tongue like an old friend.

"Chr— Did you just… did you," Sean's jaw dropped in astonishment.

Chris's head turned back to face forward and the two now noticed what Chris was standing in front of.

Guards.

About 100 guards remained in the resting house, still clad in their pajamas as they stared at Chris with a mix of fear and anticipation.

"Chris, walk away slowly," Sean murmured under his breath, his eyes trained on the guns that were in many of their hands. "Chris, let's go or they'll kill you."

"They won't," Chris shook his head.

The two stared at him in confusion – how was he so sure that they wouldn't shoot him when they were completely capable of doing so? Hana now noticed the device that was in Chris's closed fist, and her eyes slowly widened in realization. It was a hand grenade. "Chris, don't."

Chris shook his head again, "It's too late."

Hana eyes zeroed in on the pin that lied on the ground, and her breath got caught in her throat. "Chris, please."

"You should leave," Chris whispered, a small tear escaped from the corner of his eye and slowly rolled down his dirt smudged face.

"Chris, don't do it," Sean shook his head, a sudden panic surging through his chest. He reached forward to take the grenade from Chris, but Chris blocked it with his other hand.

"Sean please," Chris's voice shook as he turned to stare at him. His eyes were swimming with tears and he was trying his hardest not to let any more of them fall. "I have to do this."

The two continued to stare at each other, years of silently communicating with their eyes told Sean all he needed to know.

"No you don't," Hana pleaded as she pulled at Chris's arm. "You don't have to do this, Chris, let's just go, okay? We can all go and live happily in our little house, and we can all be together and –"

"Hana," Sean whispered as he placed a hand on the girl's shoulder. "Let's go."

Hana's spun around to face Sean and she stared at him incredulously, "Sean! Are you crazy?! You can't just – This is Chris!"

Sean's face set into a straight, rigid line as he stared at Chris. He wrapped his arm around Hana and began to turn around, "Let's go Hana."

"Sean!" Hana exclaimed as she pulled away from Sean's grip. She was confused. She was angry and confused. How could Sean even suggest to leave Chris alone like that? No matter what his reasons were, he couldn't just leave him to die! "We can't leave Chris!"

"I said let's go," Sean responded in a hard voice. He picked Hana up off her feet and gently hung her over his shoulder, ignoring the kicks and punches she threw at him. "He'll die! Sean! Stop it he'll die!"

Sean turned around to face Chris, and his voice cracked as he softly spoke, "Goodbye, Chris."

Chris nodded his head, an endless stream of tears now running down his face. He sloppily wiped them away with the back of his arm and sobbed noisily as he watched Sean and Hana depart. He whispered under his breath, "Thank you for everything."

"Sean please, Sean please stop," Hana begged as Sean continued to walk away. "Sean don't leave him. Sean, Sean! Sean let me down! Chris! CHRIS!"

Chris tore his gaze away from the pair, and focused his attention once more on the guards in front of him. Chris recognized so many of those faces, for those were the faces that haunted his nightmares, his dreams, and his reality. They were the ones who sent shivers down his spine whenever he saw them turn the corner or walk in his direction. They were the ones who laughed at his face, who ignored his cries for mercy, who whispered profanity into his ears as they touched him in unspeakable places.

They were the ones who stole his voice.

And now they were the ones who would pay for it.

"He won't do it," one of them sneered loudly in Chris's direction. "If he kills us he'll die too and he's too scared to do that."

Chris could see the way the corner of the man's mouth quivered in fear.

"He's too much of a coward to do it," he continued, his hand tightening against the stock of his gun. "He's too much of a coward to let himself die. I bet that's a fake bomb. It's a fake, isn't it, huh? You're just trying to scare us when it's actually fake."

Chris smiled.

He held the grenade up in his hand and recited the lines he had heard whispered into his ears too many times to count,

"Now, why don't you be a good boy and keep quiet?"

* * *

"The others should be coming soon," Sean murmured as he placed Hana back down on her feet once they reached the end of the 5th hall.

Hana spun around on her heels, her face twisted into an expression of rage and desperation.

"Sean!" Hana screamed, tears running down her face as she slammed her fists repetitively against Sean's chest. "He's going to die! Why did you do that, we could have saved him!"

Sean stood there silently taking all of the hits without even flinching. He clenched down hard on his jaw to stop himself from breaking into tears as he recalled the look on Chris's face. After a few minutes, he caught Hana's thin arms easily with his hands. "You're going to hurt yourself," he murmured as he stared down at the sobbing girl.

"Why di-did you d-do th-that?" Hana cried as she fell to the ground. She sobbed loudly into her hands. "Why didn't you save him?"

Sean stared down at her, his heart clenching tightly in his chest at the sight of the heartbroken girl and the thought of Chris.

"Because this is his way…" Sean's voice cracked as he swiped at his eyes with the back of his arm, "This is his way of saving himself. This is his way of ending the years of torment he suffered through."

"What happened?"

Sean and Hana both looked over at Kai who had just arrived.

"Kai, Kai, Chris's… Chris's going to!" Hana cried, wrapping her arms around Kai's waist as she cried into his chest.

"Hana? Hana, calm down," Kai responded with a worried voice as he patted the girl's back. He glanced at Sean, "What's wrong with Chris?"

"Chris won't be coming," Sean explained in a strained voice.

Kai bit down on his lip, not knowing what to say. He cared for Chris like a brother, but he knew he meant the most to Sean. "Sean… I—"

"Sean! Kai! Please help me! Aiden's –!" Luca's voice echoed against the hallway, and all three of their heads shot to the direction of his voice.

Luca was slowly making his way down the hall with Aiden's arm thrown over his shoulder. Aiden's shirt was drenched in blood and he let out grunts of pain as he pressed his hand against his wound.

"He was shot, he was shot in the leg," Luca explained frantically as Kai and Sean helped pull the male off of the smaller.

"Re-relax, Aiden, you'll be al-alright," Hana reassured the other as she wiped the sweat off his forehead. She took a deep breath to calm her nerves – she couldn't afford to get over emotional when there were others in danger.

"You're okay," Aiden groaned as reached over to pat Hana on the head, his eyes crinkling as he flashed her a small smile.

"Ye-yeah, and y-you will b-be too," Hana gave a shaky smile before examining his leg. She let out a sigh of relief after checking the wound, "It's j-just a flesh wound. The b-bullet grazed his side but he'll be okay. We'll get you p-patched up once we get home. Just bear with it for now."

"Where's Jaymes? He should have come to get us by now," Kai exclaimed with frustration as he pressed cloth against Aiden's side to stop the bleeding.

"Is everybody else here?" Luca asked as his head darted from side to side. His face twisted in horror as he realized the absences. "Where's Chris? And Chase?"

"Chris's right here."

Heads darted up at the voice, and they saw Jaymes making his way down the hall with Chris trudging behind him. His clothes were ripped and torn, and there was blood splattered against his clothes, but altogether he remained relatively unharmed. His face was gaunt, and his eyes remained dull and empty as he recalled the scene that had happened just minutes prior.

"Ch… CHRIS!" Sean shouted as he sprinted forward to wrap his arms around the elder, Hana not far behind him.

"Chris you're safe," Hana cried, a fresh batch of tears streaming down her face as she cupped Chris's face with the palms of her hands. She pressed kisses against his forehead and sobbed as she pulled him in for a hug. "I thought you were – I thought – "

"I'm here," Chris's soft voice whispered into her ears as he slowly responded to the hug. "I'm here."

"Yeah," Hana replied in a mix of laughter and crying. "You're here."

"What happened?" Sean whispered as he stared at the elder, trying to convince himself that Chris was really there in front of him.

Chris turned rigid, and a few tears rolled down his cheeks as he slowly murmured, "Chase... he... he..."

"Chase saved him," Jaymes answered as he placed a hand on Chris's shoulder. "But in the process..." He didn't need to continue his words for them to know what had happened.

"We need to leave," Kai called out. "Aiden's bleeding a lot even if it's just a flesh wound."

"I have the car parked right down the next hall, let's get going," Jaymes informed them as he placed a hand on Hana's shoulder. "I... I'm glad you're safe Miss Hana." He would have seemed almost indifferent if his voice hadn't cracked at the end of his sentence.

"We can save the reunions for later, let's get out of here first," Kai demanded once another explosion shook the building.

"Come on," Jaymes nodded as he led them in the direction of the car. Once the seven of them were buckled down, with Aiden stretched out across the back seat, Jaymes immediately got the engine running. Government officials would arrive any minute now, and they weren't about to be caught at the scene. At this point, hopefully most of the Noyes had fled the grounds.

Hana watched through the window as the car quickly drove them away from the chaos left behind. She felt Sean wrap his large, warm hand around her own and she glanced at him with a small smile. She turned back around, and continued watching the Noye house until all that was left in the distance was a flickering orange glow.

"It's over," Luca's shaky voice interrupted the pregnant silence that had taken over the car. He let out a small laugh, as if he couldn't believe what he was finally saying.

"It's all over."

CHAPTER FOURTEEN: RESILIENCE

resilience [ri-zil-ee-ence] n. - the ability to become strong, healthy, or successful again after something bad happens

"Hana, wake up."

"Hana, it's just a dream."

"Hana," Sean called out loudly as he shook the sleeping girl's shoulders. "HANA."

Hana's eyes snapped open and she jolted up in her bed, nearly slamming the top of her head against Sean's. Her chest heaved up and down as her heart beat rapidly against her chest. Her hands clenched the sheets tightly below her, "Sean..."

"Hana, it was just a dream," Sean reassured her as he wiped away the sweat that layered her skin, "You're okay; it was just a dream."

"S-Sorry," Hana murmured as she pulled the damp blankets away from her body. "Sorry for waking you."

"No, don't apologize," Sean shook his head as he pressed a soft kiss against her forehead. "Did you have another nightmare?"

Hana remained silent as the images of that night flashed through her head once more and she gave her head a slow shake.

Sean stared down at her with disappointment, "You can tell me that you had a bad dream, Hana. I won't make you tell me about it."

He let out a sigh when she refused to respond, and the bed creaked as he stepped back onto solid ground. "Do you want to take a shower?"

"Yeah," Hana answered in a soft voice. She pushed her hair behind her shoulders and slid down until her toes touched the cold floor. She glanced up to see Sean staring at her with concern, "Is something wrong?"

Sean opened his mouth to response, but reluctantly closed it as he glanced away. "Nothing, I'll go make you some tea."

Hana stared at the door to her bedroom that he had left ajar and bit down on her bottom lip. Sean was frustrated with her, she knew that.

She just wasn't ready to get everything off her mind.

Hana pulled a fresh set of pajamas from her dresser before stepping into the bathroom that lay adjacent to her bedroom. She ran her hand against the wall until her fingers pressed against the light switch, and her eyes immediately squinted to adjust to the sudden brightness. She shed her clothes, tossing them carelessly to the side before stepping into the shower. Her body immediately relaxed as the warm water pattered against her skin, washing away the sticky sweat.

She pressed her forehead against the cold tiles as the water continued to rinse off her perspiration. "I'm sorry," Hana whispered quietly.

Seven days had passed since the Noye rebellion, and the news that headlined the papers every day didn't reveal anything in their favor. Tens of hundreds of Noyes had been recaptured already, and there were faces she recognized among the photos published: Skyler, Archer, Logan. Sean had slammed his fist against the wall when they had seen Ethan's face in yesterday's paper.

That wasn't why Sean was frustrated with her, however. He was angry that she hadn't spoken, not a single word about the anguish she felt or the nightmares that plagued her dreams every night. He was frustrated that she retained her stoic expression, even when all the others shed tears.

"I'm sorry," Hana repeated as she closed her eyes; the water erased any evidence of her tears.

She couldn't afford to cry or break down, not now, not at a time as crucial as the one they were going through. If she broke down she wouldn't be able to pick herself up. If she broke down, she wouldn't be able to continue her façade in front of the public eye, wouldn't be able to fight for the rights of the Noyes, wouldn't be able to secure their freedom.

"Just a little longer," she nodded her head, slowly opening her eyes as she turned the faucet to cut off the stream of water.

After drying off and putting on a new set of clothes, Hana stepped into the kitchen where Sean was waiting for her. To her surprise, both Chris and Luca were sitting quietly at the counter as well, each with a mug of what Hana could only presume to be tea in their hands.

"Sean told us you couldn't sleep either," Luca nodded his head as he gestured to the mug that was sitting next to him.

Hana offered him a weak smile as she took the spot and burned her tongue when she took a sip.

"You should know by now not to do that," Sean scolded as he took the mug from her hands. Hana watched as he blew at the top in an attempt to cool it down, and her heart swelled as she stared at him.

"There's another court session today, isn't there?" Luca whispered.

Sean nodded in confirmation as he handed the mug back to Hana after he deemed it chilled enough.

"Are you going to go too, Chris?" Luca asked as he glanced over at the elder who sat quietly at his side.

Chris nodded his head rather than supply a verbal answer. He still wasn't used to speaking, and tried his best to avoid vocal responses.

"I want to go too." Their heads turned to the new voice that interrupted the silence and they watched as Kai stepped out of his bedroom.

"You know why you can't," Sean responded disapprovingly.

"Yeah, but I still want to," Kai shrugged as he stole Hana's tea from her hands to take a sip.

Hana gave him a small smile before shifting her gaze to the small boy who was sitting one seat away from her. Chris had his sleeves pulled over his hands that were wrapped around the large mug. He held his tea so close to his face that the steam directly hit his skin, causing it to turn a light shade of pink. His eyes were swollen and red again, just like how they have been for the past seven days.

Chris caught her gaze and gave her a smile, "Is something wrong?"

Hana was mildly taken aback by the sound; she was still unfamiliar with the elder's voice. She shook her head and returned the smile before taking another sip of her tea, flinching when the liquid scorched her tongue yet again.

"Well, I'll be going back to sleep," Luca nodded as he pushed himself off of his chair. "Aiden's going to wake up soon and throw a fit if I'm not next to him." He gave Hana a kiss on the top of her head and waved goodbye to the others, rolling his eyes when Sean shot him a dirty look.

The four glanced to the side when the sound of a door clicked open, and Jaymes paused, momentarily taken aback to see all those who had waken before him. He cracked a tired grin and stole the seat Luca had just abandoned, "Looks like nobody can sleep, huh?"

Hana hummed in agreement, deciding to give her tea another try.

"I'm going to bed," Chris announced as he pushed his tea away from the edge of the counter. His feet hit the ground with a soft thud and he said his goodbyes to everybody before disappearing back into the room he now shared with Jaymes. Luca and Aiden had taken over his room.

"He still thinks about Chase, doesn't he?" Kai asked in a low voice once he was sure Chris was out of earshot.

"Mumbles his name in his sleep," Jaymes nodded in confirmation. "I don't think the poor kid will ever forget what that guy did for him."

"Chase…" Sean murmured. "We never got to know him very well."

"Chris did," Kai shook his head as he stared down at his hands. "They'd always talk, or at least, Chase would talk to him."

"That makes it all so much harder," Jaymes frowned. He let out a loud groan as he stretched his limbs above his head. "Well, I'm going to get myself ready for court later on. I'll wear my lucky socks and hope for the best," Jaymes smiled, attempting to lighten the mood.

It was in vain.

* * *

Hana met eyes with Henry the second she walked into the courthouse and she grimaced at how smugly he stared at her. He leaned over to whisper a few words into the ear of his attorney and they both glanced in her direction before letting out a chorus of obnoxious laughter.

She wanted to rip his face off.

"Ignore those assholes," Jaymes whispered as he placed a comforting hand on her shoulder. "They won't be laughing at the end of today."

Hana glanced gratefully back at him before letting out a small breath of air, "You think we can beat them, Jaymes?"

Jaymes nodded his head confidently, "There's no way we could lose this, Miss Hana. Not with the amount of preparation you and Adrian have been doing this past week."

Hana smiled, reassured by the words the other gave her.

"Ah, Hana!" Adrian called out as he stepped forward, nodding his greetings to the other three boys that stood behind her.

Sean watched as Adrian and Hana immediately got engulfed into a deep discussion as to what they were planning to do. He knew it would be hard to keep track of what was happening with all the legal terms and sophisticated arguments that would be thrown around. Sean wasn't stupid, but his education under the Noye house could only take him so far.

Sean resisted the urge to push up the sleeves of his suit after already getting scolded by Hana several times. He hated the uncomfortable clothing and he honestly couldn't understand how people could wear such constricting outfits every day.

Chris, on the other hand, enjoyed the elegant wear. He felt refined, even with the excess layers piled on top of his skin. With his suit on, one could hardly differentiate between him and the other men.

"We should take our seats," Jaymes nodded to a row near the front of the room. "I won't be able to explain to you what is happening, so you two will have to try your best to follow along."

"It's fine," Sean shrugged, jerking his head in Henry's direction. "I can just watch Henry and see how everything is going by how he reacts."

Jaymes chuckled at the thought and nodded his head in agreement, "That sounds like a good solution as well."

He watched as the jury members began to file out of a door and take their respective seats on the side of the room. "It's beginning."

It was hard for the pair to understand what was happening, for much of the debate consisted of laws being read out of a large book and arguments that were too complex for them to follow. Still, Sean could get a sense of the debate by the look on Henry's face. The frown that had been stretched across his lips for the past few hours was a good sign.

Chris nudged him gently in the ribs with his elbow, "Hana's going up."

His words immediately got Sean to snap his attention back to the front of the room and he watched with pride as Hana took a seat with her back facing the audience. As calm as she might have appeared to the naked eye, Sean knew she must have been shaking on the inside. He didn't understand most of the words coming from Hana's mouth, but that made her appear even more intellectual in his eyes.

Sean couldn't help but feel a surge of pride burst inside of his chest. If it had been the Sean from a few weeks ago sitting there, the view would have had a tremendously negative effect on his self-esteem. How could he manage to keep up with a beautiful girl of such high intellect? The Sean now, however, knew better than to think such things.

He was hers, and likewise, she was his. Sean couldn't help the grin that spread across his face.

"Are you smiling because you understand what's happening or because you like looking at her?" Chris asked quietly with a cocked head.

"The latter," Sean answered without even a beat of hesitation.

Chris rolled his eyes and slumped in his seat, "Of course."

Sean ignored his tone and continued to train his eyes on Hana's back. The girl remained in the front for only a few minutes, and as she turned to head back to her seat she caught Sean's gaze. Sean's jaw dropped slightly in surprise when Hana flashed him a curt wink. His cheeks flamed at the bold action, and his gaze immediately fell down to his lap.

"You're like a teenage girl," Chris chortled under his breath.

Sean liked it better when he couldn't talk.

By the time the day was over, Sean had lost feeling in both of his legs. He shook the numbness out of his limbs as he nudged Chris awake. He had gotten tired of the words and arguments he didn't understand, and had been snoring softly at Sean's side for well over an hour.

"Is it done?" Chris murmured as he rubbed his fists sleepily against his eyes. "Did we win?"

"This goes on for a few more days, remember?" Sean shook his head. He paused for a few seconds and smugly jerked his head over to where Henry was seated, "Judging by Henry's expression, however, today has gone rather well in our favor."

Chris followed his line of sight and nodded his head in agreement, "He looks like he's about to kill somebody or cry." He tugged at Jaymes's sleeve to catch his attention and asked, "Did today go well?"

A bright smile flashed across Jaymes's face and he held a thumb up, "Extremely."

Sean didn't know whether Jaymes was telling the truth or not, but he decided to trust the other's judgment. A similar smile stretched across his face and he grinned proudly up at Hana who was still conversing with the other attorneys. The three of them waited patiently for Hana to conclude her discussion before finally making her way over to them.

"You did great," Jaymes grinned proudly as he quickly engulfed her into a tight hug. He released her after a few seconds, however, not wanting to test the impatient boy beside him.

"You must have been bored, huh?" Hana laughed as she gave both Sean and Chris a quick hug, eager to get back home to rest.

"No, not at all!" Chris shook his head enthusiastically. "You were great!"

"You'd be more convincing if you didn't have dried drool on the corner of your lip," Hana teased. She glanced down at her watch and nodded her head, "Let's hurry and head home for an early dinner."

"Let's pick something up on our way home," Jaymes suggested.

Hana nodded in agreement. "I'm going to go to the restroom very quick, so wait for me at the car."

She gave them a quick wave before heading towards the hall, tapping her chin lightly with her finger in an attempt to remember where the bathroom was located.

A loud slap echoed through the abandoned corridor, immediately catching her attention. Two figures stood at the far end of the hall, one with his head hung in shame, the other with an outstretched arm of fury.

Hana recognized the pair as Henry and his father. It had been quite a while since she last saw Michael, and the man appeared as if he had aged years in those few weeks.

"You insolent bastard! You're going to let this stupid, this stupid _girl_ get the better of you?" Michael hissed angrily, the palm of his hand meeting painfully with Henry's cheek once more. Henry offered no words in response, and hung his head as he dealt with his father's blows.

Hana stared at the father son pair with indifference, and was about to move on until Henry crumpled to the floor. Michael didn't stop there, and continued to stomp his foot angrily onto his son, "You – worthless- filth!"

It was then that Hana felt a foreign tug at her heart – one she had never felt for Henry ever before. Henry could have easily, _easily_ defended himself against his father's blows, yet he still refused to do so.

Hana tore her gaze away from the sight, and after using the restroom, she silently joined the others who had been waiting for her outside.

"There are two men having a brawl in the left corridor," she whispered quietly to a security guard. "Please subdue the situation before it gets out of hand."

Hana climbed back into the car to see Sean already in a state of disarray. His blazer had already been thrown somewhere in the trunk, and his tie hung loosely from his neck. "This stuff is more uncomfortable than the rags they made me where in the Noye house," Sean huffed as he tried unbuttoning the cuffs of his sleeves.

Hana laughed at the sight, but fell silent once she caught sight of Henry trudging out of the courthouse. The pair made eye contact through the car window and Henry immediately averted his eyes.

Hana let out a soft sigh before she turned back to Chris and Sean to distract herself. Still, she couldn't get rid of the thought that was tugging her mind back to Henry.

There were always two sides to every story.

Likewise, there were always two sides to every person.

Hana wondered which side she saw of Henry was the true side.

* * *

Hana pressed her ear closer to Sean's chest to listen to the rhythmic beats of his heart. The two of them had been lying in bed for quite a while now despite the fact that the sun had set long ago. The events that occurred earlier that day completely exhausted them, yet they still couldn't find themselves giving into their fatigue.

"Can I ask you something...?" Sean asked, interrupting the lull.

Hana hummed in agreement, paying more attention to the invisible lines she drew onto Sean's large hand. It was interesting to see the vast contrast in size, for Sean's hand was nearly twice as large as her own.

"Why did you do this for us?" Sean asked, his tongue darting out to lick his suddenly dry lips. Hana stilled her movements with Sean's hand and he quickly continued, "The rebellion, I mean. Why were you willing to sacrifice everything for people you knew for less than a month?"

The silence after his question burned into the air.

"Can I... can I tell you the truth?" Hana asked quietly.

"Yeah," Sean nodded his head firmly. He watched as Hana pushed herself into an upright position. She turned away from Sean, fearing that she wouldn't be able to finish her words if she was staring at him. The silence continued to stretch on and Sean propped himself up with his elbows just enough so could see the girl, "Hana?"

"The reason I did this… the reason…" Hana murmured as she ran her hand through her long hair, disheveled from lying on Sean's chest for the past few hours. She took a deep breath of air to calm her nerves.

"Because... Because this rebellion, it wasn't just a rebellion for you all. It was, I guess you could say a rebellion for myself as well; a rebellion against the world I had grown to hate. I wanted to tarnish the world's perfectly operating society," Hana explained slowly, her words beginning to pick up pace as she spoke, "I hated my life at the time. I hated the servants that would greet me whenever I came home. I hated the expectations and responsibilities bestowed onto me by my father. I hated acting like the perfect child I knew I really wasn't."

Hana glanced over her shoulder, but averted her eyes. Her palms began to sweat and she quickly wiped them against her pajamas.

"And then you guys came along and I... I guess I saw it as an opportunity. I was so eager to run away from the life society had dictated for me that I carelessly put all of yours in harm's way. I was just being a selfish, rebellious teenager who used money and power to get everything she wanted; I didn't think I would grow as emotionally attached to everybody as I am now," Hana chuckled bitterly. "I'm not as selfless as you guys think I am, you know. I've been saying that from the start."

She tensed at the uneasy silence that answered her, and stole a glance at Sean's expression, "Do you hate me now?"

Sean's eyes widened at her words and he quickly waved his hands back and forth to deny her claim.

"No I'm actually kind of satisfied that you initially did this for yourself," Sean admitted after a beat of silence. Hana turned to face him with eyes widened slightly from disbelief. He chuckled at her reaction and reached out to touch her arm. "That means you got something out of this for yourself too."

Hana pursed her lips and tapped his forehead, "Yeah, I got you."

Sean let out a loud snort. "You have a way with your words, you know that?" Sean muttered lovingly under his breath as he pulled Hana into his arms. He rested his chin comfortably on top of her head, "All of that doesn't matter to me, Hana, whatever your initial intentions were."

Sean flushed a bright color of red as he murmured his next few words, "It… it makes me love you even more, to be honest, because it makes you human. I don't want you to be perfect, you know."

Hana's heart pounded against her chest as his words processed through her mind. It was the first time Sean had verbalized his affection for her, other than the time he had confessed, and the word love sounded so foreign to her ears.

"I'm embarrassed so don't look at me," Sean muttered as he tightened his grip around her. He flushed even darker when the sound of Hana's tinkling laughter met his ears, "Don't laugh."

Hana laughed even harder at his childish antics, and wrapped her arms around his waist, "Do you know why I chose you Sean? That day in the hallways? It was because you had the defiant look in your eyes that I wished I could have in mine."

She pulled away from his chest and wrapped her arms around his neck to stare into his eyes, "And I was right. You are beautiful."

"Boys don't want to be called beautiful, Hana," Sean responded pointedly, "We want to be called handsome and manly."

Hana hummed in agreement as she pressed her lips against his. Despite her consistent nagging for him to start using chap stick, she still felt his chapped lips mold against her own. Still, she didn't mind it, for she loved everything that made Sean who he was – chapped lips and all.

Surprisingly, it was Sean who pulled away first. "We have a long day tomorrow, so we should get to sleep. If we continue this any longer I don't think I'll be able to restrain myself." He wrapped his arms around her waist and pulled the both of them down to lie across the bed.

"Night, Hana," Sean murmured as he pressed a kiss to the top of her head. He hesitated for a few seconds before shyly muttering, "Love you."

Hana closed her eyes, enjoying the sound the word made in her ears. She took Sean's large hand into her considerably smaller one and intertwined their fingers. Bringing their hands up to her lips, she pressed a soft kiss against the back of Sean's hand.

"I love you too, my handsome and manly Sean."

CHAPTER FIFTEEN: FINALE

finale [fə-'na-lē] n. - the concluding event of a sequence

"Hana's not home?" Chris asked as he seated himself beside Sean who had been attempting to read a book. After watching Sean remain on the same page for the past ten minutes, he had decided to relieve the younger of his torture and give him a reason to set aside the novel.

"Yeah," Sean huffed, unconsciously glancing over at the front door.

"You're like a puppy," Chris cooed as he disheveled Sean's hair. "Waiting for your master to come back from work, are you?"

Sean's eyes narrowed at the elder's teasing and he swatted him gently away, "I am not a puppy."

"You know, I was wondering," Chris piped up as he tapped his chin thoughtfully. "If you and Hana get married, are you going to take her last name or is she going to take yours? Because normally the wife takes the husband's last name, but Hana is clearly the man in this relationship."

"I'm going to kill you, I swear to god I will," Sean growled.

Chris hummed happily in response, pretending that he hadn't heard a single word the other had uttered.

Sean observed the light expression that was draped across Chris's face. "You've changed," Sean smiled lightly. "You're happier now."

There was a pause of silence.

"Yeah?" Chris asked softly. He tilted his head back and gazed up at the ceiling. "Chase."

Sean turned to him with a confused expression, "What?"

"Chase," Chris repeated, his face falling just the slightest at the name. He glanced at Sean from the corner of his eye, "Before he died, he told me to live my life happily so I wouldn't have any regrets."

He stretched an arm and waved up at the ceiling as if he could see Chase himself, "So I am. So when Chase watches me from up there, he won't regret giving up his life for me."

The pair of them fell silent for a few minutes, Chris's arm dropping limply back to his side with a quiet thud.

"Were you... were you and Chase close?" Sean asked slowly, glancing quickly at Chris's face to gauge his reaction. It was the first time any of them had discussed the older male with Chris. None of them wanted to reopen wounds that weren't fully closed, and had been waiting for Chris to be the first to initiate the conversation.

Chris pursued his lips thoughtfully before shaking his head, "No, but I guess that I was the closest to him out of all of you guys. He used to talk to me, you know? He used to tell me about the life he never really had."

Sean arched an eyebrow of confusion, "What do you mean?"

Chris kicked his legs up onto the coffee table in front of him and let out a quiet hum, "I wonder if he'd be okay with me telling you this. He never said that I couldn't tell anybody, but to be fair, at that time I didn't speak so I couldn't tell anybody even if I wanted to."

He glanced at Sean, "Still, I think he'd be okay with me telling you. He knew how close we were, anyways."

"Chase's parents abandoned him when he was ten years old," Chris began, folding his hands together on his lap. "He was sent to an orphanage after that, but he ran away after three years. The place was so overrun with kids that the supervisors wouldn't have even noticed – that's what he said, at least. He wandered the streets for a good two years, working odd jobs for shady people. When he was 15 he began working for a gang; he said the work was dirty but the pay was enough to feed and clothe him."

"He said he stuck with the gang for a good three or four years – by then he didn't even really bother keeping track of time. Then there was one job that he messed up, badly, from how he described it to me. I never knew the details, but it must have been bad enough for them to want to take his life for it," Chris continued. "He hid out in a ditch from that point on. He said he'd just lie there for hours, and get food from the dumpster. It was right next to a restaurant, so he thought that luck was finally on his side."

"Can you believe that?" Chris let out a bitter chuckle. "He scored food out of a restaurant dumpster and thought he was the luckiest man alive."

"Anyways, he didn't know how long he lived like that, but eventually officials from the Noye house found him and took him in. Said that with a face like that, he'd live a better life becoming somebody's Noye," Chris murmured as he raked a hand through his hair. "Personally, he said, he didn't want a rebellion. He said that he'd just end up back on the streets with an even bigger price tag on his head."

Chris's hands clenched into tight fists, and his body began to shake as he recalled the painful memory, "That night, he came to me. He came to me and he wrapped his hand around mine to make sure he was still pressing down on the grenade before slipping it out. He didn't even say anything. He didn't explain why he was doing it, but I still let him."

Chris let out a round of forced laughter, "Talking this much after several years of being mute is really tiring, isn't it?"

"You don't have to look like that," Sean spoke up in a low voice.

Chris froze, glancing nervously over at Sean, "What do you mean?"

"Chase wouldn't be happy to know that you're forcing away your grief to pretend to be happy," Sean answered thoughtfully.

Chris blinked, and then he cried.

Sean gazed at the elder with a soft expression, watching as Chris bawled at the top of his lungs like a child crying for his mother.

A good fifteen minutes passed by before Chris's cries finally died down. He flinched when he heard the sound of a door opening, and groaned to himself; the others had been home to hear his tantrum.

"It was about time you stopped crying," Kai muttered as he rubbed his temples. "No offense, but you sound like a dying whale."

Luca jammed his elbow into Kai's ribs. He turned to Chris and offered him a kind smile, "I'm glad that you finally released your emotions."

Chris sniffed, refusing to glance over at the pair.

Luca cleared his throat awkwardly and turned to Sean in an attempt to change the topic, "I uh, wh-when's Hana coming home?"

Sean shrugged in what he hoped was a nonchalant manner before coolly picking his book back up, "How should I know?"

Luca blinked, "Are you trying to look indifferent? Because it's not working, you obvious brat."

Sean flushed with embarrassment and threw his book at Luca.

"You little shit I'm older than you!" Luca barked as he dodged the flying object.

"Who are you calling a little shit?" Hana piped up curiously as she popped into the living room with Jaymes trailing closely behind her.

"I bet it's Sean," Jaymes commented with a grin.

Hana noticed the tears that stained Chris's cheeks and she glanced at Sean. He gave his head a brief shake, signaling not to ask about it for now. She stared at him for a few seconds before mouthing, "Chase". He hesitated, but nodded his head in confirmation.

"We brought you guys take out today," Hana announced as she held up the plastic bags containing the dinner for the night.

Kai's eyes widened with delight and he let out a cry so gleeful Hana had to question whether it had actually come from him. Aiden heard Hana's words from the other room as well, for he too let out a happy yelp.

"You guys are offending Jaymes, you know," Hana frowned teasingly. "Are his meals not good enough for you guys to act like take out is the best thing in the world?"

Kai shook his head and clapped a hand reassuringly on Jaymes's shoulder, "It's not that. It's just that your meals are... healthy. And I mean don't get us wrong, we definitely appreciate our… nutrients, but it's very, very nice to have food completely drenched in grease and fat sometimes!"

Hana hummed in agreement as she opened the boxes of Chinese takeout and fried chicken, "I agree with Kai."

Jaymes looked absolutely appalled with her words, "Well, for who do I cook so health conscious for?!"

Hana chuckled at his incredulous expression and passed around the plates, "You guys are probably already hungry, so go ahead and start."

"With pleasure," Kai grinned as he spooned fried rice and chicken onto his plate. The others quickly mimicked his actions, eager to indulge the greasy goodness.

"You guys forgot about me!" Aiden's faint wail sounded.

Luca's eyes widened in realization and he immediately left the table.

"Anyways, why the special dinner?" Kai asked with a cocked head.

Hana paused for a few seconds, her eyes practically gleaming with triumph, "It's a celebratory dinner!"

"What are we celebrating? Kai's clear lack of table manners?" Luca snorted, avoiding the drumstick Kai flung in his direction shortly after.

"Let Hana talk," Chris demanded with furrowed eyebrows.

"Thanks Chris," Hana tossed him an appreciative smile. The boys stared at her with anticipation. "The case was settled earlier this evening. You are all officially free of your titles as Noyes."

Her words were met with silence.

A loud thud sounded across the room, caused by Luca who had suddenly let go of Aiden. The fallen male had no complaints, however, and could only gaze at Hana with shock at the sudden information.

Kai stared blankly at the drumstick that was in his hand for a few seconds before staring back at Hana, "You mean… we're…. we're free?"

Hana smiled and nodded her head, "Yeah."

"We're free," Luca tested the sound out on his tongue. "We're free."

Hana laughed and shuffled his hair, "Yes! You're free!"

His eyes lit up, finally processing the meaning behind the simple word. He threw his hands up in the air and laughed gleefully as he wrapped his arms tightly around Aiden's shoulders, "We're free! Aiden, we're free!"

"So I heard," Aiden grinned in response.

"W-Wait, but what happened?" Luca asked as he hushed down all the excitement. "What did they say exactly?!"

"According to the court ruling, all slaves that escaped from the revolting Noye house are now entitled as freemen. Those who had been captured by the city officials are also to be released from the prisons as well," Hana beamed. "The only downside was that those whom were already sold as Noyes have to remain as such." She glanced over at Sean and Chris and teased, "So I guess you two are still exclusively mine."

Chris and Sean exchanged looks at her words and responded with simultaneous smiles, "We don't have a problem with that."

"So everything we worked for paid off," Aiden breathed, closing his eyes to soak in the reality of the moment. "It all paid off, we're free."

"We're not... we're not Noyes anymore," Kai murmured in disbelief. "We're just... we're just..."

"You're just humans," Hana finished for him as she took his hands into her own. She beamed at him, "You're all just regular, untitled, humans."

The word human never made them feel so alive.

* * *

"I don't understand why I have to wear this," Sean frowned as he stared down at his suffocating suit. "I like T-shirts better!"

"Stop complaining," Hana rolled her eyes as she nudged him gently in the ribs. "Sure we won, but that doesn't mean we can suddenly show up looking like slobs."

"I think they should make a law that T-shirts and jeans are just as acceptable as suits," Sean muttered as he attempted to loosen his tie.

"I would second that," Hana nodded in approval. She swatted away his hand, "And stop messing with that."

"But it's too tight," Sean protested as he trailed after her.

"You'll live," she scoffed. Her lips immediately spread into a smile as she greeted some of the other Presidents that called her over.

"I don't understand why we have to attend this event," Sean muttered.

"Because we have to show our appreciation," Hana responded, a smile still stretched across her face as she waved politely to a group of men.

"I hope your cheeks hurt," Sean murmured bitterly.

"Just smile," Hana replied as she pinched him gently at his side. "And stop looking like you're going to murder somebody."

"I really think I am going to, Hana," Sean responded under his breath. "My fingers are twitching to wrap around someone's throat and squeeze. I think the safest way to avoid such an event happening is to leave."

"Nice try," Hana scoffed as she sent him a pointed look.

"But nobody else had to come," Sean objected, resorting to go back to his childish methods. "Even Jaymes didn't show up to this thing; that's how much this sucks."

"Jaymes had errands to run," Hana reminded him. "And I said you didn't have to come along with me, remember? You were the one who insisted on 'protecting' me against the evil rich old people."

"Well I can't let you go to these things alone," Sean muttered.

"You volunteered, so now you have to pay the price," Hana shrugged, thanking another couple who congratulated her on her victory in court.

Before Sean could respond, a loud clang echoed through the room. Both of their heads turned to see the source of the noise and Hana froze once she saw that it was Henry causing a ruckus at the front entrance.

"What the hell happened to him?" Sean murmured under his breath as he eyes raked in Henry's appearance. "He looks like he's been to hell and back." Hana had to agree.

Henry's previously golden hair now looked almost brown from all the dirt and filth that caked each layer. His clothes were torn and smudged with dirt and he held a small flask of alcohol in his hand.

His eyes locked onto Hana's from across the room and he lunged forward in her direction, "There she is! There's that witch with her little pet! How does it feel to be free, you nasty, vile creature?!" Henry hooted.

"You're drunk, Henry," Hana stared at him with a blank expression. The strong smell of liquor radiated from his clothes, tinged with the dirty scent of urine and filth.

"And whose fault is that?!" Henry bellowed. He held up his arms mockingly, "Do you like what you've done to me? Do you feel good knowing that you've destroyed my life? Do you, Hana?! DO YOU?!"

"Take him away!" Sean ordered the security guards, angry at how they could have allowed it to have gotten this far. He pulled Hana behind him protectively when Henry stepped closer.

"You're using your little pet to keep you safe, huh?" Henry laughed, resisting when two security guards grabbed onto each of his arms. "What are you doing, do you even know who I am?! Let go of me!"

Henry's eyes narrowed and he whipped his glare over to Hana, "Do you like what you see?! I'm going to get my revenge on you! This doesn't end here, Hana Acacia! I'm going to get my revenge and I'm going to win, you Noye loving freak! Why aren't you saying anything, you filthy trash?!" He threw his bottle of alcohol at Sean, and while the glass didn't shatter, the contents splashed onto both him and Hana.

"What are you doing?!" Sean shouted at the guards.

"Having your pet talk for you, huh?" Henry laughed bitterly. "You always had something to say before, didn't you? Say something now! Are you too afraid to say something since you know I'm going to win?"

"Can you not hear?! I said take—" Sean cut himself off when Hana slowly stepped forward with a blank expression on her face.

"Gonna say something now, huh?" Henry grinned crazily as he licked his lips. "Well, what are you going to say, witch? Huh?"

"When you win, say nothing," Hana murmured as she trailed her eyes over the tattered and soiled state of Henry's body and clothes. Things had changed so much in such little time. She met his eyes with her own – his swimming with anger and craze, hers flushed with sympathy and remorse.

"And when you lose, say less."

There was beat, if only a split second, of silence in the room following her words before chaos ensued once more.

"What the hell is that supposed to mean?!" Henry screamed, the guards finally having the brains to pull him from the room. "I haven't lost anything you crazy bitch! I'm the winner! I'm going to—"

His shouts faded away as he was dragged from the building.

Hana excused the pair of them from the party to get cleaned up, and they quickly moved to the backroom. She closed the door behind her, drowning out the chorus of gossip and chatter.

"What the hell happened to him?" Sean muttered under his breath as he rummaged around to look for something to clean them up with. "That guy went completely psycho."

"I feel like it's my fault," Hana admitted quietly.

"How the hell is this your fault?!" Sean asked incredulously, stopping mid step from disbelief. "It's not your fault he's a drunk piece of shit!"

Hana chuckled lightly at his insult and shook her head to clarify, "Not for pouring alcohol on us… I mean for how he turned out."

Sean glanced at her, "What do you mean?"

"I feel like… he could have been a different person, you know?" Hana murmured as she stared down at her stained dress. "He was trying to change. He wanted to change so badly, but… but I didn't give him the chance. I didn't give him the chance to change because I was so arrogantly stuck on my beliefs."

"If I had just… If I had just gotten off of my high horse," Hana muttered as she gripped the fabric tightly in her fists. "If I had just accepted him, maybe he wouldn't have turned out this way. Maybe if I had given him the chance, he would have changed for the better"

"Hana, look," Sean sighed as he crouched down in front of her. "You are not responsible for the actions of another. Whether he changed or not was ultimately up to him, and you are not responsible just because he chose the wrong path to walk down. Everybody is their own person, and no matter what you might have done to help him, he would have ended up where he's supposed to belong."

"I know the realization hurts, but at the end of the day you can't help everybody," Sean smiled gently at her as he tucked a stray strand of hair behind her ear. "You know that."

Hana stared down at her hands and gave him a small nod, "Yeah."

Sean pulled her in for a tight hug. He ran the long strands of her silky, black hair through his fingers, smiling as the sweet scent of her shampoo wafted under his nose.

Hana buried her face in the uncomfortable fabric of Sean's suit, "Sean?" she breathed out in a soft voice as she traced light circles on the cuff of his sleeve with her thumb.

"Hm?"

"Thank you, Sean, for always reassuring me and making me feel like everything will be okay in the end," Hana pressed her smile into his shirt. "And I love you."

Sean paused briefly before pulling away from her hold. He cupped his hand around her chin and tilted her head upwards until her eyes met his own. He smiled as he stared down at her face; this beautiful girl belonged to him, and likewise, he to her.

"Thank you, Hana," Sean whispered gently as he fingered the tips of her hair. He brought the strands forward and pressed a soft kiss to its ends.

"For picking me that day in the hallways and calling me beautiful even though I was hostile." He pressed his lips against her forehead, smiling when a few strands of her baby hair tickled the bottom of his nose.

"And thank you for saving Chris from those guards and protecting him after that." He trailed his lips to the tip of her nose, his breath sending shivers down her body as it brushed against her skin.

"And thank you for persuading us to have this rebellion to free the others." He kissed the corner of her lips, not missing how they immediately curved upwards at the touch.

"And thank you," he whispered, his lips less than half an inch away from hers.

"Now for what?" she asked, her voice hardly coming out of her throat. He locked his eyes onto hers, refusing to let them go with his gaze.

Sean answered by pressing his lips against her own. His arm slid around her waist, pressing against the small of her back to force her closer. Hana clenched handfuls of Sean's shirt into her hands, not caring if she was ruining the crispness of his suit. A few moments passed by before they reluctantly pulled away, each trying to catch their breaths.

Sean glanced at the blush that tinged her cheeks, and smiled happily, knowing that he was the cause of her flushed state. He pressed his forehead against hers, catching her attention once more.

"For allowing me to see the beauty in people again."

* * *

Sean woke up in the middle of the night with Hana curled up in his arms, a happy smile still spread across her face. They had returned from the celebration party completely worn out. A glance at the alarm clock told him that it was one in the morning, and the time forced him to stifle a yawn.

A dim light from the living room caught Sean's attention and he quietly stepped in its direction. He paused at the corner of the hallway once he saw Kai seated on the couch by himself. He was holding something in his hands, and with the stretch of Sean's neck, he recognized it as the framed group picture they had shot a few days before Haru had passed.

"Did you hear what Hana said, Haru?" Kai asked in a soft voice as he lightly brushed his finger against Haru's face. "We're free."

"We're free," Kai repeated himself, this time his voice cracking mid-word. He quickly pressed the palm of his hand against his mouth to muffle his sob, his entire body trembling as he cried. Drops of his tears landed onto Haru's framed face and Kai immediately wiped them away.

Sean's heart tore at the sight of Kai. He must have been hurting. Sean missed Haru, of course, and he knew that both he and the others would never forgot about the stuttering male. He also knew, however, that Kai missed him more.

While the wounds of Haru's death would never fade away from their hearts, they had all been given some time. They had all been given time to develop that thin, thin layer of skin that protected that deep wound.

But not Kai.

Kai had cared for Haru on a level far beyond the rest of them, and Sean knew that Haru's death would always be fresh. It would never, ever be even the closest bit to healing. Sean knew, because he would feel the exact same way if he lost Chris, and so would Luca if Aiden had died.

"Y-you sh-should be here w-with us H-Haru," Kai sobbed quietly as he pressed the picture frame to his chest. "You sh-should have eat-eaten dinner with us, and you sh-should have li-listened to A-Aiden's dumb jokes, and y-you should have… y-you should… god I miss you."

He buried his face in his arms to stifle his cries, not wanting to attract any attention from the sleeping others. "It-It hurts so-so much. Ev-everyday hurts s-so much with-without you, and now everybody is free and I don't k-know what to do. I'm s-so alone. L-Luca has Aid-Aiden,

Sean h-has Chris and H-Hana, and it's j-just me. I-It's just K-Kai with no-no…nobody."

Sean winced at the painful voice Kai uttered his words in. Was that how he had felt all this time? Did he really believe he was alone? Sean clenched his fists tightly at his sides as he stepped forward to reveal himself, "You're not alone, Kai."

Kai jumped at the sudden voice and he quickly rubbed his eyes with the back of his arms, embarrassed to have been caught.

"H-Hey Se-Sean, what are y-you doing up?" he laughed awkwardly. "H-Had trouble sleeping too, huh? Ha… haha…"

"Kai," Sean called out his name in a soft, yet firm voice.

Kai's face immediately dropped, and a few tears began to glide down his pale cheeks. "You heard me?"

"Kai," Sean repeated as he stepped towards the male. He offered him the warmest smile he could muster, "You're not alone."

At this, Kai let out a bitter chuckle, "I'd like to believe your words, Sean, but I don't think I can."

"Kai, you can't possibly believe that you're all alone!" Sean exclaimed as he knelt down before him. "You can't believe that we don't all care for you!"

Kai shook his head and offered him a small, sad smile, "I don't believe that, Sean. I… I know you all care for me. I just… I know you don't care for me as much as you do for one another. I'm not, and never will be your Hana, or Luca's Aiden."

"But you don't need to be, Kai!" Sean exclaimed. He forced the male to look at him, "You don't have to belong to somebody to have your place! To be important! Why must you have to mean more to somebody than the next person? Isn't it enough to know that you're cared for? You and Haru had a tight bond, but that doesn't mean you'll never develop a relationship like that again. Why are you giving up so early, Kai? Why are you giving up when everything has just begun?"

Silence followed his words, and continued on for several minutes until it was interrupted by the creak of a door. Luca and Aiden emerged from their bedroom across the living room and froze once they caught sight of Sean and Kai.

"Well," Aiden was the first to speak. He eyed Sean's hands that were embracing Kai's face, "Should this be something we need to hide from Hana… or…?"

"Aiden!" Luca barked as he smacked the other on the back of his head. "Can't you read the moment, you dumbass?!"

He sent the pair an apologetic expression, "The giant was hungry again so we were going to go to…to… were you crying, Kai?"

Kai's eyes widened in realization and he immediately turned his head. Being caught by Sean was embarrassing enough and he didn't want the entire house to know that he had been crying.

"You were," Luca continued, his eyes furrowing in concern. He propped Aiden against the door and immediately went to his side, his maternal instincts kicking in overdrive.

"Kai, what happened?" Luca asked as he sat on the couch beside the male. He wrapped his arms around his shoulders and pulled Kai's face into the crook of his neck, "Why were you crying?"

Kai shook his head, tears already beginning to stream down his face once again from the warm embrace of the smaller male. He reminded him of Haru. He clenched the back of Luca's shirt tightly in his hands, uttering a soft and broken, "Haru."

Luca's eyes flashed in realization and he glanced up at Sean who nodded in confirmation.

"Oh Kai," Luca whispered, tears beginning to spring to his own eyes. "Haru would be so proud of us. I'm sure he's looking at us from above with high spirits, Kai."

Sean glanced up when he heard another series of soft shuffles, and saw Chris and Hana appear down the hallway. Her face fell once she saw Kai and Luca in a sobbing embrace, and her eyes met Sean's.

Sean mouthed, "Haru", and that was all she needed.

"Kai," Chris whispered in a quiet voice, his heart breaking at how intensely the boy was sobbing. He took a few steps forward, fresh tears now appearing at the corners of his own eyes. Hana nudged him gently, urging him to join in on the hug she knew he desperately needed. Chris let out a loud wail as he wrapped his own arms around the pair, tears pouring down his face.

"Come on, Aiden, I'll help you," Hana murmured as she helped Aiden move from his awkward position against the door. She had him settled down on the couch next to Luca before she made her way to Sean's side.

Sean immediately wrapped her in his arms, pressing a light, gentle kiss to the top of her head as he did so.

"I-I'm sorry for making trouble," Kai sniffed once he managed to calm down. He wiped his nose on the back of his arm and stared down at the carpet with shame, "I woke up everybody in the middle of the night."

Luca shook his head immediately and took Kai's hands into his own, "Don't say that, Kai. This is what family does for each other."

Kai paused as he replayed the words over in his head. "Family?"

"Yeah," Chris nodded his head as he glanced over at Hana and Sean who smiled fondly back at him. Aiden gave Kai a reassuring squeeze on his shoulder, and leaned over to wipe away Luca's stray tears. Chris stared down at the photo graph that lay forgotten at the foot of the couch, and smiled as Haru beamed back up at him through the glass frame. He wiped his eyes and nodded his head once more with confidence, "We're a family."

"A family," Kai repeated softly, the corners of his lips curving up slightly at the sound.

They were a family.

An incompletely complete, once lost and then found, family.

EPILOGUE
TEN YEARS LATER

"Sean you little twat, it's almost 6 PM and you still aren't dressed yet!" Hana exclaimed with exasperation.

"I don't understand why I have to get dressed," Sean protested as he kicked his feet up lazily onto the coffee table, "It's just dinner."

"Kai's bringing his new girlfriend today you insensitive prick! This is the first time he's brought any girl around to show us, so you are not about to present yourself in yesterday's t-shirt and khakis!" Hana exclaimed as she flung a dish rag at him. "Now get up and get dressed."

"Fine! I'm going!" Sean whined as he reluctantly made his way to their bedroom. "But I'm not wearing a suit!"

Hana muttered profanity under her breath and sighed at how childish Sean still acted. She felt a light tug on her dress, and her face lit up when she saw Haru staring sleepily up at her.

"Is my little baby awake?" Hana cooed as she lifted the three year old up into her arms. Haru giggled happily at the sudden height and squealed in delight, "Daddy's a prick!"

Hana nodded her head in approval, "Yes he is."

"Can you not teach him to insult me already?" Sean sighed as he came out of their bedroom with a tie hung loosely around his neck.

"But you are a prick," Hana blinked innocently back at him.

"A prick!" Haru shouted as he pointed his chubby fingers at Sean.

"Daddy is not a prick," Sean answered as he poked Haru's cheek. Haru laughed loudly at the touch, and smacked him away, "A prick!"

"I hate kids," Sean muttered under his breath.

"Why?" Hana whined as she held Haru up in her arms. "Haru is such a cutie, aren't you baby boy?"

"Prick!" Haru squealed happily.

"If Luca and Aiden ask I'm going to tell them that you taught him that," Hana added as an afterthought.

"Seannie taught you that word, right Haru-Haru?" Hana cooed as she tickled under the boy's chin.

"He's going to beat my ass," Sean sighed as he tried to fix the tie around his neck. "Give me some help, would you?"

Hana placed Haru down in his high chair, "No can do. Jaymes was the one who tied all of my ties for me, remember?"

"You're hopeless," Sean muttered under his breath as he tried to figure out how the piece of cloth was supposed to work around his neck. "Your dad called when you were out today, by the way."

"Yeah?" Hana asked with a cocked head as she began placing out the tableware. "What'd he say?"

"He wanted to know if you're still available for dinner this Thursday," Sean answered, giving up on making his tie look decent. No matter what he did, Luca was going to make a big fuss and fix it for him anyways. "I told him you wouldn't miss it."

"I guess," Hana answered in her most indifferent tone.

Sean rolled his eyes, easily seeing right through her facade, "Don't try that stuff on me Miss Hana, I know exactly what you're really thinking."

"I beg to differ," Hana retorted with a scoff.

Sean shook his head and chuckled at her childishness. He glanced at her meaningfully, "I'm glad you finally agreed to give him another chance. He's been trying to schedule a dinner for months now with you playing hard to get. Family is family, Hana, and he's the last of it."

Hana spun around to face him with narrowed eyes, "What are you talking about? You're my family, Sean."

Sean sent her a pointed look, "You know what I mean."

Hana folded her arms, "I don't believe I do. My family consists of you, Luca, Aiden, Chris, Haru, Chase, Jaymes, Kai, and whomever that new girl of his is." She glanced at Haru and cooed as she patted his head, "and I can't forget about you either, can I, little Haru?"

Haru gurgled happily in response.

"What's this talk about family?" Luca's voice echoed through the halls before his face popped up around the corner.

"Luca!" Hana greeted him cheerfully by embracing him into a hug. "Sean was just bitter that he's not a so called real family member since we don't share the same blood."

Luca arched an eyebrow mischievously, "Oh? But you guys share a lot of other things, like saliva and se-"

"Why don't you say hello to Haru?" Sean loudly interrupted as he gestured to the toddler that was sitting innocently in his high chair. "And it would be nice if you stopped letting yourself in, Luca. The key we hide in the mailbox crack is for emergencies, not for you to break in without notification. And stop leaving your kid with us, we're not babysitters."

"Hello to you too, Sean. Clearly you're still fabulous at making people feel right at home," Luca rolled his eyes. He threw his arms up into the air and made a complete 180 once he headed towards Haru. "How is my baby?! Did Uncle Sean and Auntie Hana take good care of you?"

"Thanks for waiting for me," Aiden grumbled as he entered the kitchen with several bags of groceries in each hand.

"You handled it fine without me," Luca brushed him off as he placed Haru on his feet. "Daddy missed you today!"

Haru blinked at him before turning to Sean, "Up, Daddy! Up!"

"He's not your daddy, Haru. You only have Daddy Aiden and Daddy Luca, remember?" Luca explained to his son for what must have been the hundredth time. "Sean is your Uncle, not Daddy."

Haru blinked at him before turning back to Sean, "Daddy, up!"

"I swear to god," Aiden muttered under his breath. "Our kid is dumb."

"It's your fault," Luca shot him a look. "It's because you didn't explain it well enough to him the first time that he calls every male he sees Daddy. I should have known better than to let you handle important things."

"Daddy's a prick!" Haru screamed happily as he pointed at Sean.

"Sean taught him that," Hana immediately followed up.

Luca spun sharply on his heels to face the said male, "What?!"

The doorbell chimed just in time, saving Sean from Luca's anger.

"That must be Kai and his new girlfriend!" Sean smiled as he strolled out of the kitchen. "At least somebody here knows how to use a doorbell."

He dodged Haru's rattler that Luca chucked at him, and laughed obnoxiously as he went to open the door.

"Hana, I need to ask for a favor," Luca turned to her with a serious expression on his face. "I need you to murder Sean in his sleep tonight. It can be fast and painless or slow torture. I don't care what it is as long as we're burying him six feet under next week."

"Hey, hey, hey, what are you saying in the presence of a police officer?" Kai called out as he strolled into the kitchen with his new girlfriend at his side.

"At least Kai has my back," Sean sniffed dramatically.

Kai snorted, "Screw that! I want in on the plans too!"

"Kai, shouldn't you introduce your girlfriend to us?" Luca asked as he eyed the girl who was shifting nervously in her place.

"Oh right, sorry about that. I got a little too excited about the idea of wiping Sean off the face of the earth," Kai grinned sheepishly. "Guys, this is my girlfriend. Girlfriend, these are the guys, Sean, Aiden, Luca, and Hana."

Before they could exchange greetings, the doorbell chimed once more.

"That must be Chris," Hana smiled as she quickly excused herself to get the door. She flung the door open and grinned at the familiar face.

"What happened to the key in the mailbox?" Chris asked as he engulfed her into a hug. "I swear I searched for like ten minutes. Did you guys move it? It's under the turtle statue, isn't it?"

"See! I'm not the only one who doesn't use the doorbell!" Luca exclaimed. "Sorry about that Chris, I brought it in!"

"Dammit, am I the last one to arrive again?" Chris sighed as he and Hana joined the others in the kitchen. "Is Jaymes coming today?"

Hana shook her head, "He's still on his Honeymoon in the Bahamas."

"Who goes on a honeymoon for a month?" Sean scoffed. "Ours only lasted for like two weeks, didn't it Hana?"

"That's because you're cheap," Hana deadpanned. "Besides, Jaymes deserves some romance in his life after remaining single for 35 years."

"Thirty-five year old virgin," Aiden snickered as he fist bumped Kai.

"I swear to god, why does it seem like you guys mentally age backwards?" Luca rolled his eyes. He played with Haru's tiny hands, "Don't disappoint Daddy and turn out like one of them, okay?"

"Prick!" Haru nodded eagerly in agreement.

"Let's eat already! I haven't eaten since noon and I'm so hungry I could eat a small child!" Aiden whined as he rubbed his stomach.

"Aiden!" Luca gasped as he covered Haru's ears with his hands. *"How could you?!"*

Their family had branched out quite a bit in concerns to Luca and Aiden's adopted son Haru, Kai's new girlfriend, and Jaymes's new Italian wife, but still, they were a family.

For a family, a true family, didn't simply consist of those you shared the same blood with, but those who could always make you feel as if you were at home.

Hana smiled as she observed all the different things happening from the kitchen counter. Luca and Aiden were suddenly in an intense argument over who had to fold the laundry when they got home. Kai's face had flushed a bright red when Chris had not so accidentally revealed an embarrassing story to Cecilia. All while Haru gazed at them proudly from his photo frame that was situated above the fire place.

Hana glanced up when Sean wrapped his warm arms around her waist, kissing her gently on the temple with a smile. "It's always so loud when they come to visit."

And with them, she was home.